Homeless Rats

Homeless Rats

A desert novel

AHMED FAGIH

QUARTET

First published in 2011 by
Quartet Books Limited
A member of the Namara Group
27 Goodge Street, London W1T 2LD

A catalogue record for this book
is available from the British Library

ISBN   978 0 7043 7232 0

Typeset by Antony Gray
Printed and bound in Great Britain by
T J International Ltd, Padstow, Cornwall

❧ ONE ❧

The sun reached a point at the very centre of the sky and held back the reins of its chariot. No harm, the sun felt, in standing still for a while to catch its breath.

From this position the sun shot its arrows of fire, holding the earth below at its mercy: an area of scorched earth that smelt of burning. The heat turned the earth's pebbles to live coals, the sand to burning embers, and the bushes and plants, so green before, to heaps of dry twigs ready to burst into flame and smoke.

No people lived in this patch of desert – the heat was intolerable. It was the home of animals and insects. The main animals living there were the jerboas, rodents with long hind legs, which moved by leaping. Because of this the people in the country districts nicknamed them *longlegs*.

The jerboas lived in a large colony, made up of all generations: old, young and infant. The fierce heat of the sun wasn't the jerboa's chief worry – or at least not in itself. The danger came from the way this heat sent the vipers, and the other serpents, moving madly about, lifting their heads in convulsive movements, leaving behind them twisted trails where their bellies had marked patterns in the sand. The snakes would crawl on until they reached a jerboa's burrow, and there they'd wriggle in to seek protection from the sun. Snakes don't build nests like birds, and they don't dig burrows like jerboas. They just live on the efforts of other creatures. They invade the nests of the birds in spring, to eat the young and then sleep there. In summer they invade the jerboas' burrows. And this was the greatest disaster to befall the jerboas of Jandouba. For, once there, the snakes would straight away open their mouths and thrust their poisonous fangs into the jerboas' bodies, then make a tasty meal of them, along with their mates and their young.

The jerboas were clever enough to make a second opening to their burrows, so as to make a swift exit through the rear and escape the snakes. The family would follow the male, leaping upwards, bumping their noses on the stones, their long hind legs throwing up a whirlwind of dust in their terrified flight. They'd move as far as possible from their old home, till they reached a place where they felt safe, then immediately start digging a new burrow.

In this way the jerboas coped with the menace of the snakes and lived a happy life, playing and leaping over one another. They dug new burrows for their offspring, they married their young males to their young females. They were pleased when their numbers continued to increase, for their future seemed secure and sure: their storehouses filled with grain enough to feed every small mouth.

It was the harvest season, when the ears of barley had ripened, and the jerboas of Jandouba and the districts round about sent word to one another to prepare for the reaping. They managed the work in just a few days, toiling diligently until they'd gathered all the ears of barley from Jandouba's fields and stored them under ground in their burrows. And so all the jerboas, with all their families, not only ate their fill but had enough food put by for a whole year.

The sun seemed to have rested long enough now, and caught its breath. Giving rein to the horses of its chariots, it moved on across the sky's wide spaces, slowly and sedately.

Where there had been no shadow before, the wormwood and the harmel, the gorse and the *shwaal* and the thorny branches of the *nabk* trees now cast large shadows. Even the dry stalks of the harvest on their roots, the ears themselves nibbled away by the jerboas, stood upright and headless, casting their shadows too.

The sun hadn't reached its final point yet, and now, along with the shadows of Jandouba's many plants and trees and bushes, there appeared a new and different shadow. The other shadows stayed fixed in their places, only growing taller or shorter from time to time. This new one, though, moved swiftly from spot to spot. Nor was it the shadow of a pack of wolves, or foxes, or rabbits. It was large and long, the shadow of a caravan entering Jandouba: five camels, three donkeys, four dogs, one horse and forty people, made up of men, women and children.

At the arrival of these newcomers, the jerboas leaped around, seeking safety in one another. They gazed, terrified and awestruck, at the giant shadows crawling towards them. One old jerboa gloomily wrung his hands, then turned to the sons and grandsons around him.

'We must take care,' he said. 'The strangers are bringing harm to this peaceful nation of ours, ready to afflict our land with destruction and death.'

✧ TWO ✧

The line of people began unloading goods and belongings in the place chosen by their chief, Sheikh Hamed Abu Leila. He'd visited this district before, and, to save time and trouble, he'd brought his people to the selfsame spot he'd used as a settlement in the past. They were close to the course of the fertile valley with its fields of barley, and his people would, he hoped, find a source of food there.

The people pulled the camels by their rumps till they knelt, then started the unloading. Their exclamations filled the air:

'Take this!'

'Give me that!'

'Put this child where he won't get hurt.'

'Is this the time, you fool?'

'Where are you?'

'You can have a drink when we've finished.'

Hamed Abu Leila's camel refused to kneel as Zenab pulled at its rump. It lifted its head, jerking stubbornly, viciously, from side to side, then opened its foam-flecked mouth, grunting loudly every

7

so often. The slit in its upper lip seemed wider than ever, and its tongue was a dark green colour. When it finally showed signs of getting beyond control, Zenab called her father, who was busy answering his people's questions. Where, they were asking, could they graze their animals, and where could they find wood to make a fire? They wanted to know, too, where the barley fields were. He told them he'd answer all their questions when they'd finished unloading their belongings.

Many years had passed, Sheikh Hamed said, since he'd been here last. He'd need to look around before he could give any answers. Then he went off in response to his daughter's call for help, striking the camel hard on its front feet till it finally knelt, grunting in pain.

Aunt Maryouma unloaded her belongings from her donkey's back, then sat down on her folded tent to get her breath back. Her dog Marzouq was, she saw, looking towards the horizon, eager to explore the nearby hills. He barked loud and long, but not with his usual fierce barks. He was clearly greeting the place that was to be his home for the harvest season. This raised Aunt Maryouma's hopes, and she gave thanks to God.

'Aunt Maryouma,' she heard someone say, 'your old dog's so happy he's ululating with joy!'

She laughed.

'If I wasn't so tired out,' she said, 'I'd do the same, now we've reached this land of blessing and plenty. God protect Marzouq, he's done it for me!'

Everyone was busy unloading the camels and donkeys, and the land, silent for so long, was suddenly awash with echoing voices. Each family was bustling around its own heap of belongings and making ready to pitch the tents.

Hamed Abu Leila took his camel, and the rest of the men followed him, driving their camels and donkeys towards the furrows and grooves made by floods long before. The place they had chosen was far from the vegetation and barley fields. Still, to make sure their beasts wouldn't stray and trample the barley, they tethered the camels and bound the donkeys' feet. Then they returned to help their womenfolk pitch the tents, driving the pegs into the ground with their hammers, then pulling the ropes and erecting the poles on which the tents would rest.

The dogs ran about, sniffing the ground, looking for something to eat – they were always hungry. Some lay down, too, testing the ground to see if they could sleep comfortably on it when the time came.

As for the little boys, they were as curious as the dogs about what there might be to eat. Aunt Maryouma had sent her son, Miloud, off with the other boys, and they were poking the ground here and there to find out what the place was like, this place where they were to settle. The children wanted to see if there were any edible herbs or plants, and were thrilled to find some *khubayz* and *qeez*, along with some *fuqaa* plants which they took for their mothers to cook for them.

Soon the land was the site of ten black tents with their entrances facing the valley. They were pitched close to one another, just a few metres apart. The sun had finished its journey and vanished beyond the distant horizon. Darkness began to fall and envelop their patch of earth. The air, so hot and oppressive before, grew suddenly cold, pricking their bodies like sharp needles.

The people began to enter their freshly pitched tents. The children had been running around, playing and rolling in the sand. Now, with darkness fallen, they felt cold and hungry and ran back to the tents. Their clothes were covered with sand, even their eyelashes and the hair under their caps were filled with it. They shouted as they ran, telling their mothers how hungry they were, how the shrubs and herbs hadn't filled them up at all.

Leaving the womenfolk to arrange their belongings, the men went off in search of firewood. As they came back with it, their minds were full of this new land where they'd settled. What work, they wondered, would they find, so as to feed their families? Many of them, used to walking barefoot, didn't feel the thorns on the ground. They even trod on them deliberately, to prove to themselves that their soles had grown as tough as the soles on any shoes!

The dogs, tired at last of wandering around the new land, began barking incessantly, and were answered by the howls of distant wolves. Finally they sat down outside the tents. Aunt Maryouma's dog didn't bother to look for his mistress's tent, but settled outside the nearest one. He stretched his weary legs and panted, his tongue hanging down from his open mouth, every hair on his body quivering with each breath he took.

❧ THREE ☙

The earth shook as a giant's feet trampled the peaceful city, destroying it utterly, till it vanished into the depths of the earth. Thousands of ants living in this city had fallen victim to the disaster, while others had managed to escape death by fleeing, terror-stricken, in all directions.

Several hours passed before some of these, recovering at last from their fearful ordeal, began to assess the situation. Those ants recruited for combat, whose duty it was to deal with the consequences of the disaster, returned to their stricken city and sent out patrols to search for those that had fled. They urged their scattered population to reassemble once more beside the ruins of their city, for the humans who'd come to Jandouba and committed this crime had now disappeared. It was, the patrols assured the citizens, safe to return once more. Everyone must play their part, now, in rescuing the victims trapped beneath their city's ruins.

Swarms of ants that had survived the disaster moved the earth and pebbles, pulling out the victims, some of them still alive despite exhaustion. Many were unconscious, having been trampled by the heavy feet of men, camels and donkeys.

The ants supervising the rescue had hopes that the city's lower layers, which had been very strongly built, might have escaped destruction. Luckily the home of the queen ant was in one of these layers: a great mansion with many spacious halls, where the queen received her visitors and met with her government officials. It had a large bedroom too, where the queen laid her eggs, built so as to withstand, up to a point, the disasters liable to afflict the ant dominions.

The walls of the queen's mansion were covered with leaves and fibres to protect her and the other ants, should disaster strike, from death beneath the mounds of earth and pebbles. The lower layers had storerooms too, for the grain the ants had gathered and set in place for the winter season.

As the rescue squads carried out their duties, moving pebbles and rescuing the ants beneath, another troop was commanded to break into the lower layers; not through the old entrances, destroyed now, but through freshly dug tunnels. Their aim was to reach these layers with all possible speed, so as to assess the damage and rescue the queen.

A band of more than a thousand ants, trained in digging, made three tunnels. One led to the queen's residence, a second to the food storerooms, while the third led to the houses adjoining the queen's residence, where her ladies-in-waiting lived.

These ants spent most of the night at their exhausting task, and by daybreak the three groups had reached the lower layers of the city, which were quite devastated apart from a few odd corners. Half the granary had been destroyed, and further ants were assigned to transfer the buried grain. The queen's mansion had been destroyed too, but the queen was still alive, along with some of her ladies-in-waiting, thanks to the protecting leaves and fibres.

The queen of the ants had received no reports of the disaster. It had been sudden and ruthless, the city destroyed in a brief moment, and there'd been no chance for her to send word to her officials. When she learned from the rescue squads how it was all the fault of humans recently come to Jandouba, she wasn't in the least surprised. She'd suspected all along that humans had been responsible for the calamity; for the only knowledge ants have of those giant creatures is of being constantly trampled and destroyed.

✧ FOUR ✧

The Captain was the first to feel the morning come. The land was wrapped in a dim light, the early morning air refreshing and cool. He didn't need to change his clothes to go out, for he never took off his old military suit except to wash it. Apart from that he wore it night and day.

He slipped out from beneath the bedclothes and poured some water from a jug to wet his face and hair. He brushed the drowsiness from his eyes, then, feeling wider awake, went outside and on to the large tent where Sheikh Hamed received his guests. The Captain was responsible for making tea for these guests. Standing there in the open air, he stretched out his arms and breathed deep, taking in air damp with the morning dew and the fragrance of the fields. He felt the delicious taste of apples in his mouth, and, for all the previous day's hunger, felt satisfied, his thirst quenched. His heart was at peace, and he wished this sense of tranquillity could last for ever.

He moved towards one of the sand dunes and climbed it to see what the surrounding land was like. Golden fields of barley swayed there before him, as far as the eye could see. Joy swept through him. He felt, in those early morning hours, as though the fields laden with barley ears were his and his alone, as though he'd ploughed the lands, then scattered the seeds in the furrows himself.

He clapped his hands in childish pleasure. Then, suddenly, he heard a movement from the tents next to his own and realised the people there had woken and were moving around. He stopped his laughing and clapping abruptly, thanking God no one had been near enough to see him and hear him. They would have thought he'd gone mad!

The Captain hadn't waited to eat a morsel of bread, or a date, or to drink a glass of strong black tea. A feast far more appetising awaited him, one that lay in the fields, whose fragrance he'd breathe in, whose colour, lovely and glowing, would live on in his imagination. He'd fill his two hands with the ears of barley, feel the pricking of the husk as he rubbed the ears to separate the grain from the chaff. Then he'd eat the small green grains. What breakfast could ever be tastier than that?

He raced off towards the fields, to make sure none of the newly woken people – dying as they were to discover what this new land had in store for them – could get there before him. He stopped for a moment on the way, to catch his breath and look back, to make certain no one would share his discovery, that no one would arrive at the same time as he did in front of those wondrous golden blocks of barley.

The Captain decided to play a little game with himself. He closed his eyes and stretched his arms out in front of him to walk on slowly and sedately, as if performing some religious rite. Treading over the soft ploughed earth, he felt his feet sinking in. As he crushed the stalks underfoot, a fresh, green season of spring sprouted in his own heart and the birds chanted joyfully around him. With the yearning of a lover about to embrace his beloved after years of separation, the Captain stretched out both his hands to the barley, hardly able to believe he was about to gather its ears after three long years of drought. He scarcely knew what he'd do with them. He'd smell them, taste them, then return with a bundle to the people in their tents and say: 'Here's this morning's surprise!'

The ears of barley had always been the people's main source of food. It had vanished from their lives, though, over the past three years, as their land was struck by drought. There was no harvest without rainfall. What would his comrades do when he showed them the barley plants after so long!

Closing his eyes, the Captain opened his hands and grasped the plants to pluck them up. He took an excited breath, then opened his eyes to enjoy the marvellous sight. He laughed as he opened them. Then, as if a corpse lay there in his hands, his laughter turned to horrified fear. His eyes bulged, his features lost their firmness. Trembling violently, he saw how the barley he'd plucked up was mere root and stalk and leaf, without one ear of barley on it. It was as though some blight had attacked the plants, leaving them bare of ears. He tossed the stalks aside and went further into the field, looking for barley that would calm his fears, ease the grief already weighing heavy on his heart. Up and down the valley he walked, through the midst of the fields, and found not a single ear on any plant. He fell exhausted on the ground, his heart broken. He wept long and bitterly.

He realised, suddenly, that the other people in the camp were quite unaware of this dreadful discovery. They'd all fallen asleep the night before, in the hope of harvesting the ears of barley next day; and now it had fallen on him to bring them the truth of the disaster. His news would be a shock to them, but not as bitter as the shock by which he'd been struck himself. He must get to the camp as quickly as he could, before the people came to the fields.

The Captain ran as if ten dogs were behind him, sinking their teeth into the tail of his military jacket. At last he reached the guest tent, where the men were gathered discussing their plans for the day's work. Sheikh Hamed Abu Leila had advised them not to approach the owners of the barley fields separately. They'd come to Jandouba together, and they should stick together now as they went to negotiate over wages, working hours and periods of rest. That way they'd be guaranteed better terms than if each went on his own.

Sheikh Hamed stared at the Captain in astonishment. The man was standing there in front of him, silently hanging his head, wiping away, with the edge of his jacket, the tears that flowed from his eyes.

'What's the matter with you?' he asked. 'Has a snake bitten you?'

Maybe, Sheikh Hamed thought, that was why horror was so clearly written on his face. Perhaps some big snake had struck at him. No, stammered the Captain, it wasn't a snake, or a scorpion either. The plants had sprouted no ears of barley this year.

Seeing the looks of amazement on his hearers' faces, he made things clearer still.

'The fields are barren. There's not a single ear of barley on the plants.'

No one had really taken in the Captain's words. The plants in his hands, though, proved the truth of what he'd said. There were roots, stalks and leaves, but not one ear of barley to be seen. The fields must be barren. What other explanation could there be? The stalks were tall, strong, covered with golden leaves – but had not an ear on them.

The Captain had prepared them for the bad news. Even so, their dismay was no less when they reached the fields and saw the truth for themselves. The fields were like a golden carpet, stretching as far as the eye could see. No one, seeing it from a distance, could ever have imagined the plants had produced no ears. Had the men not gone there themselves, had they not held the stalks in their own hands, they would never have believed the bitter truth. Still more amazing was the fact that no one, to all appearance, had used a scythe to reap the harvest. The plants stood tall and straight, their leaves swaying in the morning breeze.

'God have mercy on us!' one man cried. 'What's happened here?'

'The owners must have found some new way of reaping the harvest,' another man replied.

'This is a disaster,' a third man lamented. 'Here we are, standing in the middle of the fields, and every ear of barley's been harvested and threshed! The chaff's been blown away by the wind and the barley's been stored in granaries. And we thought the harvest season hadn't started!'

Haj Abu Hamama took a plant in his hand and, totally silent, examined it for a moment from its top to its roots. He knew enough to see the reason for these barren fields.

'Jerboas,' he said. 'Only jerboas could have done this.'

For the first time since their arrival the people became aware, suddenly, of the presence of these rodents with the long hind legs. There they were, with their forelegs tucked close to their bodies, and their big eyes, black and round and bright. The jerboas were,

15

they saw now, leaping around everywhere in the fields, even where the people themselves were standing.

Abdel Aaly the woodcutter was seized with hatred for these cursed creatures. He was tempted to start chasing them, to kill every last one of them. The only thing that stopped him was the sight of his companions, their heads sunk in despair. He gazed at their gloomy faces. They seemed, suddenly, much shorter than they'd been just a few minutes before.

The sun had risen in the sky now, sending a long, pale shadow that covered them where they stood. Each time they moved, the shadow split apart, as if engaged in some endless conflict. As always, the sun began its day pleasantly and calmly enough, letting the early morning breeze blow gently, caressing the people's faces. Then it rose a little above the horizon and began its assault from the sky, scorching the earth, pouring floods of fire on the creatures of the land.

The men had to act quickly, before the sun's heat became unbearable. They explored the land in every direction. Surely, they thought, there must be fields in the lowlands, or in the higher parts of the valley, not yet harvested or ravaged by the jerboas. They must search for these fields. If they failed to find them they'd be trapped by the disaster, with no hope of salvation.

And so Haj Abu Hamama took the old rifle he'd used to fight the Italians, slung it over his shoulder, mounted his feeble old horse and rode down the valley in search of ears of barley, on any plant. If he found any, he told the men, he'd fire three bullets in the air. Then the womenfolk of the camp could ululate in celebration of the good news.

The Captain trotted off in his own chosen direction. He turned right and left, in a zigzag course, as though dizzy and suffering from sunstroke. As for Aunt Maryouma, when she heard how the barley had been nibbled away by the jerboas, she joined the men in helping look for plants that had survived the blight of these rodents. She looked towards Sheikh Hamed.

'I'll take the path to the high ground,' she told him, 'and if I find any plants the jerboas haven't eaten, I'll climb to the top of a dune and ululate at the top of my voice, so everyone will hear the good news.' With that she walked off, followed by her son Miloud and her dog Marzouq.

Amer ben Sheeha had gone to the well to fetch water, returning after the dismal news about the barley had broken. He fought down his urge to take a nap, having been up so late the night before. He'd started off towards Sheikh Hamed's tent in the hope of seeing Zenab, since most of the other men had gone off. Then, realising what he'd been about to do, he felt a sense of shame – this wasn't the time to show his love for her. He went off, along with the rest, in search of barley.

✤ FIVE ✤

'According to humans,' the queen ant said, 'a camel eats in one mouthful what an ant stores in a whole year. There's a clear danger for us in the people of this camp and their camels. Now that our city's been destroyed, and thousands of our kind trampled helplessly under their feet, we've no choice but to leave our land. We must move to some other place, where the feet of these humans and the hooves of their beasts can do us no harm.'

The queen ant was issuing this command to her nation in a temporary camp, to which the ants had moved on the invitation of the jerboas. Prepared by the rescue squads, it was situated under a large, thorny *nabk* tree, which served as a temporary protection against the forces of evil and aggression.

The queen ant addressed the jerboa who'd come to offer his nation's condolences.

'I thank you,' she said, 'for the help received by our nation from the rats and jerboas of this valley. We could never have settled here, under this shady *nabk* tree, but for the generosity of our friends the jerboas, for they were the first creatures to build their homes beneath it. We and our friends the jerboas,' she went on, her tone growing more serious and solemn, 'have been subjected to the same ordeal. Together we must make a plan to evacuate this place. We must agree, too, on the new place to which we intend to move.'

The idea of leaving their land had never occurred to the jerboas' delegate. Such a possibility had never been discussed by his fellows. For all the jerboas' terror at the oncoming humans and their camels, none of them had actually been harmed. He addressed the queen ant.

'As you know, your majesty,' he said, 'the jerboas are most attached to their land, and they consider it a disgrace to abandon their home.'

'But, my dear jerboa,' she replied, 'utter destruction threatens us all because of these people.'

'Better total destruction of one's homeland than living apart from it.'

The queen ant gazed at the jerboa, pitying his foolishness.

'How ignorant these jerboas are,' she said to herself. 'They've no notion of the power humans have to harm, what power to kill and destroy.'

She went on, not caring whether or not the jerboa heard her:

'You'll regret this, my young jerboa – when it's too late!'

❧ SIX ☙

This wasn't the first time the people of Mizda had come to Jandouba. It was one of their traditions that some of them should come to Jandouba's fields for the harvest season, as their ancestors had done before them. They'd always been on the best of terms with the people here, who, in their turn, had always received them hospitably when they came in years of drought and famine, employing the people of Mizda to reap their crops.

Stories had been told, endlessly, of the fertility of Jandouba's great valley, of its blessed earth in which a single grain formed roots, then sprouted into a plant bearing ears of wheat or barley to fill a whole sack.

Whenever drought, then, struck the people of Mizda, they turned towards the lands of the north, and especially to Jandouba, which had always delivered them from their plight. It was a journey of four days to Jandouba. Even so, this was the nearest fertile land to their village. The fertile strip on the north coast, whose harvests varied with the seasons, was a full ten days away. The younger members of the tribe had never before experienced these seasonal trips to Jandouba in search of food. The older members, though, had been here many times before.

More than half a day had passed before the men returned from their search for plants not nibbled by the jerboas. Quite worn out, they felt as though they'd been on a journey of a thousand miles. Their dark skin had grown even darker, and their faces seemed longer, gaunter, than when they'd set out. Gloom was written on their faces, and their bent backs and drooping heads brought them closer to the ground. They panted through dried lips, as if the fruitless search had lasted a year.

From the midst of the sky the sun poured its fury on them, and the sweat flowed from their foreheads and necks. Their throats parched, they entered the camp and looked for the first vessel of muddy water to gulp from and quench their thirst.

They flung themselves on the ground in the middle of the guest tent. Sheikh Hamed Abu Leila's voice was faint and weak, very different from his usual commanding tone. Though he'd drunk from the muddy water, his throat and mouth still felt parched and dry.

'What are we to do, men?' he asked.

Hardly ever, he knew, had he asked such a question. He was the one of whom questions were always asked, who always replied to them. He was trying to take his men by surprise, asking them this question before they confused him and embarrassed him by posing it themselves. Looking at them, he saw how their gaze was fixed on him, how their eyes accused him. He, after all, had persuaded them to leave their homes to pursue a mirage.

He received no answer. Instead more than one voice repeated his question:

'What are we to do, men?'

As they asked, they gazed at one another in despair, pretending to forget who'd been responsible for bringing them to this place.

'There's only one really practical thing to do,' Haj Abu Hamama said sarcastically. 'We must say, "there is no god but God, and Muhammad is the prophet of God" – then lie down and die.'

Sheikh Hamed contemplated Haj Abu Hamama's words. When disaster had struck their village of Mizda, they'd refused to submit. Rather, they'd left the village, travelling over the land to provide food for their families. Now, though, those castles built in the air had toppled. They'd lost their last hope, in the fields that stretched out before them from one end of the sky to the other.

The tent was wrapped in a despair that freed them from the need to think about what should be done, and at that moment Sheikh Hamed viewed the despair as a kind of relief. His people's death from hunger was a possibility now. He'd seen more than one famine in his village, when people had died in great numbers. The handful of flour or few dates they'd managed to find hadn't been enough to keep people alive.

'It's a dreadful thing,' Sheikh Hamed thought to himself, as though addressing his people, 'to have to die far from home, in this land that's failed us. Starvation. A fierce and painful death. Yes! There's peaceful death and there's death that's fearful, terrifying, like this one waiting for you, members of this camp. You'll know the time of death when it comes. You'll hear death's footsteps as it comes closer, then you'll see it. A person who dies of hunger doesn't die straight off, or even in a day. He dies little by little, over many days. He sees death as he breathes each breath, as his pulse grows ever weaker. He dies gradually as death destroys the cells of the body one by one, with its hateful darkness. The one who dies will be buried by the one not yet dead. Then the land that failed you in life will be forced to take you into its depths. We'll all meet again here, after we die, to knock at God's doors, to complain to Him of the injustice, the affliction we suffered in this world. And, after all the misery we've endured, we'll be close to God.'

He brushed aside these ramblings of his mind.

'God forgive me,' he murmured. 'God forgive me!'

He was afraid these thoughts passing through him might have shaken his faith, and he deeply regretted now the way he'd given up hope. He gazed into the men's faces in front of him, fearing they might have read his thoughts. Gloom, though, was still written all over his people, as they hung their heads in despair. Still their eyes were fixed on Sheikh Hamed, waiting for him to say anything at all.

Striving to collect his scattered thoughts, he spoke to his men and himself alike, in an effort to chase despair from all their hearts.

'We mustn't panic,' he said. 'We must think calmly and clearly. Then, God willing, we'll find a way out of this plight we're in. He who believes in God must never let despair enter his heart, for God is just and protects the creatures of the universe. I know,' he went on, gazing at the men, 'our situation's critical. But Jandouba isn't the end of the earth, and its fields aren't the only fields. This valley stretches from the foot of the West Mountain, watered by the rains of the Nafousa and Atlas mountains. I suggest we assemble groups of men to follow the valley, beyond the fortress, staying to the west and searching the smaller valleys, till they reach the mountain passes of Gharyan to the east. They should look there for fields not attacked by the jerboas. What's to stop us doing that, even if it takes us a day, or two days, to reach the places?'

There was little enough hope, everyone felt, of finding these fields. But they agreed with Sheikh Hamed. What else could they do, except wait to die of hunger? There was one problem, though, that they'd all forgotten in their concern over reaching barley fields left unravaged by the jerboas. Suddenly one of them voiced it.

'What are we going to eat now, Sheikh Hamed?'

Every head turned towards Suliyman, who'd asked the question.

Suddenly they all realised they were hungry, with no food in their tents. They'd eaten all their provisions on the journey from Mizda to Jandouba. When they'd left their village, they were sure the fields of Jandouba would be ripe with wheat and barley waiting to be reaped by their scythes. One of the fields' owners had assured them of this when he passed through their village. This year's harvest, he'd told them, was excellent, and he'd invited them to come and reap it as in previous years.

Suliyman addressed Sheikh Hamed.

'My wife,' he said, 'couldn't find anything to cook for the children yesterday, except for some *khubayz* herbs she'd picked on our way here. It wasn't enough to feed them, and, as for me, I don't know how to bear these pangs of hunger any longer.'

He rolled up his shirt to show the stones he'd tied around his stomach, then added:

'I'm not the only one, I know, who's done this. And my wife isn't the only woman looking for edible herbs. This, Sheikh – in case you didn't know it – is the state your people are in.'

Gloom, dark and heavy like a cloud of black dust, enveloped them all. Without a word, Sheikh Hamed stood up and walked off. He moved in the direction of his tent, sighing deeply, as though wishing his sighs could blow the cloud of gloom away. His face was marked by a resolute determination, that of a man about to make the most important decision of his life. He looked at the men lying exhausted on the ground. Then, as he stepped out of the tent, he said:

'God willing, you'll all eat tonight. I'm going to slaughter my camel for you.'

A murmur of hope arose. Then it was replaced by a dismal silence wrapping them round once more. They hung their heads, embarrassed and ashamed. They knew well enough Hamed Abu Leila's camel was all he owned in the world, and the only means of livelihood for his family in these days of need.

✺ SEVEN ✺

The ceremony of slaying the camel was completed just before sunset. Some of the men, out of compassion for their chief, had begged him not to slaughter his beast. Those who had food, they said, should offer it to those whose provisions were exhausted, till Almighty God brought relief.

But Sheikh Hamed insisted on carrying out his decision. There was, he knew, no other way out of their plight; and now no one would sleep that night on an empty stomach. He was the one who'd led them on this journey, brought them to the land of the jerboas. Of course their troubles couldn't be solved in a single night. Had it been a question of the one night, he would have agreed to put off the slaughter of his camel. But there would be a second night, and a third, and a fourth, before they could be sure of the barley fields they were seeking.

Everyone in the village of Mizda knew of the closeness between Sheikh Hamed and his camel. They all remembered what had happened ten years before, when he'd come back to Mizda from Fezzan carrying a load of dates on the beast's back. A sandstorm had blown in Al Hamada Al Hamraa, for more than three days, and most of those making the journey had lost their way and died of thirst. Hamed Abu Leila had been one of the few to survive, trusting to his camel's instinct and tying himself to the beast's back, leaving him to follow the route he chose. The camel had saved him from the perils of the desert, leading him to a place where he found water. It was the camel that had saved Sheikh Hamed from the fate of his companions.

The members of the camp felt what he was doing was wrong. How could he sacrifice his comrade, who'd served him so loyally and even saved his life?

Men, women and children left their tents, and stood watching at a distance. The Captain went to where the camels were grazing, to bring the camel due to be slain and lead it to the circle of men standing in the camp, ready with their knives, to slaughter the beast and flay it, then cut up the meat and divide it out.

Hamed Abu Leila meanwhile had slipped out of his tent and gone far from the camp, to the hills on the other side of the valley, so as not to witness the camel's slaughter. He sat there on the ground, waiting for the sun to go down so he could perform his sunset prayers. Hearing the camel's groans as the knives stabbed into its neck, he could not hold back his tears. Great fountains of blood gushed from the neck. To Sheikh Hamed it was as though the blood had reached him even in that distant place, soaking his clothes. He looked down, panic-stricken, to see the blood with which he felt he must be drenched, then realised he'd imagined the whole thing because of his grief at losing the camel and his guilt at having given the order.

He invoked God in a loud voice, begging His forgiveness. Then, solemnly raising his hands in front of his face, he recited the opening verses of the Quran and asked God's mercy for his slain camel's soul.

The slaughtered beast was transformed into piles of meat, which Haj Abu Hamama then divided into equal portions for everyone. Each family was given an amount according to the number of its members, including the camel's intestines and other entrails. Suddenly Masoud Al Roumany cried out in terror that the camel's head was crawling towards him along the ground from where it had lain, its mouth wide open ready to bite him, and people fled.

Masoud had been the first to thrust his knife into the camel's neck, and he believed the slaughtered beast was looking to take its revenge. His terrified shrieks frightened the women and children, but the other men who'd taken part in the slaughter made fun of him and called him a coward. He shouldn't, they said, have volunteered to take part if he couldn't stand the sight of blood. They told him, too, that he should put the camel's head in the fire and eat the first piece of roasted head himself, so he could be sure it wasn't alive and hadn't crawled towards him with its gaping mouth.

In front of each tent the flames rose high into the sky, while the smoke formed a great cloud over Jandouba. Each wife had lit a fire in preparation for the great feast, and they were carrying their bowls in which to put the camel meat broth for their families. The cooking pots were set above the stones of the fires, and the delicious aroma of meat enveloped the camp, recalling previous years of plenty when they'd eaten meat once a week – or once a fortnight at least.

The full moon shone above them, and the heat of the day gave way to a refreshing breeze that almost tempted everyone to step out of the tents and sit in the open air, beneath the moon's silvery beams. That night they enjoyed a feast the like of which they hadn't seen for many years. All, though, firmly resisted the temptation to leave their tents, out of sympathy for Sheikh Hamed Abu Leila – or, more precisely, from the embarrassment they felt at his order for his camel to be slain to feed them. Actually, only the adults felt this sense of guilt. The youngest members of the tribe felt none at all, and, having finally eaten their fill and chewed the bones to enjoy the marrow, they ran out into the open air, playing hide-and-seek in the quiet moonlight.

The children's parents never let them play far from the camp at night, and so they played in front of the tents or between them. Some even played inside the tents, trampling their fathers and mothers and raising a mighty din.

Only Sheikh Hamed Abu Leila took no part in the feast, unable to bring himself to eat the flesh of the creature that had been faithful to him till death. He satisfied his hunger with a few dates, then asked the Captain to make tea and sat staring up at the moonlit sky with its scattered stars. He called back many memories of his companion, who had carried him constantly from one place to the next. Many nights, he remembered, just like this night, he'd spent with his camel in the open air. He'd never felt lonely, even though there'd been no person with him, for the camel had brought comfort and security.

Sheikh Hamed had always relied on his camel, and would never have embarked on this particular trip without him. Without the camel he wouldn't have been able to travel along with his family and his belongings. What, he wondered, would he do now? How could he face life without his camel? How would he carry his belongings? He decided, at last, to leave matters in the hands of Fate; for God never closes one door of sustenance without opening others.

The Captain had spread a mat for Sheikh Hamed outside the guest tent, and he sat there in his favourite spot near where the animals were, by the entrance to the tent. While the Captain was busy making tea, two children dashed into the tent to hide. Then, before the Captain could turn them out, three more ran noisily in looking for them. It was as though the shouts of the children tempted Sheikh Hamed to come out from his isolation, to think of something other than his slain camel. He called the children over and gave them some dates, then told them to go to all the other tents and tell the men he was waiting for them in the guest tent.

The men had been expecting the invitation. After a few minutes they began arriving, one by one, at the tent where Sheikh Hamed sat and where the Captain was preparing the first round of tea. To start with they all felt deeply embarrassed, but their sense of guilt began to die down as Sheikh Hamed's words broke the ice.

'We came to Jandouba,' Sheikh Hamed said, 'in search of food for our families. And instead of relief we found disaster. Now we need to find a way out of our plight.'

'We used to call Jandouba,' one of the men agreed, 'the land of bounty and blessings. Now it's Jandouba the land of affliction.'

'You wouldn't say that,' Sheikh Hamed replied dryly, 'if you were a jerboa. It's a paradise for jerboas!'

The men all laughed loudly to hide the embarrassment they felt right through the evening. Their sheikh, they felt, had recovered from the loss of his camel. When Sheikh Hamed saw them laughing, he joined in, and suddenly his sorrow over the camel became lighter and easier to bear. He was glad to see them happy.

Coming to Jandouba would, Sheikh Hamed had been convinced,

save them from starvation. Other groups from Mizda, hearing of the harvest in the valley of Suf Al Jeen, had gone off to Bani Waleed, but Sheikh Hamed had led his followers here to Jandouba. Through barren mountain passes they'd come, using up all the flour and oil and dates they'd brought with them. As for tea and sugar, no one but Sheikh Hamed had such precious commodities. He couldn't imagine life without tea. Thirst he could endure, and he could go without food for many days, but he couldn't begin his day, or his afternoons or evenings, without first drinking tea. And so, before selling all the goods in his shop in Mizda, he'd put aside the two boxes of tea and the sack of sugar for himself, refusing any amount of money for them.

From the very beginning of the journey, he'd never grudged inviting the men to drink tea with him each morning and evening. After the ceremonial drinking of three rounds of tea, the Captain would boil the leaves for the fourth time, then offer it to the women in their tents. Finally he'd take the last remaining leaves and give them to any children who happened to be around, and they'd suck at the leaves, enjoying the taste of sugar in them.

Sheikh Hamed had first come to Jandouba as a boy, along with his father, during one of the droughts that had struck Mizda. The drought years came periodically, sometimes after a few years, sometimes after many, but come they always did. The one sanctuary for the people of Mizda, in these times, was Jandouba, where the land was always fertile and drought never struck. The abundant rain of the coastal areas blessed Jandouba too, by creating a fertile district that became barren only on its southern borders. South of this was the region of hunger, of which Mizda was the centre.

Sheikh Hamed had often heard his father call Jandouba blessed. Once, he'd told him, a devout and pious man called Abu Al Uyoun had come down to these plains from the mountains, in search of land to till. The people of Jandouba had welcomed him among them, giving him a piece of land and helping him plough it. When harvest time came, they found that, the moment they reaped the ears of grain, new ears sprouted in their place. The pious man took what he needed from the harvest and told them to take the rest. And so they filled their houses and granaries with barley. So plentiful was it, indeed, that the people of Jandouba had no room to store it all. The devout, pious man then told them to bury the barley that still remained in a mound facing the valley, where it would always be under his care.

Even when it didn't rain in Jandouba, the valley still flowed with water from the streams and valleys of the Atlas Mountains. The rain pouring on the mountains, days and weeks from Jandouba, eventually reached here too, making the land rich and fertile.

Sheikh Hamed Abu Leila had returned to Jandouba when he was a man and head of his family. Twice before this he'd come with his wife Khadija, before this present journey which she called 'the third emigration'. Even after some of the others had gone from Mizda to Suf Al Jeen, still he'd chosen to come here, believing what his father had said about Jandouba being a land blessed by God. He'd often wondered why his ancestors had never settled in this fertile land; why they'd been content to live in a place that was threatened by drought always, where it rained one year then was dry for three.

In fact the original ancestors, according to the story handed down, had their reasons for returning to Mizda. But what of later generations, whose offspring had increased while the means of livelihood decreased? Why hadn't they moved north from Mizda and settled in Jandouba, when the land there had belonged to God alone and wasn't owned by people who fenced their property round?

Sheikh Hamed remembered Jandouba as he'd seen it last. Its fields had seemed endless with their ripe ears of barley awaiting the reaping. They were paid better here too, more generously than in other lands, where it had always been the custom for the owners to take personal responsibility for the harvest, reaping it themselves, then threshing it and packing it into sacks and bags. There any men hired to help would be given one fifth of the harvest. In Jandouba things were quite different. Here the owners had no time to reap or thresh the harvest, being too busy selling the produce of their vineyards, olive groves and fig trees. They only tilled the land at all because it took just the one day to plough. Reaping and threshing, on the other hand, took months, and so the reaping and guarding and threshing were assigned to incoming labourers. Then, when the barley had been packed, the owners gave the workers a full half of the harvest.

But now the fields of Jandouba were mere dry stalks; there was no harvest. The jerboas had joined with the drought. His people had fled the drought in Mizda, and now he'd led them into this disastrous trap. As he recalled past memories, he was brought back to earth by the Captain's loud roars of laughter.

'Can you believe it?' he said. 'One of our village dogs has actually had a big piece of meat to eat. I've just seen it, with my own eyes – Aunt Maryouma sharing her meat with her dog, Marzouq. Can you believe that? She ate a piece herself, then gave a piece to him!'

The men laughed at the extravagance of the old woman, who'd fed her dog with meat she knew she'd need the next day. They themselves had all saved some.

Still, for all the Captain's comic remarks and the meat they'd eaten with such relish, they couldn't forget their troubles. With the second round of tea they became gloomily silent, reflecting on the fate that awaited them.

It upset Sheikh Hamed that Aunt Maryouma's old dog had eaten part of his cherished camel. The dogs would have no trouble finding food in any case – there were plenty of old bones and insects to keep them alive. As for the camels, they'd find enough food from the stalks of the harvest and the leaves of the shrubs and trees, and the donkeys, too, could share the heaps of hay and straw that lay everywhere with the wolves, foxes, rats and other creatures. But what of his people? What would happen to them after a day or two, after they'd eaten all the meat?

They couldn't, he knew, return to Mizda. They had no food to keep them alive for the journey, and the parched land in their village had nothing to offer them in any case. Even the well around which the village was built had dried up – the buckets had been pulled up empty except for a little mud. The only people who'd stayed there were government employees on salaries, or those whose sons were employed in the British army camps and earned a few piastres from there.

Should they move on towards the coast? Hamed Abu Leila, who'd travelled to the coastal cities before, knew better than any of his people the hardships of such a journey. Between them and the coast lay mountains stretching, like a great barrier, from one horizon to the other. This was the western mountain range, which their donkeys and camels, weak and exhausted as they were, would surely never manage to cross. And if, by some miracle, they crossed the mountains, there was no guarantee they'd find work on the other side.

A few years before, many people from Mizda had gone to Tripoli in search of work and had come back regretting they'd ever set out. Those who'd stayed had lived abject lives, either as servants in the houses of Italians or as beggars outside the mosques. Only strong, sturdy men had been engaged as porters and labourers in the harbour. The men who'd come to Jandouba were all responsible for womenfolk and children, who'd most likely perish from hunger before they'd gone a quarter of the way to the coastal cities.

These people might even follow in the footsteps of their ancestors many generations before, who'd been afflicted with drought and famine, all doors of sustenance closed in their faces. When the head of a family was no longer able to feed his charges, and they were on the point of death from hunger, the family had gathered in a single room of its house, having first blocked the front door and windows with rocks and mud. Then, in the darkened rooms, they'd lain on the floor with their faces turned towards the Sacred Kaaba, reciting verses from the Holy Quran, and awaited death – a slow death within the mud-blocked house that had become a large grave.

Hamed Abu Leila remembered, suddenly, how he'd seen such a house himself when he was a small boy. It was close to the old mosque, and it was totally blocked with mud, on every side. He'd heard stories of how this family, before he was born, had entombed themselves in their home so as not to have to beg, and to preserve the honour of their womenfolk, making sure they didn't give in to hunger. He told those sitting around him of this family.

'I don't recall its name,' he added. 'I only remember the place was called the Ogre's House, because, whenever people went to perform their dawn prayers in the mosque, they'd hear moaning and groans coming from behind the blocked-up doors and windows.'

Who, today, had the courage of these ancestors, so brave that they preferred, even in affliction, to bury themselves alive rather than be forced to beg? Gloom fell over them all, for not one would be able to bear such a dreadful fate for himself and his family. Before finishing, they discussed a plan they would put into action the next morning, to look for new fields of grain. Then Hamed Abu Leila gave them hope as he wished them good-night.

'Don't despair of God's mercy,' he said, 'and don't forget to recite or read some verses from the Quran before you sleep. That will drive away despair and open the doors of hope for tomorrow.'

Hope, though, stayed in their hearts for only two days more. They'd sent Abdel Aaly the woodcutter to the east and Amer ben Sheeha to the west, to look for fields still uneaten by the jerboas. Both had gone off on their camels. There'd been no point in sending anyone south, where they'd come from and where, they knew, there was nothing but desert, while the north, with its mountains, stood as a barrier in front of them. After two days the men returned and gave their reports. The whole harvest had been eaten by the jerboas.

✣ EIGHT ✣

The dogs of Jandouba hadn't supposed any other dogs existed in the world. One of these dogs' ancestors might once have met a dog coming from the south with the harvest season caravans and so become aware of others. But if so, it had been generations ago and was quite forgotten now.

So it was that the dogs of Jandouba were astonished to hear the barking of the camp dogs, and above all by the noise of Aunt Maryouma's dog Marzouq, who, as the oldest, regarded himself as their leader. His gruff, hoarse barking sounded strange to the Jandouba dogs – they'd never heard anything like it before. Being very curious about it, they answered with their own incessant barking, and waited to see if the original barkers would get in touch. When, though, two days passed, and no strange dog appeared, the dogs of Jandouba decided to send a delegate to assess the situation.

The next morning this delegate, a female dog, left the foot of the mountain, and the orchards, and the houses dug in the ground, and the three shops around which Jandouba was set, and made for the fields from where the strange barking had come. At length she reached a spot near the tents of the camp.

The female barked in a way that conveyed a welcome, but the difference of barking accent caused some confusion and misunderstanding in the southern dogs of Mizda. These latter put their heads together, consulting as to whether the barking they'd heard was a welcome or a threat. Finally, though, the delicate, courteous nature of the delegate's bark reassured them it was a welcome. Four dogs went out to meet her. She told them, on behalf of the dogs of Jandouba, that they'd be most happy to become better acquainted with these visitors from the south, and to become their friends. She explained, too, the reasons for her astonishment, and that of the dogs she represented. Never before had they heard the barks of other dogs, nor had they had any notion dogs so much as existed outside Jandouba. All they'd ever heard was the howling of the wolves who roamed the wilderness and mountain passes. The dogs of Jandouba were the wolves' enemies, and they stopped them invading the orchards or the houses at the foot of the mountain.

The delegate of the Jandouba dogs was most happy to learn from those of the camp that dogs enjoyed a high status among the animals of the world, and lived in every part of it, having survived the perils threatening other species in the animal kingdom. The perils in question had sprung from that tyrannical creature man. The genius of dogs, though, had enabled them to form a historical friendship with man (that source of endless disaster!), thereby guaranteeing safety for themselves and their offspring, in perpetuity.

'Well may you rejoice, most beautiful of females,' said Marzouq, gazing into the delegate's lovely face, 'and take pride in your species; for dogs are the kindliest of animals in their treatment of one another. You may rest assured that the meeting between the dogs of Jandouba and the dogs of the south will be a great one in the history of our species. And a day of dread it will be for the wolves, for from this day on they will know no peace from us.'

The delegate of the Jandouba dogs had a slim and beautiful face, and eyes that shone with charm. In a soft, gentle voice she expressed her gratitude for all that had been said, adding that she was confident warm relations would be forthcoming between the dogs of Jandouba and the dogs of the south.

Marzouq gazed at her, his eyes filled with desire; he was drooling, his whole body quivering as if in a fever. And all the while a group of jerboas watched the scene in silent suspense.

❦ NINE ❧

Fatima woke with a start in response to her husband's repeated urging. She raised her head, rubbed her eyes and looked around, but could make out nothing in the darkness of the tent.

'What's the matter?' she asked. 'It's still the middle of the night.'

'I'm not staying here another day,' Abdel Aaly replied, 'in the middle of all these jerboas. They've been jumping about between my feet all night. I want to go back to Mizda.'

Fatima realised her husband hadn't slept. She knew too that, ever since his return from his expedition, when he'd failed to find any plants left uneaten by the jerboas, he'd been plunged in a mood of depression and gloom. When he'd stretched himself out beside her on the mat, it was to toss and turn continually, as though he was sleeping on a bed of thorns.

Now, exhausted from lack of sleep, Abdel Aaly was trying to wake Fatima, to deprive her of sleep, too.

'It'll be much easier to talk about that in the morning,' she said, trying to stop him disturbing her.

'Travel by night,' he answered, 'and you'll always make it.'

'You mean you want us to run off like thieves? Isn't it our duty to wait? To see what the others are going to do?'

'Let them stay here and die if they want to.'

'And what are we going to eat on the journey?'

Fatima wanted to go back to sleep, but her husband gave her no chance to close her eyes. He kept repeating how stupid he'd been to believe a foolish old man like Hamed Abu Leila and follow him to Jandouba. He should, he said, have stayed in Mizda, or else gone to Suf Al Jeen like some of his friends. Still he talked on, but Fatima gave no answer. All this complaint, she decided, was his way of disturbing her, of forcing her to share his sleeplessness and keep him company in the restless state he was in. She tried to arouse his passion, placing her bare leg on his, to stop him harping on his worries.

Fatima had realised before this moment that her husband had come to regret joining the people of Mizda on their journey to Jandouba. Because of this, he'd felt the shock of their disaster more than his comrades. His circumstances had been different from theirs. Unlike them he could have stayed in Mizda, free from the fear of hunger that had spurred the others on to leave.

Abdel Aaly was a woodcutter. He could have stayed on in the village, collected firewood, loaded it on his camel and sold it for enough to buy a handful of barley each day, enough to feed himself and his wife. However straitened people's means might be, there were always government employees who needed firewood.

Abdel Aaly had come to Jandouba dreaming of a plentiful, bountiful livelihood. He'd thought he'd eat better food, reaped from the fields of barley – and, in seeking to better himself, he'd found himself faced with starvation.

'Get up, woman!' he yelled furiously. Fatima withdrew her leg, turned her back on him. She couldn't, she saw, make him forget his troubles. And since he couldn't spend all night talking to a sleeping woman, he got up and went out of the tent. There he stood, amid the silence and darkness, not knowing what to do with himself. He saw his camel kneeling on the ground, about to stretch his long neck, close his eyes and sink into sleep. Abdel Aaly walked up to him and poked him in the side till he woke. He hadn't managed to wake his wife, but at least he could wake his camel! His wife and the camel were the two creatures dearest to his heart, and one of them at least ought to share the troubles and worries that were keeping him awake. He put the saddle on the camel's back, along with some empty water bags and a bucket. Then he rode the beast towards the well.

The moon vanished and a host of glittering stars appeared to light up the darkness. Abdel Aaly felt himself beneath a ceiling so much lovelier and more spacious than the top of his tent. At least he was doing something useful during these hours he couldn't sleep. Glancing towards the camp, he noticed a new tent had been pitched during the night, and he wondered whose it could be. A camel was standing outside it, and, as he approached, he saw the beast was grey with a black patch on its neck. At once he remembered who the owner was – Burhan, the man who called himself the religious scholar of Mizda, though Abdel Aaly called him the false prophet. What, he wondered, had brought Burhan to their camp? His mind was filled with suspicions as menacing as vipers' heads. Had Burhan come there after Fatima? He'd kill the man and drink his blood if he made so much as a movement or gesture that was suspect. He thought of putting off bringing the water till next morning and going straight back to his tent, then changed his mind once more as he realised he'd need more water than ever now, for the return journey to Mizda. Burhan's arrival compounded his resolve – he wasn't going to stay in the same place as the false prophet.

Under starlight, the nearby plateau seemed like a giant tent, pitched amidst the even plains stretching as far as the foot of the West Mountain. Behind this, in the distance, a chain of mountains loomed, set one above the next like a wall towering up to meet the sky. Here and there, between the bare rocks, appeared green circles: the fig and olive groves where the mountain dwellers lived.

The well was set in a limy hollow, and Abdel Aaly had been sure he wouldn't find anyone there at this time of night. There might not even be anyone there during the day, after everyone had left this land ravaged by the jerboas. When he reached the well, though, he found a bedouin who'd got there before him. The man had brought the five camels he'd driven from Sinawun to drink from the well and graze on the surrounding land, which was useless for anything but pasture. The bedouin left Abdel Aaly to squeeze a way through the camels, which were drinking from the trough alongside the well.

Abdel Aaly muttered some expressions of sympathy for the owners of the fields, who'd lost their crops on account of the jerboas. But the bedouin just laughed, saying the jerboas hadn't been an affliction at all but a blessing; and when Abdel Aaly couldn't understand this riddle, the bedouin went on to explain the matter. The fields' owners, he said, had been blessed when they complained to the British Military Governor in Gharyan. They'd exaggerated their loss, and, as a result, every owner had been compensated with a sum of money worth five or six times the price of their crops.

'The people of Jandouba,' he went on, 'fooled the British Governor completely. They all came back with so much money they married new wives and held weddings and feasts!'

What did all this have to do with the people of Mizda, who'd suffered the pangs of hunger and lived in terror of snakes and scorpions, and been victims of the south winds on top? Three whole years they'd been without rain, unable to find water even to drink, and no governor, British or Arab, had learned of their plight. No one, Muslim or non-Muslim, had hurried to save them, to earn their reward from God for keeping the people alive.

Abdel Aaly didn't, of course, give voice to any of these thoughts passing through his mind – the bedouin could have been no help to him. In any case, he regarded it as abject to complain to any but God. He left his camel to drink as much as it wanted, then filled the bags with water and hung them from the beast's back. Fearing the camel might stumble, he led him over the ground muddied by the water spilling from the troughs till he reached the sandy land nearby. Then he mounted to return to the camp, thinking of the jerboas, and the British, and Burhan the false prophet.

Abdel Aaly had married Fatima a year before, more than two years after the death of his first wife Burniya. Seven years he and Burniya had been married without having children, and he'd married Fatima in the hope she'd bear him the child his first wife had been unable to bear. Besides, Fatima was his paternal cousin. It had been his duty to protect her honour. Fatima's father had requested Abdel Aaly to ask for her hand when it began to be whispered through Mizda that Burhan had cast a spell on her, and that she would end up as other women had done; for it was rumoured Burhan seduced women, married them for a few months, then divorced them. Fatima's father had accordingly refused Burhan's proposal of marriage and swiftly married her to Abdel Aaly.

Abdel Aaly approached the tents of the camp as daybreak, with its bright hues, was just tinting the rim of the sky. Suddenly a figure emerged from Burhan's tent, and Abdel Aaly, coming closer, saw it was Burhan himself. He was dressed in the *jilbab* commonly worn by religious scholars, and he had a white skullcap on his head. He stood there in front of the tent, staring at the horizon tinged with its various colours. Then he raised his voice, calling the people to dawn prayers:

'Allah Akbar! Allah Akbar!'

Burhan's voice rang out in the early morning stillness, echoing back resoundingly from the nearby hills, so that his voice seemed to be coming from the four corners of the earth.

The sound of the voice drove Abdel Aaly into a fit of rage. This impostor, he thought, was calling the men to prayer with that strong, resonant voice of his, and he'd be their imam, leading them as they prayed. In this way he'd control the people of the camp. For the past three days the people had not felt the need for a call to prayer or for anyone to lead them in praying. Each had the right to arrange his own relations with his Creator in the way that suited him best. Each could pray inside his tent, without anyone to supervise him. There was no need for Burhan the impostor.

The members of the camp were wakened by the call to prayer. Burhan repeated the traditional declarations following the call, as he'd always done in the mosque in Mizda. Three times he repeated: 'Praying is better than sleeping!' Then he announced his intention to lead the prayers communally.

The people, woken by the prayer call, left their tents to see what was happening, and found that the scholar Burhan and his old mother had arrived in the camp. The mother lit a fire and swept the ground in front of her tent with a dry branch, ready to pray on it. Burhan had also brought his widowed sister and her two sons with him to Jandouba.

Without further delay the men of the camp stood in a single row behind Burhan, who called them to perform their prayers. He turned towards the East, in the direction of Mecca and the Kaaba, then raised his hands to begin praying. Abdel Aaly was the only one who failed to attend this communal prayer, held in the camp for the first time. He stayed there in his tent, refusing to have any part in prayers led by a man like Burhan.

❦ TEN ❧

Hajja Khadija, the wife of Hamed Abu Leila, was the only woman in Mizda who'd travelled to Mecca to perform the pilgrimage. This had been more than five decades before, during the lifetime of her blind father, who'd been famous for his recital of the Quran. When his splendid reputation for this reached the ears of Rajab Pasha, the Turkish Governor of Tripoli at that time, he'd been invited to recite in the Citadel's Assembly, and the Governor had later appointed him a member of the Pilgrimage Mission, which travelled by sea that year. The old man had taken his daughter Khadija, then seven years old, to act as his guide during the pilgrimage.

From that day on she'd been known as Hajja Khadija, and the people of Mizda had looked on her with the utmost veneration and asked for her blessings. The women of Mizda had gone to her home when she was still just a child, to ask her to describe the Kaaba in Mecca and the Mosque of the Prophet, blessings and peace upon him. They'd asked her, too, to describe Mount Arafat and the other holy places she'd visited. They never tired of hearing about the religious rites, and Khadija never failed to answer their questions, giving a detailed account of her journey to and from the Holy Country. So often had she been asked to repeat her story that she'd come, at last, to describe things as though repeating the words of a book she'd learned by heart. Even now, after the passage of half a century had made her an old woman, the other women visited her ceaselessly to hear her account of the Holy Journey.

From her childhood, too, Khadija had been taught by her father to recite the Holy Quran, which she'd learned by heart at an early age. This had still further increased people's respect for her, and encouraged the other women to visit her and ask her opinion and advice on many of their problems. She had, by God's will, borne only daughters, all of them married now except for the youngest, Zenab. Zenab's maternal cousin, Amer ben Sheeha, had asked for her hand in marriage, and the proposal had been accepted, but the marriage itself had been put off on account of the drought. It wouldn't be consummated till they'd been blessed with rain.

Khadija had always hoped for the blessing of a son, and had invoked God in her prayers to realise her hope. Still, this good woman had accepted God's will and her own destiny. In the larger family of her brothers and sisters the number of females was, she saw, equal to the number of males, a sign that life was arranged according to the will of the Creator of the universe, which far transcended the petty concerns of individuals in their limited world.

And yet Hajja Khadija's prayers to Almighty God had not been wholly without fruit, for He'd blessed her with a grandson – the son of her eldest daughter – whom had been named Ali after Hajja Khadija's father. Khadija had taken Ali to live with her as soon as he was weaned. Now, here at Jandouba, Ali was six years old, but his speech and behaviour were those of an older boy, and he recited as much of the Quran as an older boy would do. Hajja Khadija loved him dearly, but couldn't control his energy. She'd try treating him gently, then, if that didn't work, she'd resort to various forms of cunning. She never complained to his grandfather unless she really had to, for fear he'd treat the boy severely.

Ali would never go to sleep till his grandmother had told him one of his favourite bedtime stories. Before the sun set that evening, Hajja Khadija had seen him with a stick in his hand, sitting between the ropes of the tent and scratching at the ground for roots of the *tameera* herbs that bury their small white berries in the ground. These berries were very sweet, and the little boy loved them. As the sun began to set and darkness started to envelop the place, she'd tried to lure him away with some of the dates that made up their supper, but he'd paid no attention to her, and so she'd left him there while she performed her sunset prayers. Then she'd taken a kerosene lamp to give him some light outside the tent, till he'd found the first sweet berry; after which she'd finally led him away from the hole and washed the berry, which he'd nibbled happily.

Before Ali had time to ask his grandmother if he could go back to the hole, to look for another berry, Hajja Khadija had started telling him the story of Um Basseesy the sparrow, and the mouse that stole the milk; and how the sparrow had punished the mouse by plucking his tail from his body.

Hajja Khadija knew how fond her grandson was of this story, which he'd insisted on hearing for the past two nights, refusing to listen to any other. No doubt the mice and rats and jerboas they were seeing day and night had aroused the boy's curiosity. He

40

wanted to know more about these creatures that had become part of the life of the camp.

Hajja Khadija told Ali how the mouse had wept and begged the sparrow to give him back his tail, as he couldn't dance or sing at weddings without one. The sparrow, though, refused to return the tail, for she couldn't live without her milk and couldn't forgive anyone who'd stolen the provisions vital for her life. The sparrow told the mouse to go to the nanny-goat to fetch her some milk. Then, she said, she'd give him back his tail.

It wasn't hard now for Hajja Khadija to persuade Ali to put off digging for more berries till the morning. She took him to lie down beside her on the mat, and he listened eagerly to the rest of the story that had become such an important part of this new life he was living.

Hajja Khadija went on. The mouse, she said, rushed off to the nanny-goat to ask for some milk, saying:

'Beautiful, noble nanny-goat, daughter of a fine family, please give me some warm milk from your udder, so I can give it to Um Basseesy the sparrow, so she'll give me back my tail, so I can dance and sing at weddings.'

The nanny-goat was a thick-skinned creature, and the mouse's flattering speech left her quite unmoved. In an unfriendly tone she told the mouse, that, if he wanted any milk, he'd have to bring her *nabk* from the *nabk* tree. With that the stubborn nanny-goat turned away, refusing to hear another word.

The mouse ran off to the *nabk* tree.

'Blessed, generous *nabk* tree,' he said, 'the finest tree in all the land and the kindest to mice, strangers and wayfarers. Please give me some of your *nabk* to give the nanny-goat, so she'll give me some milk to give to Um Basseesy the sparrow, so she'll give me back my tail, so I can dance and sing at weddings.'

The *nabk* tree told the mouse plainly, in a way you might expect from her thorny covering, that she wouldn't give him a single *nabk* till he'd brought her some water from the valley. The mouse, scorched now by the sun's heat, ran panting to the barren valley

41

that had water only in winter. He addressed the valley in broken and humble tones:

'Oh great valley, you who make this district fertile. Please give me some water, so I can give it to the *nabk* tree, so it can give me some *nabk*, which I'll take to the nanny-goat, so she'll give me milk, which I'll give to Um Basseesy the sparrow, so she'll give me back my tail, so I'll be able to dance and sing at weddings.'

At this point the boy fell asleep, and it was time for Hajja Khadija to leave him and perform her evening prayers. She fell silent, and was about to get up when Ali, waking again, asked her to tell him what the valley had said to the mouse. The valley, she said, had told the mouse how the keepers of the floods, who lived in the high mountains, could only be woken by the sound of happy, joyful ululation. Then they'd send out the water to irrigate the fields, and the mouse had the right to make use of the water – if he could make the women ululate joyfully on the banks of the valley.

The mouse, breathless with anxiety, ran to the women, who knew how to ululate loudly and joyfully. He addressed them from some way off, not daring to approach and reveal his disgrace at not having a tail.

'Oh women,' he said, 'you who attend glad occasions in God's name, please ululate happily, joyfully, for such is the desire of the great valley, so it will give me water for the *nabk* tree, which will give me *nabk* for the nanny-goat, who'll give me milk to give to Um Basseesy the sparrow, so she'll give me back my tail, which I have to have if I'm to dance and sing at weddings.'

The women, who went to weddings, knew all about the mouse and the part he played at them. They'd be happy, they said, to see the mouse singing and dancing at weddings again, but they were weak from hunger and couldn't ululate unless they were given bread to eat.

The mouse was weak and exhausted now, from running here and there. Still, he had to complete his task if he was to have his tail back. So off he went to the baker.

'Oh generous baker,' he said, 'who bakes bread and delights the hearts of hungry people, please give me one loaf of bread, so I can give it to the women who go to weddings, so they can ululate joyfully, so the valley will give me water to give to the *nabk* tree, who'll give me *nabk* to give to the nanny-goat, who'll give me milk to give to Um Basseesy the sparrow, so she'll give me back my tail, so I can dance and sing at weddings.' The baker told the mouse he couldn't give him a loaf of bread till the mouse first brought him barley from the field.

The little boy fell sound asleep at last, so there was no need for Hajja Khadija to finish the story. What happened was that the mouse, who went to the barley fields to beg for some barley for the baker, realised begging wouldn't solve his problems, and so he decided to use his teeth and claws and take all the barley in the field for himself. That way he'd never be forced, ever again, to beg for help from any tree, or stone, or bird, or human, or any other creature of the desert, but would rather be master of his own life.

When Hajja Khadija was sure her grandson was fast asleep, she prepared the bedding for her husband, Sheikh Hamed, on the other side of the tent. It was his habit to stay in the guest tent till after evening prayers, after which he'd come in to sleep. She left the other tent flaps, which stayed open all day long, for her daughter Zenab to close before she went to sleep herself. As for Hajja Khadija, she stayed up some time longer, reciting sections of the Quran and praying voluntary prayers. Finally she lay down next to her grandson and slept soundly till just before daybreak.

She'd been used, ever since childhood, to waking at that time. She took her pitcher and, in the dawn silence, went to relieve herself behind the sand dunes, then completed her ablutions. Then, before the call to dawn prayers, she performed voluntary night prayers and waited for day to break. She recognised Burhan's voice as he called the people, for it was he who called them to prayer in the mosque in their village of Mizda. She heard, too, from the neighbouring tents, the voices of those who'd been woken by the call. Her husband, Sheikh Hamed, woke along with them, and she didn't need to rouse him as she usually did each day. When, she asked him, had Burhan arrived? He didn't know himself, for Burhan had arrived late, when everyone was asleep.

Sheikh Hamed Abu Leila performed his ablutions and left to join in the communal dawn prayers, while his wife stayed in the tent, listening to the sounds of life that announced the birth of a new day. After a while Burhan's voice rang resonantly out, as he invoked Almighty God to deliver them. Behind him the assembled men repeated his 'Amen!', loudly and in unison. It was as though the echo of their voices were the echo of all the creatures of the plains and plateau, as these repeated their own invocations.

Hajja Khadija ended her prayers to find her grandson approaching like someone walking in his sleep. He asked her for a piece of wood, so he could go on digging the hole he'd started the evening before. All night long, he told her, he'd dreamed of those delicious berries lying hidden in the ground. His grandmother poured some water over his face, so he could wash it, then pointed to a piece of wood he could take to dig for berries. Then she spread a mat at the entrance to the tent and waited for the sun to rise.

The Captain had saved her the trouble of preparing a fire and making tea – that was his job whenever they were staying in the desert. And so she was able to spend the precious time after daybreak praying and invoking her Creator. The amber rosary her father had left her shone between her fingers, as the light of the sky spread like molten gold. No sooner had she seen the tip of the sun appear from behind the horizon than she stretched out her arms, opened her hands and invoked the Creator of the universe in humble and pious tones:

'Oh God, Light of the earth and heavenly Lord of sun and moon and stars, and the planets turning in the dim depths of space; oh Creator of this universe that has no limits, whose mysteries are known only to the One Everlasting Refuge; send us relief in our plight and deliver us from this disaster fallen on us. You know us better than we know ourselves. You know what lies concealed in our breast, and in our conscience, and You know what is to befall us tomorrow. Save us, oh God, and have mercy on us, for Your mercy enfolds all things.'

Hajja Khadija's distress was not for her family alone. She was deeply moved by the misery of all the people who'd followed them to Jandouba. She'd helped her husband persuade them to throw off their apathy and leave Mizda, urging them to make a proper effort, according to God's command, to seek their daily bread.

They must, she'd told them, leave the narrow boundaries within which they'd lived. God's earth was wide. No living ever came to man unsought, it was rather for man himself to seek it out. Hajja Khadija felt no sense of shame in making this special petition to God, though it was something she'd never done before. Before she'd prayed in a general way. Now, though, in their present plight, she felt they were in dire need of God's help, even if that were just the barest amount of food to keep them alive.

'All each of us needs, oh God,' she went on, 'is a morsel of barley bread to keep us alive. That's all people ever need, whatever their age, whether they're as old as Aunt Maryouma or as young as my grandson.'

'Just a morsel of bread.'

'A morsel of bread for each of us.'

'Grant us this, oh bountiful Lord.'

'Do not close your doors against our prayers.'

'Your will shall be done, before and ever after.'

'Whether You bless or deny us, praise and thanks are due to You.'

So moved was Hajja Khadija that the tears flowed from her eyes. Her voice trembling, she ended by reciting the opening *sura* of the Quran. Then, for a few moments, she stayed silent, without moving, feeling at peace now she'd poured out her heart in her invocations. Suddenly she remembered her grandson and looked for him between the ropes of the tent, but he was nowhere to be seen. Her heart pounded in fear. Then she saw a cloud of dust from inside the tent. The roots of the plants had, she realised, strayed under the tent and her grandson was digging there. She went in, and there was the boy, lying face downwards on the ground, digging for berries.

45

Hajja Khadija gazed, in wonder, at the golden heaps lying around the boy. Could they – could they be ears of barley? She hardly believed the evidence of her eyes. Heaps and heaps of ripe grain covered the mats, the blankets, the place where she and her grandson had slept, where her daughter Zenab was sleeping still. The barley grains glistened in the sunshine filtering into the tent. What had happened? Where had all this bounty come from? Could the angels of God have worked this miracle, when the ages of prophetic miracles were so long past?

Still the woman could hardly believe what she saw there in front of her. Even the kings of the jinn, who move around invisibly, would have needed a helper versed in the mysteries of Solomon to bring these stacks of barley ears, in the few minutes in which she'd turned her face to the heavens.

Before seeking to find out just what had happened, Hajja Khadija prostrated herself twice, giving thanks to Almighty God for His blessings, glorifying His greatness and majesty.

☙ ELEVEN ❧

The bands of ants sent out by the queen, to explore the countries round about, returned with good news. They'd found many ant kingdoms ready to welcome her emigration, and that of her nation, to their own domains, now that their city had been destroyed by the human incursion.

These ant kingdoms were in secure districts, chosen with care by earlier generations that had themselves fallen victim to unjust human invasion. In the past, too, they'd been subjected to floods that submerged their cities, drowning whole nations of ants. The only survivors had been the queens, who could fly, and some winged male ants who'd managed to flee the flood with them.

New kingdoms had then been founded from the offspring of three or four queens who'd survived the ordeals of humans and floods. They'd built their cities in safe spots, in the rough, rugged land of the plateau or on the outskirts of the valley. They only came down into the valley to find provisions, before returning to homes set far from floods and human caravans.

These scouting bands conveyed to their queen the messages sent, by word of mouth, from the queens and leaders of the cities visited. They informed her, too, of the anger and grief felt by their new friends at the brutality to which their brother and sister ants had been subjected. Such was the fury of one of the queens they'd met that she'd expressed her longing for the day when all the ant nations would rise up together in fierce war against the brutal humans. She had, she added, already prepared a mighty army of bold and fearless fighters, who would defend, valiantly and dauntlessly, the right of ants to exist and survive.

There are, though, no recorded instances of such wars, for in reality the ants would have had to retreat from any encounter of this kind. Ants saw humans, by and large, as another form of natural disaster, alongside floods and hurricanes, which couldn't be fought. The sentiments conveyed by the scouting bands were therefore somewhat strange, reflecting a new spirit of rebellion on the part of the younger generations. The only battles ants remembered had been waged in years gone by, against beetles and spiders and grasshoppers. But these battles had been fought for food and survival, and the insects lived in peace, side by side, now there was grain enough for all and the struggle for life was no longer necessary. In any case, most of the soldiers of the ant kingdom were grinders of grain, and the present plentiful stock gave them quite enough work without thinking of war.

The ants had accordingly become friends with their neighbours, who included beetles, spiders, worms, grasshoppers and scarabs. Friendly relations existed, too, with other, stronger neighbours, like hedgehogs, rats, jerboas and hares. And now relations had been cemented still further through the threat of humans arriving in Jandouba.

The sense of common danger had been heightened when the

humans pitched their tents and settled in their camp. The insects and animals had considered leaving their homes and moving to the nearby plateau, or to more distant highlands indeed, to ensure their safety. Even the jerboas, whose burrows were dug deep in the earth and mostly covered by thorny trees and bushes, were as terrified as the other creatures.

None of the animals or insects living in the fields saw any good in this human invasion of their land – except, that is, for the desert moths, who were drawn to light and loved celebrations. They alone flapped their wings joyfully, even as others were fleeing to the highlands. They sang and danced as the humans unloaded their belongings and pitched their tents, then lit their fires. The sight of these glowing fires was one the moths had missed for a very long time, so much so that their colour, derived from the gleam of the flames, had almost faded. Whenever the moths saw flame, they'd leave the fields, rushing to dance around the fire.

✺ TWELVE ✺

The fourth day had begun. How would the people of the camp face it? And how would they face the fifth day, and the sixth and seventh after that? They'd learned finally, the day before, how the jerboas had left not an ear of barley on any plant. That was the thought turning in their minds after dawn prayers were over. They sat there in front of Burhan's tent, reflecting on their critical plight.

Burhan, after arriving the previous night, had had no difficulty finding the camp, for he'd been to Jandouba once several years before. He'd only just learned, from the men coming to pray, how the jerboas had eaten the crop, and now he was feeling the same shock the others had felt when they realised the disaster first.

He wrung his hands in despair, regretting now that he'd ever come to the place. There must, he felt, be some curse hounding them. How could such ill fortune have struck otherwise, right here in the most fertile land in the country, which had been delivered from drought? The land had been irrigated by the rainwater sweeping through the valley from the distant mountains, and the crops had grown and ripened. Yet all had come to nothing, for the jerboas, knowing humans were on their way to the fields, had devoured the harvest.

A desperate voice addressed the pious man.

'What are we to do now, Sheikh Burhan?'

What could a man who wrote charms for barren women say? All he could do was bring a brazier from his tent, put some incense in it, then murmur incantations, walking among the people with his brazier to drive out ill fortune, and the evil spirit that steals the sleep from children's eyes and fills the hearts of adults with despair, their nights with fearful dreams. Such spirits hounded humans wherever they might be, poisoning the wells and burning the fields, making their lives wretched.

Burhan told them to repeat, after him:

'There is no god but God!'

'Help us, oh Prophet!'

But Burhan's invocations and murmurings failed to answer the crucial question. How were they to feed their families that day? Sheikh Hamed had slaughtered his camel to feed them the day after they'd arrived, but would any other man with a camel be brave and generous enough to slay his beast for them, when everyone knew a man's camel was his sole means of livelihood?

The meat from Sheikh Hamed Abu Leila's camel wouldn't have lasted three days had the people not resorted to sleeping most of the day to keep the pangs of hunger at bay. They ate just the one meal a day and drank as much water as they could. The lucky ones still had some flour, which they kneaded with water and made into *zumeeta* to supplement their meal. There seemed no hope, however faint. Nothing, surely, could help them beat their hunger.

What were they to do? They couldn't stay in their camp, for there was no harvest to be reaped. Nor could they go elsewhere in search of work, since they had no food to eat on the journey.

'We can't stay here,' one man said, 'and we can't go anywhere else. We can't fly over land and sea like birds, to find a place where there's plenty of food.'

Another man remembered there was an agency in Gharyan that bought scrap iron. Often men from Gharyan had driven to Mizda in their lorries. They'd picked up the heaps of barbed wire, which had lain on the outskirts of the village since the time of the Italian occupation, then sold it to the agency. Only when the scavengers had carried everything off had the people of Mizda learned of the profits to be made from barbed wire and other scrap.

'And where are we going to pick up iron for the agency,' another answered, 'here in this wilderness?'

'You can find scrap iron anywhere,' the first man retorted. 'All we have to do is go to the towns. We'll find plenty of it in the rubbish dumps. Then we'll load our camels and donkeys with it.'

'And even if we do decide to search through the dumps, do you think we'll find anything? What about those people who risk their lives in the minefields? Wouldn't they have taken everything from the dumps first, before they were ever forced to go and look there.'

'All right then. Let's go to the minefields too.'

'And have you thought of all the problems? First, the minefields are all a long way off, and we'll never reach them without food for the journey. Second, you need experience for work like that. We haven't got it, and there's no time to learn how to go about things. Third, nobody's ever been into a minefield without losing an arm or a leg – or even his life.'

'No one ever said it's easy to earn your living.'

'Some people live by stealing,' Haj Abu Hamama said, 'and robbing people of their money. Do we have to follow their wicked example? Or should we try and earn a living in some way that's decent and honourable?'

And how, the men asked him, were they to earn an honest living? It was their duty, Sheikh Hamed put in, to find some way. As for Haj Abu Hamama, he was sure what they should do.

'We can reach Al Urban in two days,' he said. 'The villagers there are from the Jaafira tribe, and they're related to us by marriage. There's a shop in the village that buys the *halfa* people gather from the land round about. We'll find work the first day we arrive, and that will get us our food.'

Haj Abu Hamama didn't have to tell them how much strength it took to pull up *halfa*, the reeds that were sold on to make paper for banknotes and other things. Only the strongest men could manage it. To reach the *halfa* they'd have to climb over mountain paths, and besides, it wasn't as plentiful as it had been, because others facing poverty from the drought had resorted to gathering it too. It was hardly worth the toil of pulling it up. All the men knew this, but they knew, too, that any other option was just as exhausting.

Haj Abu Hamama waited, to see if anyone would agree to his suggestion. But only gloomy faces met him.

'I thank God,' he said, 'I still have the rifle I used fighting the Italians. I'll always be able to shoot a lark or a sand grouse, or a hare, to feed my family. But it's not just a matter of me and my family. There are forty mouths to feed in the camp.'

Little by little the men came to realise they might after all be saved from starvation – something which, in the shock of finding no harvest, they'd supposed at first was inescapable. Sheikh Hamed suggested another option, besides uprooting *halfa* from the high- lands of Al Urban. Abu Ghara, he said, through which they'd come on the way, had been the site of a famous battle between them and the Italians, and there were plenty of tamarisk trees there.

'But those trees don't have any fruit on them,' one man said, 'and their seeds are no good for anything except tanning leather.'

'And leather,' put in another man, 'comes, as we all know, from slaughtered animals. So what are we going to do with the seeds? What use are they to us?'

'I hate the thought of having to cut down trees,' Sheikh Hamed went on, ignoring these remarks. 'But if you can't make a living any other way, then that's what you have to do. People in other valleys have cut down trees that don't have fruit, then burned the wood to make charcoal. We'll do the same with the trunks from those trees. We'll sell the charcoal to the middle men, and they'll take it off in their trucks to sell in the towns.'

These middle men would, Sheikh Hamed knew, pay just a few piastres for the charcoal then sell it at many times the price. He realised, too, what a great crime they'd be committing by destroying these trees in whose shade their ancestors had reclined. There it was that their forbears had taken their midday naps, while the leaves had provided fodder for their animals. And yet it was only a matter of time before the trees were destroyed in any case; for, if they didn't cut them down, other hungry people from other villages would come and do it instead. Their ways to survive were limited. They could work in the minefields, or they could go to Al Urban and clamber up dangerous mountain paths to pull *halfa*. If those possibilities were too difficult, then their only course was to make charcoal.

The real problem, whatever they decided, was the time it would take before money and food were forthcoming. All they could do for the moment was follow the example of Suliyman's wife and Aunt Maryouma, who'd gathered herbs and boiled them to eat. But could you really call that food?

Sheikh Hamed, like everyone else in Mizda, had eaten this kind of thing when drought struck. They'd all eaten boiled herbs, with a crust of dry bread or a few dates added. Or else they'd swallowed the herbs down with a glass of goat's milk. Eating them without other food could only stave off hunger for a while, and often, too, it made the stomach swell up. This, in turn, often led to diarrhoea and then death. Sheikh Hamed knew all this well enough from past experience, over the many years of drought afflicting the land. In fact several of his relatives had perished in just this fashion.

A clamour of voices rose, as people argued over which course to follow. The uproar only died down, finally, when Burhan's mother came with a large loaf of hot bread she'd just baked. They shared it morsel by morsel, envying Burhan this luxury with which he'd been blessed.

Burhan didn't tell them the truth about the loaf. On his way from Mizda to Jandouba he'd spent the night near the bed of a dried-up stream whose water had been drunk by camels. There he'd found masses of camel dung with grains of barley in it – the beasts had swallowed the grains whole and they'd passed straight through their systems. A whole day Burhan and his family had spent, removing these grains from the dried dung, till finally they'd filled a whole basket. This had then been washed by Burhan's mother and sister, before being left to dry, then ground to provide loaves of bread.

Suddenly Ali, Sheikh Hamed's grandson, appeared.

'Grandfather!' he shouted. 'Hey, grandfather!'

The boy, barefoot and covered in dust, ran up to Sheikh Hamed. His grandmother, he said, wanted him to go to their tent at once.

Sheikh Hamed rose, his anxiety written on his face. Excusing himself from his comrades, he put on his shoes and took his grandson's hand, murmuring anxiously:

'May the news be good news!'

❧ THIRTEEN ❧

Hajja Khadija was still lost in utter bewilderment, thanking God again and again. Sheikh Hamed asked her why she'd sent for him so urgently, when he was in the midst of a council with his men. Saying not a word in reply, she simply pointed her finger to the inside of the tent, where the barley was heaped up in piles on the mat. First the man looked at the ears of barley, then he looked at his wife, waiting for an explanation. But still she said nothing.

'Who brought all these ears of barley here?' he asked, his voice choked with astonishment and emotion. 'Who in the name of all the prophets brought them here?'

Three whole days he'd just spent looking fruitlessly for barley left uneaten by the jerboas, and the effort had worn him out. It was hardly surprising he was dumbstruck to find barley there in his tent!

'I just don't know what happened,' Hajja Khadija said. 'God knows I didn't leave the tent, and no one's come in or gone out.'

'But this is unbelievable!' Sheikh Hamed said.

'Almighty God, may He be praised, has power to do anything,' his wife said simply.

Sheikh Hamed went further into the tent, filling his hands with the ears of barley. He smelt them, then rubbed them to see the grain itself inside, paying no attention to his daughter, who'd just woken up and kept asking what the matter was, or to his grandson, who'd gone back to looking for berries in the earth.

Then, all of a sudden, Sheikh Hamed realised where these ears of barley had come from. There in front of him, his grandson took some more from the hole he'd dug, then, in a tantrum, flung them on the mats because they'd stopped him finding the berries he loved so much! Sheikh Hamed took his grandson in his arms, kissed him on the forehead, shook the dust from his shirt, then told the lad to stay there alongside his grandmother.

The man took the earth from the hole, and there, inside, saw ever more ears of barley. He told his wife what he'd found. This, he said, was a burrow where the jerboas had stored the barley. And now their grandson had found it while looking for the berries he loved to eat. This meant, he added, that the barley harvest was still there. It had been reaped and then put in underground granaries, waiting for whoever might find it.

Hajja Khadija hugged her grandson and covered him with kisses, for it was he who had brought good luck to his family and his people. Meanwhile Sheikh Hamed inspected the burrow, then thrust his hand inside to fetch the rest of the ears. Next he told his daughter to bring an empty basket and help him fill it with the heaps of barley, for this was a blessing they must grasp. But how, he asked his wife, could the long-legged jerboas have dug this on flat ground where there were no plants? Everyone knew, after all, that jerboas always chose a thorny *nabk* under which to dig and

54

conceal their burrows. But Hajja Khadija told him how, before they'd pitched their tent, they'd cleared the ground of some thorny bushes; and he realised the burrow must actually have been dug beneath them. They'd only had to scratch the ground to find the store of barley.

Now, too, Sheikh Hamed understood what had puzzled him all along: just how the jerboas could have 'eaten' all the ears of barley from fields stretching as far as the eye could see. If only someone had told them of the jerboas and these underground storerooms of theirs, and saved them from the fearful despair they'd known since arriving in Jandouba!

No one, he reflected, could remember the last time such a disaster had happened. Certainly he himself could recall nothing like it. And so no one could possibly have known of these tunnels full of barley ears, discovered now by sheer chance. He called down God's blessing on his grandson Ali, for, but for him, the shadow of starvation would have hovered over them still, when the grains of barley were there beneath their very feet!

Sheikh Hamed had left the men looking for some way out of their plight. How would they react to the good news? His thoughts were suddenly interrupted by Abdel Aaly the woodcutter, who came and greeted him. Sheikh Hamed saw he was, with the help of a boy, carrying a water bag, which he now set down in the fold at the entrance to the tent. Sheikh Hamed thanked him, realising it was water for the guest tent, where the Captain had lit a fire and begun to prepare the tea. Abdel Aaly didn't want to have to sit in the tent and wait for the Captain to bring the first round of tea. He was, he said, in a hurry, and had something important to tell Sheikh Hamed before he left. It was highly unusual for anyone to pass up the chance of drinking tea with him, but the sheikh made no comment, simply waiting to hear what the man had to say.

Abdel Aaly said there was no point in staying there with jerboas all around, and so he meant to return to Mizda straight away. He wished, he added, that Sheikh Hamed would see the point of this, so they could all return together just as they'd come to Jandouba.

He spoke nervously, staring into space and avoiding the gaze of Sheikh Hamed, who decided to have a joke with him before telling him of the secret he'd discovered that morning.

'And do you think there's any difference,' the sheikh asked, 'between staying here and going back to Mizda? Either way we need God's help to deliver us from this trial, and when God's salvation blesses us, it will bless us whether we're here in Jandouba or there in Mizda.'

Abdel Aaly stood in gloomy silence. How was he to tell the sheikh he'd made up his mind to go back to Mizda? That he'd told his wife to pack their belongings, and that there was nothing left to do but fold his tent, put it on his camel's back, then leave this land of jerboas as fast as he could?

The *nabk* on the *nabk* trees hadn't ripened yet, but, while out searching for barley, he'd gathered some that were almost ripe and would help them survive their return journey. There was a chance, too, they might come across some terebinth trees that still had some of their sweet green fruits; or else they could eat any herbs they found on the way. He wasn't in the same situation as the large families with their many sons and daughters. Whatever bare nourishment could be found would be enough for his wife and himself. In any case, whether they found food or not, nothing was going to stop him going back to his home in Mizda. Suddenly he heard the sheikh's voice, and felt his hand patting him on the shoulder.

'Cheer up, Abdel Aaly,' the sheikh said. 'God's delivered us from our trial.'

Abdel Aaly smiled, but didn't believe him. The sheikh, reading his thoughts, asked him to bless the Prophet and take the tea from the Captain, then wait for a while for everything to be made clear to him. Abdel Aaly sipped the tea as quickly as he could, while Sheikh Hamed told the Captain to go to Burhan's tent, beside which the men were gathered, and tell them all to come to the sheikh's tent.

The Captain rushed off, leaving a cloud of dust in his wake. The best way to break the good news, Sheikh Hamed had decided, was to take them to see for themselves another jerboa burrow he would uncover, to show them the ears of barley. He went towards the valley, while Abdel Aaly walked alongside in bewildered silence, waiting to see the reason for this mysterious behaviour.

When all the men had arrived, Sheikh Hamed went to the first *nabk* tree he saw beneath which the jerboas had made their home. A number of jerboas ran off the moment the men's shadows fell on the branches of the trees. Sheikh Hamed stood by the tree with his scythe in his hand, while the men, standing round him, gazed at one another in wonder. The sheikh hacked away the thorny branches, and the opening of the jerboas' burrow appeared. Then he began to take the earth away from its surface, and the astonished men craned their necks to see the result, like an audience watching a magician.

Sheikh Hamed didn't disappoint them. Gradually, as he took the earth away, the grains of barley began to appear inside the jerboas' burrow. The ears were arranged as neatly as if they'd been stacked, perfectly and precisely, by a skilled human hand.

Sheikh Hamed put down his scythe, filled his hand with the ears of barley from the burrows, then, without a word, offered them to the man nearest him, his face glowing with triumph and pride – for the barley spoke more eloquently than anything he could have said. He heaped a second handful of barley, then a third, and a fourth, into the rough, stretched out hands of the spellbound men. Still he doled out the barley from the burrow, till there was nothing left there. Only then did the men realise the barley was real, and not some trick of their eyesight!

❧ FOURTEEN ❧

Jerboas take pride in living in the desert and the countryside, rather than in towns, which they never even go near. There had been a complete severance of relations between them and the rats and mice of the cities and towns, for the jerboas considered themselves superior in appearance and cleanliness alike. City mice and rats weren't just dust-coloured and ugly, they were stupid too, ending up, always, being caught in traps. On top of that they'd lost their pride, being content to lead abject lives in the dark, plague-ridden corners of cities, where they stayed till they met their deaths, through poison, or through being caught in traps, or torn to pieces by cats.

The reason for their fate was that they'd never, from the beginning, tried to establish peaceful relations with humans, who hated them as a result. And so they'd brought endless misery on themselves. The jerboas of the countryside and deserts had no wish to take sides in this conflict, not wanting to live in constant fear of death at the hands of humans. If jerboas competed with humans in reaping harvests – well, didn't humans compete with one another in matters of the kind? And even then jerboas didn't invade humans' houses, or steal their food, or infect them with plagues. This way of life had delivered them from any harm from humans.

The jerboas had chosen to live in wide, open spaces, for they loved their freedom, and they were clean in their habits. They were keen, too, to live at peace with their neighbours, whether human, animal or insect. The jerboas were active creatures, and all of them, male or female, young or old, worked diligently at the hardest tasks, like reaping the harvest, or digging large burrows, which were their underground homes and had many entrances. They also dug big storerooms under the ground, with the aim that every member of the community should live a decent, healthy life in the open air. Recreation played an important role in these creatures' lives, and it was rare to find them sick or sad. They invariably worked together; and the sole desire of the jerboas of Jandouba, when the people of Mizda came to pitch their tents, was to continue the good relations they'd always enjoyed with humans, and not to have these humans treat them, mistakenly, as they treated the city mice and rats.

Most of the jerboas, then, were content with their lives in these steppes, and had no wish to live anywhere else – especially after they'd united with the many branches of their species from which they'd been split off before. When the strength of their union was known, they came to hold a high status among the other creatures of the district, who recognised the jerboas' power and submitted to their authority. The abundant crops the jerboas reaped and stored helped ensure a high standard of living, and they lived a happy, contented life in consequence.

That morning, though, having witnessed a certain incident, they'd all become deeply anxious, and the older jerboas began to feel their happy state of affairs wasn't destined to continue.

The occasion of their packed assembly was one of the many weddings they held during the harvest season. The atmosphere was cheerful and noisy, and jerboas of all ages had come to play their part in the celebration by dancing and singing. The bride-groom, arm in arm with his bride, walked proudly among the guests – proudly, because he'd managed to win the prettiest, most graceful, most intelligent female jerboa. He'd loved her passionately and fought hard to win her love, in the face of many rivals. The first of these was her neighbour, the second a relative of hers, the third her brother's friend. The fourth was one of her colleagues. The victorious jerboa came, himself, from a family of lower social status than his bride, for she was from the original inhabitants of Jandouba, whereas his family had only recently come to settle there. Although a fraternal spirit existed among the jerboas, the higher class to which the bride belonged was inclined to look down on newcomers to the area.

The bride's father had objected to the marriage, having hoped to persuade her to marry her relative. Yet, in the face of every obstacle, the love born at first sight had eventually triumphed. This love gave the bride strength to speak up for herself and tell her father, who opposed the marriage more than her mother did, that it was her life and her future, and that he should let her choose her own husband. This reasoning had finally won him over, and she thus had every right to rejoice at marrying her bridegroom.

To the strains of music, the bridegroom led his bride among the dancers. They danced cheek to cheek, and he found himself powerless to resist the charm of her wide, bright eyes and long black lashes.

Ever since that morning there'd been news of how the men of the camp had destroyed some of the jerboas' homes. The whole jerboa community had been deeply shocked, and they wondered if the matter had been accidental or if it had come about by design, part of a policy the humans would go on pursuing.

The older jerboas used the wedding as a chance to meet and discuss the matter, choosing a place far away from the noisy rejoicing of the celebration and dancing, so as to converse about the incident and the evil it augured.

Already, since their arrival in Jandouba, the newcomers had destroyed the cities of the ants, who were the jerboas' closest friends. Those ants that had survived had been forced to leave their land and homes. The jerboas had been much upset by this, on account of the many close bonds existing between them and the ants. Both were rich in resources, both well organised, united and diligent. Both lived near the barley fields so as to eat the grain, and built their storerooms and homes underground to ensure their survival through the various seasons. For this reason the jerboa community had been more distressed than when beetles, or grasshoppers, or scorpions, or lizards, or other desert creatures had abandoned their homes. Most of these had fled because they'd felt there was no future for them anyway, there in the midst of humans.

'There's no future for us either,' said a jerboa who'd just recently come to Jandouba, 'with all these humans here.'

An older jerboa, one of the original inhabitants of the place, grew furious on hearing this opinion from one he felt had no roots in the land.

'And where,' he asked, 'do you suggest we go?'

'Anywhere where we'll be safe,' the first jerboa replied.

'And what about our children's food, which we spent so much time and trouble gathering and storing up safely? Who are we going to leave that for?'

They might, the old jerboa pointed out, be able to dig new homes in another land. But where would they find another harvest to reap and so fill their storerooms? And just how were they going to move the ears of barley, which had taken so long to reap, to some other place? They'd reaped those ears one by one. Were they to give all that up now, and go off and live as best they could?

The old jerboa heard another youngster say they should abandon Jandouba, that this was the only way out. The old jerboa slapped him down too, all the more since he was another newcomer, related to the one who'd first voiced the idea. He rounded on him furiously, addressing, through him, all the other weak-willed jerboas.

'The spirit of submission,' he declared, 'has spread among the younger generation. This land's ours. It belongs to us and no one else. We've dug the land with our claws, set down our roots here. These humans won't always be here. They've come today and tomorrow they'll be gone. But we'll be staying here forever.'

Besides, the old jerboa added, though the destruction of their homes was certainly a crime, the humans hadn't killed a single jerboa, nor had they ever done so in the past. When had the youngsters ever heard, from their fathers or grandfathers, of humans killing jerboas? What had happened to the ants and the other fleeing insects and creatures would never happen to them.

There were some who supported the old jerboa's argument. Others, though, were adamant they should abandon their land at once, before it was too late. They wouldn't be safe as long as these humans remained. No good would ever come of such cunning, treacherous creatures.

The old jerboa was saddened by this evidence of rift in the stable community of which jerboas were so proud. He turned to one of his supporters, who was nearly as old as he was.

'Don't you reckon,' he whispered in his comrade's ear, 'that the ant community's wiser than we are?'

'Why's that?'

'Because they've chosen a queen to lead the nation, and when she gives an order they all obey her.'

Close to this serious and solemn meeting, a group of happy jerboas danced and sang and clapped their hands, eager to seize the chance to be joyful. They cared nothing about what the future might hold.

❧ FIFTEEN ☙

The tender, pale green ears of barley, which had been kissed by the sun's heat, had a special taste, one that could only be enjoyed after they'd been roasted, then rubbed to separate the inner grains from the chaff. The grains took on a darker green when roasted, and the resulting dish was called *makhdour*. It was specially linked to the harvest season, when people ate nothing else. The dish didn't need any addition, like oil, or tea, or milk, which were needed when barley was eaten in other ways.

The children who'd never known a harvest season before, or had been too young to remember the taste, loved it. As for the older members of the camp, the taste of *makhdour* called back the days of plenty, when there'd been enough food for everyone. They remembered harvest seasons past, and did not worry that that *makhdour*, and *makhdour* alone, would be their breakfast and dinner and supper for many days to come.

Their absorption in the work of digging out the jerboas' burrows, and their eagerness to eat the roasted barley, made them forget their first outburst of joy at the discovery of the barley ears. The first day passed without any celebration, but by the next, when everyone had had enough to eat, the zest for digging began to wane. There were, they all believed, countless burrows filled with the crop. A few days would never be enough to collect it all – it would take several weeks to finish the job.

It was then the people realised they hadn't celebrated this change in their fortune, which had delivered them from the threat of starvation. At sunset they went back to their tents and roasted more ears of barley; and then all at once the celebration started without any prior arrangement. Masoud went to fetch his musical instrument. Masoud was called Al Roumany by everyone in Mizda, though that wasn't his family's name; he was dark-skinned and most definitely not descended from the Romans. This instrument had stayed in his tent for the past four days, not because he didn't want to play it, or because there was anything wrong with it, but because of the shock that had struck everyone when they found there was no barley. He'd thought of the feelings of the people, who'd been in no mood to listen to his music.

Now, Al Roumany realised, there was nothing to stop him playing the instrument he'd loved since he was a child. By the age of ten he'd become the most skilled player of the bagpipes in Mizda. He took his pipes now, went to stand by a series of sand dunes with a group of boys clustered round him, and started to blow, moving his fingers over the holes. The small skin fixed to the pipes, tucked under his armpit, became filled with air, swelling ever more as his breath grew stronger.

He sang as he played, making the tune now low, now loud, happy or sad, quick or slow. After a few minutes all the men and women and children of the camp were clustered round him and joining in his song. As at traditional weddings, the men sat on the sand to one side, in a half circle, while the women and children sat in a half circle opposite, with Al Roumany sitting in the middle. Young men of his age accompanied him, beating bowls with sticks to keep the time. As for the women, they vied with one another in giving out the longest and loudest ululations, a sense of joy enveloping them all.

Amer ben Sheeha chose to sit at the far end of the men's half circle, and Zenab sat opposite him at the end of the women's. They were quite close to one another, and could look at each other and talk together without attracting any attention in the din of the celebration.

As if it were a real wedding, Aunt Maryouma, who regarded herself as the mother of them all, brought kerosene lamps from her own tent and a few others, and asked some of the girls to take part in the celebration. She spread a mat for them in front of the women's half circle, then told them to take off the veils covering their hair, to let their hair down, then shake it in time to the music and the beats of the sticks on the bowls.

Fatima, Abdel Aaly's wife, sprayed some orange blossom water on the girls' hair, and its scent added a touch of glamour to the celebration. The singers and those making the music became ever more enthusiastic, and Aunt Maryouma spurred Zenab on to join in the festivity, urging her to take off the veil covering her lovely long, black hair. Zenab, though, told her she must ask her mother's permission first, for she'd been forbidden to join the other girls in loosening her hair and shaking it during celebrations.

With that Aunt Maryouma went straight up to Hajja Khadija and told her there was nothing wrong with what the girls were doing. These were, she said, the customs and traditions of their fathers and mothers, whenever there was a joyful occasion like a wedding or a feast. She added that interfering with such customs and traditions, which had been handed down through the generations, would bring bad luck.

'The people of the camp,' she went on, 'are all one family, and they've come together to celebrate the bounty God has blessed us with. Your daughter will be sitting with the girls, and there's a good distance between them and the men. There's nothing to worry about. Why stop your daughter joining in? Any more than you should stop yourself watching it and enjoying it!'

Aunt Maryouma wouldn't give up till she'd finally persuaded Hajja Khadija to go and watch the celebrations with her. As for

Zenab, she was overjoyed at the chance to take part. She put on her silver rings and bracelets and sat in the midst of the girls, as lovely as a bride on her wedding night. Then she knelt down on the mat and swayed her head and hands in time to the music. Her hair flowed, now right, now left, in harmony with her hands shining with the rings and bracelets.

Amer ben Sheeha, entranced by Zenab's grace as she moved in time with the music, went to where Al Roumany and his comrades were sitting and sang a fresh song, while the rest of the people joined in, clapping their hands to the music.

Still, they meant to gather the barley crop from the jerboas' burrows underground. And, on the third day, it became vital to organise matters, so as to avoid what had happened during the first two days. Then, they'd run through the fields in all directions, digging, haphazardly, under every *nabk* tree or thorny bush where the jerboas had dug their burrows, hacking these down with scythes and even hatchets, with no regard to the amount of barley that might be wasted or spoiled. Their one thought had been to collect as much barley as they could, as quickly as they could – then roast it and eat it as soon as they could.

Some of the men, rather than wait till they returned to their tents, had lit fires close to the fields to roast the barley there and then, not even bothering to keep normal meal times. They'd missed too many meals in the past, and now they were going to make up for it, especially as the food was there in such abundance!

Now, though, they all agreed these wasteful ways must stop. They must organise the gathering of the barley, then how it should be consumed. Only a very small amount should be eaten now. The rest should be stored, to last them right through the year till the next harvest came round. They ought to be at least as wise as ants and jerboas!

Sheikh Hamed and his men also agreed that they should deal very cautiously with any strangers they encountered, making no mention of the buried barley. They should take every precaution in their camp, and when they went to water their animals at the well, and when they went to buy anything from Abu Zayyan. Their secret must remain a secret. No one outside the camp must ever know; for, if other hungry people did come to hear of it, these people would come and take the blessing God had granted to them alone.

Every man had warned his family of this, first the children, then the old people. The need to keep the secret of the treasure they'd found had the effect of drawing them all closer together. They'd made this journey together, from one village, and were living together in this camp. They'd all been subjected to the same ordeal. Now they must all keep the secret hidden in their hearts, safe from any stranger.

The next morning they were put to their first test, when a flock of sheep with its shepherd came from behind the rows of sand dunes and moved on towards the valley. This shepherd, they knew, was liable to discover their secret, for he'd pass close by the camp and his sheep would graze in the fields between the *nabk* trees and the stalks of the harvest, where the men and women of the camp were digging for the ears of barley. If the shepherd saw them, he'd know everything and spread the news of it east and west through the land.

Whispers sped from one person to the next, that they should stop digging, stop collecting ears of barley, if so much as the shadow of a stranger appeared. Even the camp dogs seemed to share their masters' notions, barking ferociously and chasing off the sheep, till finally the shepherd drove his sheep away from the place.

Then there was the question of what to do with the ears of barley they'd collected. They couldn't store them in barns as they'd done in previous harvest seasons, for that would be to proclaim their secret to the world and invite others to come and take the barley the jerboas had hidden. There was only one way. Each must make room for the barley in a corner of his tent, and they must go on piling it up there till they'd finished digging out the burrows and collected everything. These were vital precautions if newcomers and passers-by weren't to discover their secret.

Then, they decided, after they'd collected all the barley, they'd take it to threshing floors, where they'd thresh and winnow it with the help of the wind, before finally packing it in sacks and bags.

Their consciences were eased by the fact that the fields' owners had been so liberally compensated for their ravaged crops by the mandatory government. This good news, which Abdel Aaly had passed on to them, meant the owners wouldn't harry them even if they learned the truth of the situation. The people of Mizda had a far better right to the barley than the jerboas did!

Now, after the haphazard digging and piecemeal gathering of the past two days, Haj Abu Hamama was put in charge of organising the work. His military experience, as a non-commissioned officer in the army of resistance, was a great asset in this 'assault' on the jerboas' homes.

Haj Abu Hamama divided the fields into squares, as they always did when harvesting, then assigned a particular group of people to each part, telling them how to move from one part to the next when they'd finished gathering the ears of barley. Nor did he simply plan and organise the work. He supervised it personally, making sure all the burrows had been dug and every ear of barley collected. He also told them to count the number of burrows before they started digging. They'd learned, from their mistakes of the past two days, how easy it was to hide the openings to some burrows beneath heaps of earth, by digging other burrows haphazardly.

Every family in the camp had brought the equipment needed to reap the harvest, such as scythes, two-eared baskets and ropes. They should, they agreed, begin the digging and gathering straight after dawn prayers, working on, as they always did when reaping, through the early morning. Then they'd rest during the midday heat, in their tents or under the tamarisk and *batm* trees, before resuming once more following afternoon prayers and working through till sunset. Haj Abu Hamama's organisation gave everyone the equal chance to work and take the fruits of their work. No one would take anyone else's share, and people who were lazy would have only themselves to blame.

Although Sheikh Hamed Abu Leila was the head man of Mizda,

and so the chief of the Jandouba camp, he disliked having to organise or to issue orders. He was in the habit of leaving such things to Haj Abu Hamama, who was his half brother, and the latter now sometimes went on his horse to inspect the work in the fields. He'd volunteered to do this and spent half his time at the task. He wasn't worried about missing out on his share of the barley, for he had a large family, and they made up for the time he spent overseeing and making sure all was well.

He gave directions that families shouldn't allow children younger than ten to dig the burrows, since he was afraid they'd spoil the ears of barley. But he let them be used to carry the barley to their tents. He also let the men and women work together, on condition the women covered their faces with their veils.

The unprecedented situation obliged him to permit this licence. Because the spiny bushes covering the burrows made it difficult to reach the bottom where the ears of barley were stored, the women had to ask for the men's help in removing the branches and thorns. Hajja Khadija wasn't upset when Amer ben Sheeha rushed to aid her daughter Zenab, clearing, with one stroke of his hatchet, the thorns that had covered the opening. Without his help Zenab could never have collected the barley beneath.

Hajja Khadija wanted to see Zenab and Amer ben Sheeha married. Amer had asked for Zenab's hand three years before, but her father was determined his daughter's wedding shouldn't be a poor occasion – he wanted to slaughter sheep and provide everyone in Mizda with the finest food at the ceremony. As for Amer, who'd inherited a small grocer's shop, his position was no better than Sheikh Hamed's. For all his diligence and his popularity with the people of Mizda, his trade had slumped because of the drought. His shop was empty like all the others in the village. There were no goods and no customers.

Hajja Khadija was worried about her daughter, who was still unmarried and getting older with every year. But there was no will except God's will, and He'd opened the door of bounty for them. This, she hoped, meant a new time of weddings and rejoicing, and that she might soon, God willing, see her daughter in her bridal gown.

The voices of the men rang out as they sang the well-known harvest song:

'In Your Name, oh God, we come to reap the crop,
And Your gracious Prophet we bless indeed.
Oh, may You most divinely bless
These plants of bounty in our hands!'

✺ SIXTEEN ✺

Haj Abu Hamama's supervision of the work didn't stop him using his scythe or hatchet, along with everyone else in the camp, to dig the burrows where the ears of barley were stored – though only when he was sure everything was going to plan. This he did even though he was nearly seventy years old.

If Sheikh Hamed, his half brother on his mother's side, had left the overseeing to him, it was because he was sure Haj Abu Hamama would enforce better discipline than he could himself. Haj Abu Hamama had been a soldier in Suliyman Al Barouny's army and fought in one of the most important battles against the Italians here on this very land – the Battle of Jandouba. He had an especially close relation to this earth, drenched with the blood of so many of his comrades.

Sheikh Hamed, too, often joined in the work, clearing the thorns from the trees and bushes, accompanying the village men in their battle against the jerboas, to gather the ears of barley from their granaries. The two old men would work during the mornings, then leave the fields and sit in the shade of a great *batm* tree that grew on the side of the valley, far from the tents of the camp. They talked of the recent happenings, and about the old days, then usually played a game of draughts, which the old men of Mizda greatly enjoyed.

That morning Haj Abu Hamama had made a quick tour of inspection, then left his horse to eat the dry stalks and straw with the camels and other beasts. He would, he decided, make the most of the rest of the morning by adding to the barley his family were gathering, before the rays of the sun began pouring down their fire. Suddenly he saw Sheikh Hamed, with his scythe and basket, walking towards the *nabk* tree in the area he'd marked out for him. When Haj Abu Hamama reached him, Sheikh Hamed was already digging at the roots of the tree. Then he saw one of the men come hurrying up to address Sheikh Hamed.

'If any stranger saw you working here in the field,' the man said, 'they'd think we were criminals – leaving our village chief to dig out the jerboa burrows.'

'Working's a kind of worship,' Sheikh Hamed replied, 'and God rewards and recompenses every step we take to win our daily bread. I've no wish to lose out on this world's reward, the barley, or on my better, everlasting reward in the hereafter.'

'Look,' Haj Abu Hamama broke in, 'we don't want strangers to see anybody from the camp, Sheikh Hamed or anyone else, working in the fields. And besides, these burrows full of barley are a blessing bestowed on us by God. Anyone who doesn't do his utmost to gather it in is a miserable wretch.'

The two old men went on to talk of the present situation. Who, they asked one another, would have dreamed that this harvest, which they'd come to reap as workers for wages from the owners, now belonged to them alone, with no one to share it with? By the end of the season they'd have gathered several hundredweight of barley, which would need dozens of hired camels to carry it away. In fact it might even be better to hire a truck to take it back to their homes.

This gave Haj Abu Hamama just the chance he needed to launch into his favourite topic – the Battle of Jandouba in which he'd fought. The blood of the martyrs who'd died here had, he believed, blessed the land. It was important, too, that Suliyman Al Barouny and Abdullah Al Buseify, the leaders in the battle, had been pious men and warriors in the cause of God, might they dwell in His paradise.

Haj Abu Hamama looked right and left to gain a wide view of the surrounding district, trying to recall just where the battle with the enemy had happened, and where the patriots had launched their attack. He gave a detailed description of the battle, and especially of the attacks made by a warrior on horseback, who'd covered his face and was draped in a black flag. This hero had pursued the fleeing enemy with his rifle, planting terror in their hearts. Later Haj Abu Hamama and his comrades had learned the man was none other than Muhammad Abdullah Al Buseify, who was leading the patriots in person while Suliyman Al Barouny kept overall command of the battle.

'What a difference there is,' Haj Abu Hamama concluded, 'between great men like that and us today. If there were two like them in Libya now, we wouldn't be living the way we are.'

Although Sheikh Hamed had lived through the period – actually he was only two or three years younger than Haj Abu Hamama – he'd never been near the battles. He'd been busy helping his father in his trade, transporting goods bought in the north by caravan to Fezzan, then returning laden with dates.

The two old men went on talking and digging, till at last the morning breeze gave way to waves of heat and they went to rest in the shade of the giant *batm* tree. On their way they met Suliyman, who was in a furious temper, though they could make no sense of what he was saying. They told him to wait till they'd reached the shade of the tree, then asked him why he was so angry.

Suliyman was stuttering as he tried to explain, and still they couldn't follow him. At last it came out. The ears of barley might be providing them with food, he said, but he couldn't smoke the stuff. He was used to smoking, and he couldn't go on working with all his tobacco gone. Nor, he added, had the glass of tea he'd drunk in Sheikh Hamed's guest tent been enough to clear his head, because he was used to drinking tea four times a day. He told them he couldn't wait till the end of the season to sell the barley. He needed to sell some now, so as to have the money to buy tea, sugar and tobacco. He'd buy some oil too, so he could cook his food and eat something different from the constant roasted barley grains.

Sheikh Hamed looked at his half brother.

'This is a good sign, Haj Abu Hamama,' he said. 'The problem of hunger's solved. The problem now is that we've had enough to eat!'

For all their critical situation, and the fear of their secret coming out if they threshed the barley, Suliyman's point seemed reasonable enough. All the families apart from two or three, Sheikh Hamed's being one, had exhausted their stocks of tea, sugar, oil and soap. The problem was threshing the ears of barley without arousing the suspicions of anyone passing by. There was only one solution. They'd have to thresh at night, finishing before sunrise. They'd use just the one threshing floor, and each family would put some of its barley there, in proportion to its size. It would be threshed by the camels and winnowed in the cool dawn breeze. Abdel Aaly could then take it to the market of Abu Zayyan, where he'd exchange it for tea, sugar, oil and soap, which were the goods they needed most. Anything else could be put off for the moment, except for the tobacco on which a number of men – and one woman – insisted. The woman was Aunt Maryouma, who dried the tobacco, then ground it and used it as snuff.

Suliyman was overjoyed to find Sheikh Hamed and Haj Abu Hamama agreeing to his suggestion, and he raced off to tell everyone he met of the big threshing floor they'd soon be preparing. He was so happy he hardly felt the sun's heat scorching his back. Meanwhile the two half brothers were engrossed in trying to beat one another at draughts, before sinking into their naps in the intolerable midday heat and waiting for the pleasanter sunset temperature to revive them. The cool sunset breeze would transform their discomfort to pleasurable anticipation, for it would be time for the men to gather in front of the guest tent to drink tea together.

At this hour the empty spaces around the tents became a playground for the children, while the women would go off, one by one, to Aunt Maryouma's tent to listen to her stories and poems, the last of which was a song with a lively rhythm. She'd been inspired to it by the recent events, and in it she thanked the jerboas for the service they'd done them in reaping the harvest. The song began:

> 'Greetings to you, long-legged ones,
> For we and you are neighbours now.'

While he was waiting for the men to come and sit outside the guest tent, and the Captain was lighting the fire to make the tea, Sheikh Hamed often found himself alone with his grandson. Now the old man put his arm round him and gazed up to where the stars were clustered, forming a river of light that divided the sky into two halves. He told the boy to look up at this river, then asked him what its name was, seeking to test his memory about what he'd taught him before.

The boy answered that it was the Way of the Thief of the Milk, then asked his grandfather who this thief was. Sheikh Hamed was pleased he'd managed to arouse the boy's curiosity about the secrets of the mighty universe. But how was he to answer the question? All he could think of was that some giant of space hid between the folds of eternity, ready to creep his way into the night – the night that comes to despoil the lovely, planet-strewn sky and hide it beneath endless banks of black clouds – so as to steal the divine hay made by the stars. Then, suddenly, the hours of serenity and purity take the giant by surprise. He drops the bright, shining treasures he has stolen, and this river of light is the result.

Sheikh Hamed gave a brief answer to the boy's question, then, pointing to the brightest star in the sky, asked what its name was.

'It's the Bull,' the lad answered.

'No,' his grandfather corrected him. 'It's not the Bull. It's the Goat.'

Then he explained to his grandson that the Bull wasn't a single star at all, but a group of moving stars he'd pointed out to him before. He showed him, once again, where the Bull was shining in the roof of the heavens, and told him it would descend till, before the break of dawn, it reached the line separating the earth from the sky. The Bull, he added, was always thirsty, and each night it had to reach the water on the horizon's edge before night was over, so as to stretch its neck and drink from the hot spring where the setting sun had vanished.

The old man gazed at his grandson.

'That star there,' he said, 'which looks the brightest in the sky, is the friend of desert people, because it lights their way.'

'It's the Goat,' the boy cried excitedly.

Sheikh Hamed went on explaining to the boy.

'This star,' he said, 'stays fixed in its place, while the others move around it. Because of that, it's taken as a mark to guide travellers at night. Stand here next to the tent,' he went on, 'and look up at it. If you follow it, you'll reach Mizda without fail.'

Sheikh Hamed always spoke of Mizda when talking to his grandson, because it was the only place the boy knew. He did, though, feel there was one other place of which the boy should learn, greater than Mizda and precious in God's eyes: that is, Mecca, to which Muslims turn when performing their prayers.

'If you leave this star behind your right shoulder,' he said, 'you'll be facing towards the Holy Kaaba.'

Remembering his grandson was just seven years old, he asked him which his right hand was and which his left. The boy hadn't forgotten, for his right hand was the one he used to eat with, and he showed it to his grandfather, who once more gazed up into the sky.

'Do you know,' he asked, 'the names of the four stars turning in a circle there, round the Goat? They're the daughters of Naash. And do you know why they turn round the star?'

The child, fascinated, gazed up at the sky studded with its countless stars, looking where his grandfather pointed, but said not a word.

'The Goat,' his grandfather told him, 'killed their brother, and so they've surrounded him to take their revenge on the murderer. But a fifth star, which is a good friend of the Goat's, comes to save him.

It stays close to him and turns round him, to protect him from attack by the daughters of Naash. That's the duty of a friend.'

At this point, though, the lad lost interest in what his grandfather was saying, because the other children had finished their supper and begun to play hide-and-seek in front of the tents. He didn't want to miss the game, but he knew his grandfather wouldn't keep him much longer anyway. He'd let him go as soon as the first guest came.

Haj Abu Hamama was usually the first to arrive, partly because his tent was next to the guest tent, but also because he'd been his brother's right-hand man ever since they'd left Mizda. They had the same mother, but different fathers, with Haj Abu Hamama's father coming from one of the most respected village families. It was one of his ancestors who had first founded the village of Mizda.

Haj Abu Hamama's great-grandfather had been a pious ascetic, who had left his family in Quntrara, on Mount Nafousa, and renounced all worldly pleasures. He'd wandered the plains in search of a place where no one would find him, so as to devote himself wholly to worship and prayer. After several days, in which he'd suffered the blazing heat of the sun and the scorching south winds, as well as hunger and thirst, he'd found a palm tree under whose shade he'd rested. Dates had fallen from the tree, and he'd eaten these, then quenched his thirst from a clear stream running from the rocks of the plateau.

This pious man had been well content to find such a secluded spot and had decided to follow in the footsteps of Abu Dhar Al Ghaffary, one of the Companions of the Prophet, blessings and peace upon him, who had prophesied that Abu Dhar would live alone, die alone and be raised alone on the Day of Judgement.

But in this case Almighty God willed a different fate. A dove came to perch on the branches of the palm tree beneath which he sat. Finally, used to hearing the dove's cooing day after day, the man decided he should answer; and so he recited to the dove verses from the Quran and praises in glory of Almighty God. He recited too, in her honour, verses his ancestors had made about doves.

This tame dove had wakened in his heart a longing for company and a yearning for his home, where he'd left his family and friends.

And God willed he should be blessed with a miracle that could be merited only by God's most pious and devout servants, upon whom 'there shall be no fear, nor shall they grieve'. The dove stood before him and proclaimed that there was no god but God, and Muhammad was the messenger of God; and then she was transformed into a beautiful woman. She was, she told him, a human being who'd been transformed into a dove by an old woman's black arts, and the spell had been broken after he'd recited verses from the Quran and uttered praises to God. Now, she said, she would be his lawful wife. And so he took her by the hand and recited the opening prayer from the Quran; and they became husband and wife. In time they were blessed with sons and daughters, who inherited the honour of being related to such a pious, devout servant of God.

The man's family in Quntrara had been besieged by the ruling powers, who wished to kill the religious men among them and so stifle the spirit of national resistance they were inspiring in the land. Now, learning where he was, the people of Quntrara sallied out to break the siege and evacuate the men of religion to the distant, deserted spot where their kinsman had made his home.

The good, pious man welcomed the other men of religion, and the secluded place became famous for its holiness and was named a centre of religious thought, Al Massyeda. Later this was turned to Mizda.

Over all the many years that followed, this branch of the pious man's family kept its surname; and, if ever it seemed in danger of being forgotten, they'd give this name to a child as its first name. And so it was with Abu Hamama, which means 'owner of the dove', referring to his great-grandfather and the family name. He'd inherited, too, the fame and good reputation handed down through the generations. But he hadn't inherited the village headship because he'd been engaged in the struggle against foreign occupation, leaving Mizda to fight and returning only during a cease-fire or a truce.

When the Italians learned of his patriotic activities, they confiscated his property and condemned him to death, but he fled secretly to the distant oasis of the south, where he lived under another name and married a dark-skinned woman from Fezzan. He returned to Mizda only when the war was over and the Italians had left the country.

He'd returned a great hero, but a poor one owning nothing but his camel and his horse. All his previous wealth had been confiscated, and nothing remained but the large house where his first wife lived with his children and an old maidservant, the last of a generation of slaves. This woman left a son whom she'd named after her African grandfather, Samby, and this son lived with Haj Abu Hamama, knowing no other home.

When Haj Abu Hamama reached the guest tent, he heard Sheikh Hamed talking to his grandson about the stars before the lad ran off to play, and was interested by what he'd heard.

'I wish you'd ask the stars,' he said, 'to tell us what they've got in store for us now, so we can look out for any trouble coming to meet us.'

The two men had seen many changes in their lifetimes. They'd both been wealthy and fed many people, then become poor, hardly able to feed themselves. They'd fought the Italians, and now they were fighting the jerboas.

The sight of these creatures leaping about in front of them worried Haj Abu Hamama. The number of homeless jerboas was growing daily, and they were looking for homes inside the tents.

'It's no wonder,' Haj Abu Hamama said to his brother, 'when more of their homes are being destroyed every day. It worries me to see them,' he went on, 'especially at night. I'm afraid I'll wake up one morning to find they've nibbled my leg or my arm.'

The rest of the men arrived, and they talked together about finding some solution to the problem of these jerboas, who were invading their tents, settling on the bedding and nibbling the clothes and blankets. The only way out, they decided, was to enlist the help of the jerboas' traditional foes – the cats.

❦ SEVENTEEN ☙

At the jerboas' meeting, held to decide on a course of action following the destruction of their homes, two opinions had been voiced. One section was for immediate departure, while the second recommended patience and forbearance till the danger had finally passed.

At this point a third proposal was made, by a jerboa neither from those who'd always lived in the land nor from among those who'd come to settle in Jandouba from elsewhere. He sprang from intermarriage between the two classes. The other jerboas listened attentively, and sympathetically too, for he and his family had been the first victims of the humans' attacks, and his plight was all the more distressing because he'd just started a family and had two infant jerboas. The humans' scythes and hatchets had been relentless in destroying his home, turning him and his family out with no shelter or food or honour. Even the terrified squeaks of his infants had left those cruel humans unmoved.

The others were all surprised to see this jerboa, who'd been the victim of the attack, appear before them showing no signs of the trial to which he and his family had been subjected. His head was held high, his fur was clean. He was even smiling.

'I suppose,' he said, noting the astonishment on their faces, 'you're all wondering how I've managed to get over my problems. Well, I haven't gone weeping and whining to the Committee for Relief of the Distressed, to beg for food and shelter. I've used a bit of resolution and common sense instead.'

The head of the committee in question threw the jerboa a resentful glance, ready to pitch in if he started insinuating the Committee hadn't fulfilled its duties, since its foundation, in offering its valuable services to the distressed.

'I don't mean,' the jerboa went on, 'to impugn the standing of this committee in any way, or to cast any slur on its efficiency. If I didn't resort to it, it's because my home was the first to be destroyed and the Committee hadn't been formed yet. How, then, was I to deal with the situation?'

The other jerboas strained ears and eyes, hearts and minds, to hear and see what it was he'd done. They waited breathlessly for him to go on.

'The moment our home was destroyed,' he said, 'my wife and I went to a safe place to build a new one. We chose a spot a long way from the camp, where people couldn't see it. Then, at midnight, when all the people were asleep, we made our first raid on their tents, sneaking into the places where they'd hidden the ears of barley. We carried off as much as we could, to our new home, then repeated the raids the following nights. In the end we recovered all the barley they'd taken from our old home.'

The place echoed with admiring applause for this bold jerboa, who'd shown such courage and self-respect. His course was, the other jerboas realised, the proper way out of their plight. He'd given a splendid example of resolution and leadership; they too should fight for their stolen barley and recover it. They agreed unanimously to adopt his means themselves, as a policy to be followed in the coming time.

The arrangements previously made by the Committee for Relief of the Distressed had involved finding out which families had spare rooms in their homes, in which they could receive the distressed families till new homes had been prepared for them. The Committee had been responsible, too, for providing these jerboas with food from a fund made up of donations and grants.

The situation was changed, though, in the light of their new plan, and a new committee was formed alongside the existing one, called the Committee for Development and Construction. Its duty was to make a survey of the land, with a view to selecting the safest sites for carrying out new construction projects. The jerboas decided to work hard during the day, building their homes, then raid the tents at night to recover their stolen barley.

⚜ EIGHTEEN ⚜

The night when the ears of barley were threshed was unique, quite different from any other. Men, women and children all took part in the work, so as to finish the threshing and winnowing before sunrise.

To thresh the barley as quickly and easily as possible, a suitable area of hard ground had to be found. This wasn't difficult, for most of the land, lying between the sides of the valley and the edge of the sandy part where their tents were pitched, was hard and firm.

At sunset they began preparing the ground, clearing it of pebbles and dust till it looked like the paved floor of a hall in a fine house. When the signal came that the floor was ready for the ears of barley, the people of the camp, one after another, brought their full baskets and emptied them out on the ground. Amer ben Sheeha wrote down the names, recording, by the light of a kerosene lamp, the amount brought by each family.

Very soon a small mound of barley ears appeared and the five camp camels got ready to do their work. The people waited for the full moon, which gave a brighter light than the stars, then tethered the beasts together and led them to the threshing ground, so they could crush the ears with their hooves, going round and round, again and again. The people then gathered up the ears the camels had scattered around them to produce a mixture of grain and chaff.

The people sang their customary threshing songs, to urge the camels on to work quickly and well. When they were sure all the ears of barley had been well threshed, they herded the camels away and separated the grain from the chaff by winnowing it with the help of the night breeze. Any remaining chaff was picked off by nimble hands. Then they measured out the barley, packed it into four sacks and tied them tightly ready to be sold or bartered for the goods they needed from the market of Abu Zayyan. Nor did Sheikh

Hamed forget their duty to God, putting aside two full measures of barley in a small bag for distribution to the poor people standing outside the mosque.

When the night of threshing was over, Abdel Aaly loaded the sacks on his camel, sat down himself on the sacks and headed for the market of Abu Zayyan, amid a clamour of voices urging him to bring different goods from the ones he'd agreed on with Sheikh Hamed. The women wanted combs and mirrors, while the children were demanding chewing gum and sweets. As for the older women, they were asking him to bring them benzoin and asafetida. But he waved the demands aside, telling them he couldn't buy all these items with the barley he had – luxuries like that would need more barley and more journeys. He poked his camel in the flanks, and it moved off so quickly no one could keep up with him.

Haj Abu Hamama chose not to burden him with the task of bringing back a cat. These, he knew, weren't sold in the Abu Zayyan shops, and Abdel Aaly had quite enough to do in any case, selling the barley and buying the goods, without trying to catch cats. For two or three days more, then, the jerboas would be safe from their traditional enemies, until Haj Abu Hamama himself went to Abu Zayyan, where certain families would help him catch a cat, or several for that matter. He would, he decided, pick out some fierce ones, which would solve their problems with the jerboas.

The next day, though, just before sunset, something happened that drove all thoughts of cats from Haj Abu Hamama's mind. There, on the horizon, a small truck appeared, moving towards the plateau, then circling it, disappearing behind it for a while, before once more becoming clearly visible to the people of the camp.

The noise of the truck's engine and passengers came ever nearer. The passengers were sitting on their belongings, clapping their hands and singing as though they were on a picnic. The truck came to a halt at the foot of the plateau, just opposite the tents of the camp on the other side of the valley. It couldn't go any further, over the rocky, uneven ground and the deep furrows left by earlier floods.

A number of people called out from the midst of the fields, to alert their comrades to what was happening at the foot of the plateau. They all stopped digging and straightened their stooped backs, standing upright to see this thing that had suddenly appeared there in front of them. What would happen next?

The moment the truck stopped, the passengers jumped off and started exploring the place, chattering away to one another. It seemed to meet with their approval, for they immediately started unloading their belongings; then, when everything was off, the driver started the engine and drove back and forth for a while, ready to go back the same way he'd come. The newcomers waved goodbye to him, and off he drove, leaving a trail of black fumes behind him.

Before anyone from the camp had the chance to remark on what had happened, they saw one of the former passengers come leaping towards them in his long, flowing *jilbab*. The dogs started running towards him, barking fiercely, but Haj Abu Hamama, who was standing with a group of men, turned on them and ordered them to be quiet, then went to meet the newcomer half way. The newcomer greeted them, saying: 'Peace be on the people of this camp.'

The man's accent showed he was from the east of the country – something Haj Abu Hamama had already concluded from the way he and his companions were dressed.

'Peace be on you,' he replied.

The man offered his hand to shake.

'I'm your brother Yunus,' he said, 'from the Jibreel family.' He pointed to the place where he'd left his companions, then added: 'We're all one family, and we've come from Bir Hakeem. We came to reap the harvest, but now it seems these long-legged jerboas have eaten the crop and become fat as sheep.'

Yanus laughed as he spoke, but the men's faces remained sullen. They didn't respond to what he'd said, and they didn't welcome him.

'As you can see,' Haj Abu Hamama muttered, looking around him, 'those fields there aren't good for anything except grazing our

82

camels.' He hoped these people from beyond the distant horizon, who owned neither camel nor horse but rode in trucks, would realise there was no point in staying.

'I've come,' the man said suddenly, 'to ask permission to pitch our own tents and settle near your camp.'

The men all turned pale, and Haj Abu Hamama himself was hard put to keep a normal expression. Why were they looking for permission to settle here in this district? Why should they want to stay, since the crop they'd come to reap no longer existed? The men gazed silently at one another, while the newcomer proceeded to answer their unspoken question.

'We know,' the man said, 'that people in this region don't use the jerboas for meat. For our people, though, it's one of our favourite foods.' He laughed. 'The jerboas have eaten the crop,' he said. 'Now we'll eat the jerboas!'

The men gazed at one another once more, astounded by the man's words. Then one of them said, in a tone of loud disgust:

'You really mean to say you're going to eat these rats?'

At that moment a large number of jerboas appeared, then leaped off again in all directions.

'We don't call the jerboas rats,' Yunus answered. 'We don't even think of them as rats.' He burst out laughing. 'It doesn't matter anyway,' he went on. 'We'd eat them even if they were rats!'

The newcomer told the men how he and his people had come from the eastern oases, where there was no way of finding food. They'd finished up all the desert herbs, and even eaten lizards and drunk the water they'd used to boil ants.

Haj Abu Hamama told the man he and his people had the right to pitch their tents wherever they liked. The land belonged to God, and they themselves were newcomers in the place. All human beings, in any case, were guests in this transitory world.

The moment the newcomer heard he had the right to pitch his tents on the land, he ran straight off, almost tripping over his long *jilbab* in his haste to get back to his family, who could hardly wait to feast on the meat of the jerboas.

✺ NINETEEN ✺

As the sun set, three grey tents were pitched at the foot of the plateau. They were different from the tents in the camp of the Mizda people, which were deep black and made from goat hair. Although dusk was falling, the people of Mizda saw at once, to their profound curiosity, that the number of females was double the number of males: there were eight women and only four men. Even more astonishing was the way the women mixed with the men without veiling their faces or wearing scarves over their heads. Strings of glass shone in their hair, around their necks and on their bosoms. Such a state of affairs could exist only if the men were the women's brothers. Otherwise they'd be acting against every tradition and custom of decency and morality by which the people of Mizda abided, ordained as these were by the faith of Islam.

Abdel Aaly had returned from the market with tea, sugar and oil. Each family took its share, then they busied themselves preparing a cooked supper, frying the barley in oil after eating it roasted for so many days. But their pleasure in this tasty food had been ruined by the dark shadow of the family of Jibreel.

This family, which had arrived like an unheralded disaster, was the sole topic of discussion as the men met in front of the guest tent. How, they asked one another, should they treat these people? It was the custom of the desert, one man said, to send newcomers some food on their first night.

Sheikh Hamed quickly silenced him. They were, he said, living in unusually difficult times. Nobody in the desert, or in the towns for that matter, had any food left over to give to strangers, whether they lived near them or far off. They shouldn't, the sheikh went on solemnly, mix with the newcomers or forge any sort of relations with them.

'The best thing,' he concluded, 'is to leave them to their own devices. That way they'll leave us alone too.'

The people of the camp were in agreement with their chief. Abdel Aaly, though, asked:

'Do you really think, Sheikh Hamed, that they *will* leave us alone? I'll be surprised if they do.'

He raised his head and gazed, frowning, towards the fields, which were quite dark now.

'Just look there, Sheikh Hamed,' he went on, 'and you'll see the truth of what I said.'

Even before he'd finished speaking, the dogs had all started barking and running towards the seven figures approaching the camp. Samby darted out from where he'd been sitting and ran towards the newcomers too, keeping the dogs from them and leading them to the guest tent, where they greeted the men.

'Peace be on you,' the newcomers said. 'We've come to offer our greetings to the people of the camp.'

'Peace be on you,' the men replied.

Three men, among them Yunus, who'd come to the camp before, stretched out their hands to the men sitting in front of the tent. The men of the camp stood up and shook hands, while the group of four women stood a few metres off from the guest tent. Yunus pointed to them.

'These maidens,' he said, 'have come to greet yours.'

The word 'maiden', Sheikh Hamed knew, was used by the eastern bedouins for all females, regardless of their age. He looked at the women, and, for all the darkness concealing their features, was indignant to see their faces were unveiled, and that they were making no attempt to hide them as the women of Mizda always did.

Sheikh Hamed beckoned to Samby, indicating that he should conduct the women to Aunt Maryouma's tent. As they followed the black-skinned lad, the strange tinkling of the iron and copper bracelets and anklets on their arms and legs, and the amber necklaces on their bosoms, shattered the silence of the night on the Jandouba plains.

The Captain brought an extra mat for the guests, and there they sat, separated from the rest of the men by an uncovered patch of dusty ground. They looked different from the men of Mizda, who wore red or white skullcaps. These men covered their skullcaps with a turban folded many times over their heads. The edge of the turban dangled on their chests, and this end they used when they needed to cover their faces during sandstorms.

Yunus introduced the two men who'd come with him: his brother Idris and his cousin Matouq. Sheikh Hamed repeated their names to the men.

'Although there are so many of us,' he told the newcomers, 'you can regard us as one large family too.'

'Only a few from our family have made the trip,' Yunus said. 'A lot of them have stayed on in Bir Hakeem. We didn't want to risk bringing any children because of the dangers of the journey.'

'Adults can bear hardship,' Sheikh Hamed agreed, 'but it's dreadful to see children suffer.'

'The drought's destroyed everything in Bir Hakeem,' Yunus went on. 'Our cattle died of thirst and hunger, and we would have died too but for the locusts that swept over our land. They were a blessing sent by God. They came in endless swarms, so thick they hid the sun from Bir Hakeem for a whole day almost. When night fell, they settled and slept on the plain, and we waited for the dawn light to guide us to them. There they were, pounds and pounds of locusts, sleeping under the curve of the horizon. It looked as though God's divine power had painted the rocks and lowlands with gold. Seeing it as a blessing from heaven, as I said, we gathered the locusts, then packed them in sacks and bags the way we would have done with wheat and barley. We took them to our homes, boiled or roasted them, then ate them. They staved off hunger for days on end. Then, when our food had almost run out, we came to Jandouba to reap the barley, leaving the rest of the locusts for our children and the old people who stayed there with them.'

'You came here,' one of the men said, 'only to find the land in the west more barren than back in the east.'

'We were told,' Yunus said, 'that the barley fields in Jandouba had no one to reap them.'

'Well, as you can see, they've been reaped right through. You can't beat jerboas for that.'

'It's all very strange. The sands told us we'd find plenty of barley in Jandouba. When Rabiha reads the sands, she never makes a mistake.'

'God's compensated us with the jerboas,' laughed Idris, Yunus's brother. 'They're a lot better than barley.'

He looked at Sheikh Hamed.

'We've come to take our revenge on the jerboas,' he went on. 'We set some traps for them before we pitched our tents. By the time morning comes, we'll have caught enough for a mighty feast.'

None of the men found these visitors welcome, and the mention of feasts with jerboa meat filled them with disgust, making them resent the newcomers still more.

Next Yunus began, without the smallest show of embarrassment, to talk about the women in his family. He started with Rabiha, who could tell people's fortunes, then he named the other women one after the other: their names were Qamara, Zuhra, Tibra, Fijra and Zenab. He spoke of them as if talking about the men in his family, not the women. These women who'd come with them now, he went on, were their wives, apart from the fourth, who was Matouq's sister. The other women and his cousin hadn't come to visit them because they were clearing the land outside their tents, ready for their stay.

'Is Bir Hakeem far from here?' Suliyman asked. As always, he shot out the question like a bullet from a gun to overcome his stammer.

'If we hadn't come by truck,' came the answer, 'the journey would have taken three months.'

Suliyman silently cursed the truck for bringing these people here in a couple of days instead. But for that truck, they wouldn't have been bothered by them. He wondered, too, how they could have come so far to hunt jerboas. He looked Yunus in the eye, then abruptly shot out a second question.

'Don't you have any rats in Bir Hakeem?' he asked.

Suliyman pretended, deliberately, to have forgotten these people didn't call the jerboas 'rats'. He wanted to insult them by showing his disgust at what they ate. But Yunus wasn't put out. He smiled even, as though proud of eating these animals.

'The jerboas are wild creatures,' he said, 'and their meat's as tasty as rabbit's meat. That's why people eat them. We went on eating them, through the years of drought, till there weren't any left. You can search through the valleys of Bir Hakeem for a whole day now, and you won't find a single one. Here in Jandouba, though, there are huge numbers of them. According to my wife Tibra, this is the finest hunting ground for jerboas in all the world. She's right too. We're so happy we could fly through the air with joy.'

Suliyman wished they'd fly right off, and he waited longingly for a miracle that would make them vanish into thin air. Then, when he saw it wasn't going to happen, that the people were still sitting there in front of them, he wished for something more reasonable: that they'd stop talking about eating rats and change the subject to something less sickening.

Haj Abu Hamama, who'd concealed his resentment during the meeting, found an outlet for his feelings without actually insulting the guests.

'Strange, isn't it,' he said, 'the way some people travel to your land in the eastern desert in search of food – and then we meet you here, after you've left your homes to look for food among us? Wouldn't it have been better for the people of Bir Hakeem to stay at home? Things are just the same, after all, east or west.'

He felt some relief, now he'd given these people an idea of how he felt about them and how he resented their presence. The men of the camp all laughed at the ironic state of affairs he'd pointed out. Yunus waited till the laughter died down, then said:

'Do you know, Haj Abu Hamama, why people from these lands go to the eastern desert? They go to work in the minefields, to defuse the mines there. As you know, the eastern lands are filled with mines, thousands of them, laid by the Germans and the Italians and the British.'

'And don't you have more right than anyone,' Suliyman asked him, 'to make a profit from the mines in your own country?'

He only asked the question out of the hatred he felt for these unwanted guests. Surely they deserved to work in the minefields if anyone did!

'We all worked there,' Yunus told him. 'In fact we were the first people to go in. We've had more experience than anyone in defusing them.'

The men pricked up their ears. If he'd actually been in a minefield, then that raised his standing in their eyes.

'All the men of our tribe,' Yunus went on, 'were hired for the work. It paid very well. Then fifty of our men were killed in an explosion in one of the fields. After that no one in our family dared go anywhere near those cursed places.'

He paused, then went on.

'Our people went off in all different directions, looking for food. They had to eat anything that moved on the earth or flew in the sky. They ate frogs, grasshoppers, lizards, even dogs and donkeys.'

Sheikh Hamed showed his sympathy for their suffering, in a plight to which everyone, everywhere, had been subjected. His followers shouldn't, he felt, express their disgust at the thought of these people eating jerboas, insects and dogs. That was better, after all, than people attacking, robbing or killing one another. He remembered how, in previous times of drought, when there was no authority and no security, people had become cannibals, eating human flesh.

He said, in a gentler, more sympathetic tone: 'We always supposed people in the east were luckier than us, especially during drought, because drought never strikes Jabal Al Akhdar.'

'The crops growing there,' Yunus answered, 'are only enough for a hundred families, who come each year to help with the harvest – on top, that is, of the hundred families who live there and own the land. Just imagine what it was like when twenty or thirty thousand families came to the mountains from the desert, all looking for food. Hunger's worse there than anywhere else, because of all those thousands of people.'

'Times are hard everywhere,' Sheikh Hamed said.

He only offered his guests tea that evening, for, if he'd offered them cooked barley too, this would certainly have aroused their suspicions – they'd wonder where it had come from. He'd taken care to send a messenger to Aunt Maryouma, to warn her to say nothing of the barley to her woman visitors, and to offer them no cooked barley. This was before he'd sent Samby to conduct the women there. These vital precautions would put off the newcomers' discovery of their secret, though they were sure to find out sooner or later.

How, Sheikh Hamed thought, could they not find out about the burrows filled with ears of barley? Then they'd join in the digging and gather plenty of the grain, just as the sands had predicted – for no one could deny the truth of prophesy by the sands. He just didn't want to give away any information about it. The longer they took to find out, the better for the people of his camp.

The visitors sipped the third round of tea, then rose and asked permission to leave. They exchanged farewells with the men. 'Good night,' they said. Not a man in the camp, though, believed anything good would come from these people!

Before Samby could hurry to Aunt Maryouma's tent, to tell the women their husbands were leaving, the men called out to their wives by name, with enough noise to shatter the night silence.

'Come on, Zenab! Come on, Tibra! Come along, Zuhra!'

The glass bracelets and necklaces tinkled louder than ever as the women came dashing up to their husbands. As the procession of visitors disappeared into the darkness, Haj Abu Hamama whispered in Sheikh Hamed's ear.

'I'm the only one who's got anything out of these people coming here. They've saved me the trouble and bother of fetching cats from Abu Zayyan!'

☙ TWENTY ☙

Burhan the scholar had erected a shade in front of his tent, for people to pray communally, protected from the heat of the sun. He'd driven in a number of tent poles, in a circle, then made a roof from tree branches, covering the branches and leaves with pieces of straw mat and old rug to stop the sun's rays filtering in. He'd tied the branches and mats and rugs to the poles with strong ropes, so the structure could withstand the fierce winds. He'd built it for the worship of God, but actually no one but himself prayed in this sacred place, shaded from the noonday heat. This heat, Burhan told the people, had been created by God, as a reminder and a warning of the heat of hell awaiting those who failed to perform their prayers.

The dawn prayers, performed communally with all the men assembled, took place in the cool open air. The men hadn't prayed together in this fashion since their arrival, for they'd spent the whole day digging out the jerboas' burrows and collecting the ears of barley. At midday they'd simply rested beneath the shade of the tamarisk and *batm* trees, before resuming their labours, then finally returning, quite exhausted, at sunset. They'd eaten their supper and performed the sunset and evening prayers in their own tents.

Burhan's call to dawn prayers would, Sheikh Hamed realised, be an open invitation to the newcomers to come and pray too, and give them a good excuse to come and mix with them. And since any mixing with the newcomers would harm their interests, he decided the call to prayer should cease for the moment.

Without the call, and without the men who now had no one to wake them, the pious Burhan found himself quite alone as he prayed in the sacred spot he'd prepared. He was most unhappy that the small Kingdom of God he'd erected there in the open air had, by the Divine Will, become a place of solitary prayer. But he knew he couldn't chain people and lead them to Paradise.

91

It was still early morning, and the sun had still to pour its heat down on the people's heads, when Burhan returned to his tent to put down the basket he'd used to collect his ears of barley. He changed his clothes, putting on a clean white *jilbab*, then went to the shade he'd contrived. He called this sacred spot '*Al Jawsaq*', meaning 'the pavilion'. There he seated himself, waving away the flies with one hand and holding a book in the other, its pages yellow with age. In a loud voice he read out the invocations and supplications, though he recited them more from memory than actually reading them. He'd been reading from this book for most of his life, and he knew it by heart now. Every so often he looked around him, then, seeing no one was approaching, returned to his reading:

'When You intend a thing, Your command is "Be" and it is. So glory to You in Whose Hands is the dominion of all things. You give power to whom You please and strip off power from whom You please. You endue with honour whom You please and humiliate whom You please. In Your Hand is all Good and You have Power over all things. You cause the Night to gain on the Day and you cause the Day to gain on the Night. You bring the living out of the dead and the dead out of the living and You give sustenance to whom You please without measure. Have Mercy on us, for You are the Most Merciful of the Merciful.'

Burhan had from the start divided his day into two parts. The first was during the early morning, which, having first performed the dawn prayers, he spent digging the jerboa burrows and collecting the ears of barley. He worked in the fields till some time before noon, then went to his pavilion, where, twice a week, he taught the boys of the camp to recite verses from the Quran. The pavilion was his clinic, too, where he received cases needing spiritual treatment. He wrote charms and amulets for these patients, and prepared concoctions of herbs and certain plants, along with reading spells, all in return for a small amount of barley.

Burhan had written amulets and charms in Mizda, but without any great success, for the village had believed in the spiritual powers of Misbah, another holy man, who'd earned an excellent reputation from thirty years of teaching the Quran to the village children and writing charms and amulets for men and women.

It hadn't been easy for someone like Burhan to compete with Misbah. He'd returned to Mizda after nine years away, spent as a labourer and as a guard at the granaries on the estate of the Countess in the suburbs of Tripoli. He'd been hard put to to earn his living, as he sat in the roofed entrance of his home, reading Jalal Al Din Al Siyouty's book *The Mercy of Medicine and Wisdom* – the very same book used by the holy man Misbah, whose home was crowded with patients.

Burhan had used the same sources as Misbah and taught the Quran to the village boys just as he'd done. Yet it had been more than a year before he could earn a living from this. The spiritual clinic he'd held in his home had seen no more than two or three visits a month. One of these rare cases had involved two women who complained they'd been divorced because they'd been unable to bear children. When he began his treatment, a small problem presented itself. How could he prove he'd cured them while they were still unmarried? Yet he needed to protect his name in his new profession by showing success! And so he'd married first one of the women, then the other five months later.

Although, in the past, Burhan had often shirked hard work, he found himself forced to work now, to feed the many mouths for which he'd become responsible. His mother, his widowed sister, her children and his two wives lived in a village that was starving, and so he had no choice but to break rocks and dig paths in the mountains for a company that was making a route for big lorries on their way to the desert.

After two years of this hard labour, during which he'd managed to visit his family only once every month or two, he'd had to confess his attempt to cure his two wives had failed – they should have had daily treatment, which was impossible while he was away. And so he'd been forced to terminate these two marriages, which he'd entered as a duty to try and prove his medical skill.

After leaving his work in the mountains, his wish was to present himself to the village community as a man of piety and a religious scholar. The money he'd put aside kept him from starving through the days when he earned nothing. This was the price of his aspiration. He'd stayed in the mosque till the chance came to make the call to prayer. One day Misbah failed to attend the Friday noon prayers because of some emergency, and Burhan seized the chance to take his place, then delivered the two Friday sermons, making the most of his eloquence in a way that appealed to the people. They congratulated him on his recital of verses from the Quran, and this would have paved the way for his new career as a religious and spiritual leader, and as a popular physician and writer of charms too – but for the drought that had struck the village.

The granaries were empty and people had nothing left to eat in their homes. Those with flocks of sheep or herds of cattle were no better off, for their beasts had died of thirst and hunger. The people of the desert had died too, of what was thought to be an epidemic of some kind, and a medical mission had been sent down from the capital to investigate the cause of the diarrhoea that was proving fatal. The mission had returned to the capital with good news: there was no plague or other infectious disease. The people had simply died of starvation after eating herbs and grasses that lacked the essential nutrients for life.

The mandatory government sent two truckloads of food, made up of grain, flour, oil and powdered milk, and distributed it to the chiefs of the tribes. Then it washed its hands of the whole affair.

The only way Burhan had managed to make a living during this time was by writing charms for the villagers. Unable to leave to take back his job as a store guard on the Countess's estate, he'd simply stayed put, waiting for his luck to change.

It was in this critical situation that Burhan saw Fatima and fell in love with her at first sight. It was as though an aura of light had pierced the darkness surrounding him. Her father had been taken ill, and he'd treated him, bringing herbs and writing charms to speed his recovery. Fatima had been by her father's side constantly during his sickness, and this had given Burhan the chance to speak to her and explain how the medication should be applied. The girl, he noticed, was always happy to see him, and, having told her of his wish to seek her hand in marriage, he realised she returned his feelings. But, though she welcomed his offer, false rumours began to spread of sinful relations between them. Burhan, it was said, was a wolf in sheep's clothing. He'd seduced the daughter of a sick man who'd trusted him and welcomed him into his house. These rumours now planted hatred for Burhan in her father's heart, and, fearing a scandal, he refused Burhan's proposal – supposing that, if he married Fatima, the rumours would be considered true – and immediately agreed to marry her instead to his relative Abdel Aaly.

Burhan believed in destiny, that a person could achieve only what God willed for him; and, since the Divine Will had ordained that Fatima be Abdel Aaly's wife and he her husband, there was nothing to be done. He decided to forget Fatima and direct his thoughts, till then occupied by love for her, in different directions – above all, to looking after his mother, his widowed sister and her children. Though troubled by the thought of staying in Mizda with no means of earning a living, he couldn't, either, bear the thought of leaving the village a second time. This was finally an unimaginable step, both for himself and for his mother, who couldn't endure another long separation from her son.

But now the journey to Jandouba, after so many months of unemployment and hardship, had given him the chance to change his surroundings, to break the meaningless flow of his life and create a new opening for himself beyond the bounds of his village.

Burhan had been asked by Sheikh Hamed to go off with him to work in the fields of Jandouba, and he'd prayed to God to guide him to the right path. When he'd decided good would result from this new place, he'd agreed to go, waiting only for his camel to return from its grazing place outside Mizda. The others had already left, but he followed on next day, taking the exact route he'd been given by Sheikh Hamed.

As he sat there, reciting verses from the Quran and reading

invocations, he heard a shriek from the direction of the fields. He stood up to find what the matter was and saw a number of people from the camp running towards a crowd already gathered there. Then he saw Samby running towards him, calling out for his help, then breathlessly begging him to go with him to the fields.

❧ TWENTY-ONE ❧

The women in Aunt Maryouma's tent loved to talk, nightly, about the origins of their families and the relations between them all. They were often surprised to learn they were related to families they'd never realised were their kinsfolk. Of course the members of the camp knew they'd all descended from the same ancestors, and so were related to one another in some way. Even so, they were avid to be told of the exact relationship now so many generations had passed.

The young women of the new generation made their inquiries of the older women, and were tireless in their questions to Aunt Maryouma, Hajja Khadija, Burhan's mother Sadina, Amer ben Sheeha's mother and Haj Abu Hamama's first wife, who came from Quntrara. They didn't of course ask his wife from Fezzan about these things, and she sat there amongst them, sure none of them could know about her southern ancestry, unrelated to any of the families of Mizda.

But Aunt Maryouma, who was an expert in descent and lineage, surprised them all by telling this woman her southern ancestry didn't mean she wasn't related to the Mizda families. In fact, generations before, her great grandfathers and theirs had been brothers, and their families had intermarried. Aunt Maryouma never ceased to astonish the women sitting in the tent, as she traced the ancestry of each and every one back to the seventh or eighth grandfather. Nor was she just an expert on lineage. She knew all about the battles their ancestors had fought, and told stories of these, along with the poems their ancestors had recited. She'd take a pinch of the snuff she made, then add some verses of her own; and, in response to the requests of her guests, the older women above all, she'd recite part of the epic of Abu Zayd Al Hilaly, which she knew by heart.

Aunt Maryouma wasn't just loved and respected by the women of the tribe. She was held in the highest esteem, too, by all the men in the camp, especially the older ones, who'd ask and take her advice on village affairs. This advice was good, and she was well known for her frank and forthright opinions, as she was for her courage and the way she'd struggled over thirty years to provide for her family, ever since all the men in it had been killed in a single battle. That had happened when the menfolk of Mizda had been fighting against the Italians. They'd advanced to meet the enemy at the mountain pass of Abu Ghara and managed to prevent them from re-occupying Mizda. But the price they'd paid was a heavy one. They'd lost many brave men, among them Aunt Maryouma's husband, father and three brothers.

The only people left now, in her home and her father's, were women and children; there wasn't a single man to provide for them, and so she'd taken responsibility for them all. She'd been a young woman then, in her thirties, and she'd turned her father's home into a workshop for spinning and weaving, with the whole family joining in. She bought wool from the market, then spun and wove it to make the finest cloaks, wraps and rugs. This work didn't stop her, either, from ploughing their land, and during the harvest season they'd all come together in reaping the crop. Year after year she worked on in this fashion, till at last the little boys had grown into men with families of their own, and the girls had become wives and mothers in their own homes.

Her eldest son had travelled with the caravans to Fezzan, where he'd settled and married. He'd asked his mother to go and live with him, but she'd refused to leave her home and village, just as she'd firmly rejected all her daughters' requests that she should live with them. In fact all the relatives she'd brought up and cared for had asked her to leave her old home, so they could take care of her in her old age and repay the kindness she'd shown them when they were young. But she'd refused to give up her independence, or allow anyone to provide for her. She was satisfied and content with her life, and with her youngest son Miloud, who, although thirty-five years old, had the mind of a six-year-old child. She was very attached, too, to her dog Marzouq, who was descended from dogs owned by generations of the family.

Aunt Maryouma was well known for her intelligence, and her dog seemed to have taken on some of it. The dogs her father had owned had been trained to go to the market and come back with the goods needed when the family wasn't there in the village, or during the harvest season. Her father had owned a shop, and he'd tied small packets of tea, sugar and almonds round the dogs' necks, or on their backs, and they'd delivered these to where they had to go, however far from the village that might be. Aunt Maryouma no longer had the shop, so she couldn't send Marzouq off in this way, but she relied on him in more important matters. He was the trusted guardian of her son Miloud, watching over him constantly to see he came to no harm. The dog would follow Miloud wherever he went, even when he answered a call of nature behind the sand dunes, and would take care of him during his mother's absence.

The women of the camp, who were from Mizda and knew no other village, were astonished by the appearance of the four eastern women who'd come with their menfolk. Their bracelets and necklaces and other trinkets were, they noticed, different from their own, and they had tattoos on their foreheads and on the backs of their hands, quite contrary to the customs in Mizda. They spoke with a strange accent, too, and their clothes showed a part of their legs. They talked about men, and compared them, without the least show of embarrassment, in a way the Mizda women would never have done. One of the women was divorced. She was the cousin of the three married women, who exchanged winks as they told their hosts the reason for the divorce, which was the result of something she and her husband had done in bed.

The women of the camp were deeply embarrassed by the things their guests said, listening in total silence and exchanging glances of wondering amazement. Indeed more than one of them came close to leaving the gathering. Hajja Khadija actually rose and told her daughter Zenab to leave the tent with her, only choosing to remain after all when she saw the women's conversation was taking a more respectable turn.

Things became clearer when the hosts mentioned that, in their village of Mizda, it wasn't the custom for men and women to mix together. The guests were astonished. This, they said, was quite different from the custom in their own community. They lived with their families, moving from place to place on the frontier between Libya and Egypt, where people had fled during the war in search of food and safety. Their menfolk had become peddlers and hawkers, carrying their goods on the backs of donkeys. They'd gone to and fro among the villages and small towns, only returning home to Bir Hakeem, in the eastern desert, when the war was over. They talked about this time with a yearning for the days of happiness and plenty.

Why, Suliyman's wife asked them, had their families left such a good life and gone back to Bir Hakeem?

'Our families were worried about the girls,' she was told. 'They'd reached the age to be married, and so the families went back to Bir Hakeem to find them husbands among their relatives.'

They'd all married happily, the woman went on, except for Zuhra, whom they referred to as 'the foolish cousin'. With that the women started exchanging winks once more. Zuhra was, they maintained, to blame for her divorce – her poor husband hadn't been able to meet her physical demands. What she'd needed was a husband who was virile.

'He could never satisfy her,' one woman said.

The women of Mizda turned their faces away in embarrassment, while Aunt Maryouma rose in a boiling rage, ready to turn these low, contemptible women out of her tent. They'd lived, as she said later, as homeless wanderers on the frontier, and because of that they had neither loyalty nor decency. Then, suddenly, the voices of the womens' menfolk had shattered the silence of the night, telling them it was time to return to their tents.

The conduct of these women would no doubt have fuelled Aunt Maryouma's comments for many days to come – with the verses on wisdom and chivalry she'd memorised from the Hilaly epic giving further ammunition for condemning their talk and behaviour – had she not been confronted, the next day, with something far more embarrassing.

As she was on her way to the fields, ready to go on digging out the jerboa burrows and collecting the ears of barley, some boys ran up to her and told her to go quickly to her son Miloud, who'd just been seized by a fit. She was horrified at the news, and astonished too. She'd woken her son a short time before and helped him wash his face, then joined him in eating breakfast and drinking tea. She'd asked him if he'd like to help her by carrying the basket for the barley, as he did each day, but he'd said he was going to take the vessel of water to Marzouq. She'd raised no objection, leaving him in the safe keeping of the dog that loved his company. What could have happened, she wondered, in such a short time, to cause all this uproar?

Although the woman was over seventy, she ran as if her whole body was on fire, trying to catch up with the boys who were running on ahead of her, leaping like jerboas. At last she saw her son, who'd raised his clothes, leaving the lower part of his body completely exposed. He'd put the hem of his *jilbab* in his mouth and was trying to reach the back part of a female donkey, which kept kicking him with her hind feet. Still, though, he'd get up and, panting and gnashing his teeth, try once more to have relations with the donkey, in front of all the boys who were shouting and shrieking round him. As for Marzouq, he was barking loudly, running round his master, then standing in front of him as if trying to divert him from what he was doing. But Miloud, interested only in quenching his desires, was taking no notice of anything. At last he was successful, holding on to the donkey's back part with a spasmodic grasp of his fingers. The boys had now surrounded the donkey, which, unable to escape the violation, had been forced to submit.

Aunt Maryouma, setting her shame aside, flung herself on her son from the rear, trying to pull him by his clothes, away from the donkey. He panted and groaned, making a noise like a grunting camel. He'd become a mass of inflamed desire. Several of the boys now rushed to Aunt Maryouma's aid, helping her tug at her son's clothes to pull him from the donkey, but Miloud remained rooted to the ground, becoming ever more agitated. Frenzied finally, he begged them to leave him for just a moment, as he'd started to feel the excitement.

All this became a story to be told and retold by some of the people of the camp. But for Aunt Maryouma it became a source of grief and worry, so much so that she didn't dig for barley for the rest of the day, afraid she might, in her fury, quarrel with anyone who asked her embarrassing questions. She dragged her son off to the tent and gave him a good beating with the dry branch of a tree. He screamed and started running round and round inside the tent, with his mother running after him and beating him all the while. At last Suliyman's wife came to save him, standing between the woman and her idiot son and telling her beating wasn't the answer to his problem, which would come up again if he didn't take the only medicine able to cure his condition.

The one solution, Suliyman's wife told her, was to marry the boy to Zuhra, the divorced woman from Bir Hakeem, who was looking for a husband. The woman would, she went on, jump at the chance of marrying a man like her son Miloud. Aunt Maryouma's reply to this suggestion was blunt and furious:

'Anything but that!'

✵ TWENTY-TWO ✵

Samby and Burhan ran as fast as they could towards the crowd in the field. All Samby had told Burhan was that Abdel Aaly's wife Fatima had been bitten by a snake and needed urgent treatment. He hadn't been able to tell him where she'd been bitten or what kind the snake was.

Burhan reached the spot where the men and women were crowded round Fatima and stopping the air from reaching her. He ordered them to stand aside and let her breathe, for she was in dire need of air. They moved away and made room for him to come to where she was lying on the ground, moaning, with her hand on her breast. A number of women were trying to help her, but they lacked any knowledge of first aid. All they could do was wipe the sweat from her brow and wail over her, invoking God to deliver her from her plight.

Burhan learned what had happened from one of the women. Fatima, she said, had been standing next to her when a small, speckled snake leaped into her bosom from inside the jerboa's burrow, after she'd struck the burrow with her scythe. The snake had bitten her, then slithered off, but the men had killed it with their scythes and hatchets. The woman pointed to where the snake was hanging from the branch of the *nabk* tree beneath which Fatima had been digging.

Fear took hold of Burhan's heart, fear that Fatima might die – for the snake that had bitten her was one of the most poisonous of the desert. He had to act quickly, before the venom started to circulate in her blood. He began by ripping away the part of the gown covering her breast, then, looking around him, found to his annoyance that people had started crowding in again, staring at the exposed part of her body. He shouted to them to move away, to let him do what he had to do if he was to save her.

Burhan asked just one woman to stay with him, choosing Haj

Abu Hamama's wife from Fezzan. She held Fatima against her own bosom as he got ready to extract the poison from the breast. Sitting in front of her, he took from his pocket a small scalpel used to bleed people and made three slits where she'd been bitten. Then he bent over her bosom, sucked the blood till his mouth was full, then spat it out on the ground. This he went on doing, repeatedly.

Meanwhile Samby had gone racing off, shouting, in search of Abdel Aaly, who'd been working a long way from where Fatima had been. Now the man came running in terror through the ploughed fields. His feet sank into the earth, but still he moved just as quickly as he could, scattering the earth around him, as though dragging chains of soil. Samby ran after him, but couldn't catch him till they'd almost reached the place of the accident.

There Abdel Aaly stopped short, shocked by what he saw, wishing he'd never lived to see his rival bending over his wife's body there in the field, in front of everybody in the camp, his head touching the bare part of her bosom, his lips between her breasts. The people, he knew, had meant well when they'd called Burhan to treat her. Even so, he believed the man had deliberately picked this evil method of treating her, pretending it was the only way to save her life. Surely Burhan was only doing it to take his revenge on him, to humiliate him and his wife alike. If there'd been a thousand and one ways of treating her, this was the one he would have chosen. Perhaps he was even going to squeeze her breasts in front of everyone, claiming his sinful act was a necessary part of the treatment!

Abdel Aaly didn't know whether to grieve over the pain his poor wife was suffering or over his tarnished honour. Should he bury his head in the sand, pretend he'd seen nothing, and let the humiliating minutes pass? Or should he rather fall on this impostor Burhan, thrust him off his wife's body then give him a sound beating?

But what if he struck Burhan and sent him off, then his wife died of the snake bite? Everyone would say he'd killed her, by sending Burhan away when Burhan could have saved her. He'd never, he knew, forgive himself for the rest of his days if he committed such a crime. And so he stood there in a daze, not knowing what to do. It was Burhan himself who rescued him from his confusion, as he stood up, wiping the sweat from his brow and asking Abdel Aaly to fetch him some water, so he could wash his hands and mouth from the traces of blood and poison. This meant his task was completed.

There was, Burhan told the woman holding Fatima, a good chance the danger was past. But that wasn't enough: she was liable to suffer a relapse if his instructions weren't strictly followed. His first was that she should be given neither food nor water before the end of the day.

Even as he was saying this, he realised his instructions wouldn't be followed. The old woman couldn't stay with her all day, and in any case might not even have taken in what he'd said. The one to be told about these things was her husband, Abdel Aaly. Burhan looked round and saw him standing there behind him, as still and silent as a statue. Adopting a professional manner, Burhan told him his wife should be given no more than three or four drops of water, just to moisten her lips and throat. He also told him he'd send him some herbs to be made into a paste and placed on the bite to absorb any residual traces of poison.

He had further instructions. The patient should be taken to her tent and put to bed, then left to rest, for the coming few hours would be crucial in overcoming the crisis. Abdel Aaly wasn't to worry if she sweated – indeed, this would be a good sign. Abdel Aaly had no option but to listen and carry out these instructions. When Burhan had finished, he rushed over to his wife, who was now almost unconscious, and carried her to their tent, while Samby followed behind with the baskets of barley.

Before Burhan returned to his shade, he noticed a man and a woman from the Jibreel family standing there in the middle of the people who'd been crowding round Fatima. They must, he was sure, not only have witnessed his treatment of Fatima but seen and made a note of the bags and baskets of barley ears the people of the camp had been carrying, together with the jerboa burrows that had been dug out to reveal the barley inside. The secret the people of Mizda had been hiding was a secret no longer. The Jibreel family knew all about it.

Still, these suspicions, and the fear and anxiety they aroused, didn't make him forget what was far more urgent: to make sure Fatima was going to recover. He must keep her under observation till the danger was quite past. He was sure he'd managed to suck out all the poison from her body apart from what had entered her bloodstream during those first moments before his arrival, and that should be remedied by the herbs he'd sent her and the diet he'd prescribe for her. When he'd sucked the poison from her bosom, he hadn't thought of her as anything but a patient, and he was obliged, by religious and professional duty, to treat her in a correct manner.

His patient was a woman in whose bloodstream the venom had entered, and he had to do all he could to save her from certain death, whoever she might be. Still, he couldn't forget she was Fatima, whose lovely eyes had aroused in him a passion of which he had never believed himself capable, a passion born the first time he'd seen her in her father's house. He could hardly believe that his heart, toughened by so much hardship, could have known such tender emotions, which made him shed inner tears whenever her name was mentioned. He'd always believed the love sung about in songs was no business of his, or of any man who worked for a daily wage. Love was for a small section of humanity with no problems in this world, people blessed by God with abundant income and leisure. It was only natural for people like that to consider love an essential element in their lives, something without which their happy existence in their mansions and gardens would be incomplete.

During the time he'd worked on the Countess's estate, he'd noted how love was an essential part of the Italians' lives. For them love was like the air they breathed, like the bread they ate. They held balls at which lovers danced in one another's arms to

105

the strains of sweet music, and they drank wine to one another's health.

Burhan had envied them, supposing such emotions hadn't been created for him or for other poor, toiling people. And yet his belief had been swept away the moment his eyes had met Fatima's eyes, as his whole being quivered and his heart shone with the light of dawn. He'd felt his world transformed each time she smiled at him, as a sign of her pleasure at seeing him when he went to her father's house. He'd believed, at one ecstatic moment when Fatima's eyes had lit up all the world, that her father, whom he'd cured, would give him her hand in marriage once he'd irrevocably divorced his other two wives. But his dreams had been shattered, his hopes of marrying Fatima blocked by the impassable barrier of her father's refusal. And so he'd been left with no option but to force himself to try and forget her. In this trial, he decided, he must turn to his strong faith in Almighty God and learn to accept the situation.

He'd made up his mind to regard Fatima, from that time on, as a sister, and not as the woman he'd desired to marry. He only wished Abdel Aaly would understand that, for Burham could not have failed to see the man's suspicious scowls. Burham couldn't blame Abdel Aaly, but Burham had noticed the ordeal to which the lovely, gentle Fatima had also been subjected. Now he decided to take no notice of Abdel Aaly's suspicious glances. Fatima's condition was of more importance than any doubts based on misunderstanding. And so he decided to take the herbs necessary for Fatima's recovery to Abdel Aaly's tent.

When he arrived, he found Sheikh Hamed Abu Leila inside the tent inquiring about Fatima's condition, wishing to know if they should take her to a nearby medical centre. Abdel Aaly's eyes were swollen from tears shed over his wife. He'd put her in her bed, covered her with blankets, then sat there weeping by her side. Finally he'd asked Aunt Maryouma and Haj Abu Hamama's wife from Fezzan to stay with her and take care of her.

Burhan gave the herbs to Abdel Aaly, who passed them on to the two women, asking them to make a paste and place it on the snake bite. Then Abdel Aaly went back to where the men were sitting in his tent, but he couldn't bring himself to thank Burhan. Nor, though, did he regard him with any hatred or anger. Burhan's quick and skilful treatment had clearly saved his wife's life, and there was no need now for her to be treated at any medical centre.

Visitors began arriving at Abdel Aaly's tent, among them Haj Abu Hamama and Amer ben Sheeha. They began talking about the disaster that had fallen on the camp: these newcomers who'd started their campaign against the jerboas, causing great numbers of the terrified creatures to seek refuge in the tents.

Haj Abu Hamama told them how, as he'd passed the newcomers' tents that morning, Yunus had seen him and invited him in to drink tea. He'd tried to excuse himself, but Yunus had sworn he'd divorce his wife if the invitation wasn't accepted. So he'd sat drinking tea, and there, inside the tent, he'd seen a great number of jerboas skinned and placed in a big bowl, ready to be roasted. After he'd finished his tea, Yunus had asked him if he'd like to taste some roasted jerboa meat, and Haj Abu Hanana made a hurried exit, turning down the offer of another glass of tea.

'If you go back there tonight,' Burhan said, 'you'll find something you do like, something that won't disgust you the way the jerboa meat did. They'll offer you your favourite food – *makhdour* made from barley.'

Everyone supposed Burhan was joking, though in fact he was quite serious. Haj Abu Hamama looked at Sheikh Hamed, waiting for an explanation of the remark, or looking for a chance to share the joke. In one breath the two old men asked Burhan what he meant.

'Exactly what I said,' Burhan replied.

He went on to explain. He'd seen two of the newcomers in the middle of the crowd round Fatima, which meant they must have discovered the secret of the ears of barley buried inside the jerboas' burrows. Everyone was most anxious and upset at this, afraid they'd have to share the grain with these strangers, and fearful, what's more, that their secret would now become known far and wide. If so, people would come to Jandouba in their thousands, taking all the barley and leaving them nothing to reap but misery and failure.

They must, they all agreed, think of some way to counter this new threat. Leaving Abdel Aaly to care for his wife, they went with Burhan to sit in his pavilion.

The hot sun was beginning to force the people out of the fields and back to their tents, or in search of shade under a tamarisk or *batm* tree for their noon nap. At this time of day the shade outside Burhan's tent, in his pavilion, was the best place to find some protection from the heat.

'Before anything else,' Haj Abu Hamama said, as though thinking aloud, 'we must be sure these people really have discovered our secret. We don't know that for certain yet. What are we going to do,' he went on, 'if they *have* found out?'

'Give me your rifle, Haj Abu Hamama,' Suliyman said abruptly, like a bullet shot from a gun, 'and I'll show you what we'll do!'

'What are you saying?' Sheikh Hamed cried, alarmed. 'You mean we should kill them?'

'I didn't say that,' Suliyman replied.

'Well, what are you saying then?'

'I mean we'll shoot anyone who tries to lay a finger on our ears of barley. Those burrows are ours. We were the ones who found the hoard of grain.'

'They're not our burrows, and they're not theirs either. They're the jerboas'. Don't make such a wicked suggestion again.'

It was better, in Sheikh Hamed's view, to face the facts than try and shut them out. This land wasn't their land, and the burrows where the barley had been stored weren't theirs either. They had no better right to them than these people who'd come from the farthest corners of the country in search of food. If they really had found out about the ears in the jerboa burrows, the only thing the people of the camp could do was to meet with them and make an agreement to keep the matter a secret among themselves. It wasn't, after all, in the interests of either party for the matter to become known more widely.

The young men, like Suliyman, Amer ben Sheeha and Al Roumany didn't welcome this suggestion. The decision lay, though, with the older men of the camp. It was decided Haj Abu Hamama should watch the Jibreel family that evening, to see if they were still busy hunting the jerboas or whether they'd started digging the creatures' burrows and collecting the barley.

Everyone hoped Haj Abu Hamama would bring back good news – that the newcomers were still setting their traps for the jerboas, quite unaware of what was in the burrows. That would be fair enough. Those people ate the jerboa meat the people of the camp didn't eat, so the people of the camp were entitled to the ears of barley the jerboas had stored, without having to share it with the newcomers.

They were having enough problems as it was. The ears of barley were taking up all the space in their tents, so that they were now actually sitting and sleeping on piles of barley. This meant they absolutely had to find a way of moving the barley to storage places and threshing floors, even if it meant covering them with some sort of cloth, or with the branches of trees. They needed, too, to thresh more of the crop so as to sell the barley and buy the goods they hadn't been able to buy the last time.

This was a great source of worry. How could they possibly thresh the ears of barley in full view of the Jibreel family, and within earshot of them? They had to find some means of doing it without being seen or heard – if, that is, their secret hadn't already been discovered. If it had been, they'd simply have to accept the fact and become partners in digging out the burrows and collecting the barley. And in that case they could thresh the barley openly, preparing two or three threshing floors and selling the grain to buy the food and drink and clothes they needed.

There was another problem worrying them too. If Fatima had been bitten by a poisonous snake, then other snakes might be hiding in the burrows. They'd hardly settle in the ones crammed with barley, since this would prick their smooth skins, but they could settle and lurk in the new burrows dug by the jerboas, which would be cool and airy in the heat of summer. Fatima's accident could happen to anyone. The snakes were a danger and a threat to them all, and they'd have to take the greatest possible care.

The people went back to their tents, full of anxiety. As for Burhan, he sat under his shade reading invocations and supplications till the time came for the noon prayers. He fetched a plate of roasted barley from his tent and ate his lunch. Gazing around him, he saw everything was still in the noonday calm. Not a soul was stirring and the only sound to be heard was the buzzing of flies. They seemed masters of the situation, in the wide, open spaces that shone with an intense white light reflecting the brilliance of the sun.

The silence encouraged Burhan to take a short nap, and, when he woke, he decided to go and ask about Fatima. Then, abruptly, he changed his mind, for fear Abdel Aaly might misunderstand the reason for his visit. If she'd had a relapse, he assured himself, the family would have sent for him. Since no one had come to see him, Fatima must be all right.

Burhan stayed there under his shade, but not a single member of the camp came to ask him to write a charm or ask for herbs as they'd done before, when he'd received one or two patients every day. This, he thought, must be the result of Fatima's mishap, with the women, who were his most frequent patients, spending their spare time visiting her. As for the men, they were all full of worries that the Jibreel family might have found out the secret of the barley. He could see them there in the distance, neglecting their work as they stood around in small groups, engrossed in endless discussion under the tamarisk trees.

Burhan had just finished performing his afternoon prayers. Now, stretching out his hands, he besought God to answer his prayers and cover the eyes of the Jibreel family so as to prevent them seeing the ears of barley. He recited the Quranic verse: 'We have put a bar in front of them and a bar behind them and further, We have covered them up; so that they cannot see.'

No sooner had he done this than he saw someone's shadow there in front of him; and, when he raised his head, saw a woman whose beautiful face was unveiled, a woman he'd never seen before. She was wearing a long blue *jilbab* whose colour shone in the sun's rays, so that blue sparks seemed to be flying from it. Her eyes were wide and dark brown, her lips large and tempting. She spoke in a soft, seductive voice.

'Greetings, Burhan!'

✥ TWENTY-THREE ✥

The male and female jerboas, as was only natural, looked on the destruction of their homes, the seizing of their storehouses and the terrifying of their young as an infamous and hostile crime. The humans had committed crimes against them and against all the other animals and insects living in the valley.

They were capable, even so, of setting these events in their historical context, in the light of previous relations between humans and jerboas. The present situation was, they believed, a temporary phase, one to be endured in patience and through devising a system to help them live with their plight, overcoming it through daily toil and resolution.

But the jerboas had never heard of, never envisaged such crimes as had been committed by this second group of people, who'd entered the valley in such a noisy, rowdy fashion. They hadn't followed the ways of those who'd come before them, by digging out the burrows and seizing the barley. Rather, from the very moment they'd arrived, they'd hunted and slain every jerboa they could lay hands on. The destruction of the burrows, the eviction of the jerboas from their homes, wasn't, it would seem, enough for humans. Now their inborn wickedness and bloodthirsty nature were spurring them on to slaughter the peace-loving jerboas, who'd always lived quietly here in this land.

The humans evidently had a fresh approach now, one based on bloodshed and crime, in defiance of all their previous rules on the treatment of jerboas. And these new developments had upset all the plans the jerboas had made to meet the situation. It wasn't just a matter, any more, of their homes being destroyed or their stores plundered – they could build new homes and gain back some of the crop. This was altogether more serious. They were being subjected to massacres aimed at exterminating them once and for all. This slaughter, they declared, must cease.

A young jerboa spoke, in a tone that expressed hatred and gloating joy together.

'Today,' he said, 'a snake bit one of the women in the camp. She's lying between life and death.'

Killing wasn't the sole prerogative of human beings! There were animals and insects and other creatures that could kill even more efficiently than humans could. Humans might have their traps and rifles, their scythes and axes and hatchets, but some creatures had weapons, like poison, that were deadlier still. True, the jerboas had been victims of snake venom themselves, but they went along with the famous saying: 'On me and on my enemies, oh God!'

The jerboas were willing, accordingly, to leave their newly dug burrows to the snakes, as a base from which to attack and kill humans. It wasn't, any more, just a conflict for a morsel of bread or some ears of barley. This was a struggle for survival or death, based on a new set of rules for relations between humans and jerboas, come into force with the arrival of this second group of bloodthirsty humans. Them or us – that was the rule now. And the ones to be exterminated, the jerboas decided, had to be 'them'!

Of course the challenge was a great one. There was a vast difference between their power and the power of those gigantic humans who made the earth shake as they trod it. And the humans had the advantage of tools, which they used to destroy the jerboas' homes. The jerboas couldn't possibly confront them alone, and so they'd have to seek aid from some of their neighbours and allies living on the plains. Their neighbours could not possibly ignore what the jerboas were being subjected to.

Delegates were sent from the jerboas to the other creatures, who'd either remained in the fields or fled to the mountains, inviting them to attend an urgent meeting. Lizards, beetles, grasshoppers, spiders, butterflies and worms all sent their representatives to take part, and a group of ants also attended, to show their solidarity with the jerboas – ready, they said, to wage war on the humans from that moment on.

Many things came to light at the meeting, including the fact that the lizards were in the same plight as the jerboas. Lizards had never been targets for humans before, which only went to show the bloody frenzy that had seized these people. Not a single creature living on the plains, insect or animal, was safe from their evil.

The creatures invited decided, one and all, that the jerboas' desired battle of self-defence against the humans was their battle too. From the start, though, they were against making any pacts with the two venomous creatures that were symbols of evil and treachery, the scorpions and the vipers. The jerboas had wanted to seek the support of these two vile creatures to help them annihilate their human enemy, but were finally convinced by the others that scorpions and vipers would be more harm than help, because they'd never keep their word.

At the end of the meeting an alliance was agreed among them all, to wage war against these unjust invaders. They formed suicide squads to enter the humans' tents, leap about among their clothes and spoil their food and water. They'd attack them sleeping and waking. They'd so provoke and irritate them that they'd quit the land, leaving the other desert creatures to live in peace.

The volunteers registered their names forthwith, willing to sacrifice their lives for their families' right to live in safety and peace, free from any threat of extermination.

TWENTY-FOUR

Surprised at the sight of this tall, slender woman in her shining blue gown, Burhan stood up to welcome her. He'd never seen her before today. Her figure, he noticed, was bursting with femininity, and her clothes did nothing to conceal her bosom. Her long black hair hung down on to her shoulders and back, a few strands straying down over her breasts. One side of her hair was covered with a pink scarf, while a necklace of purple agate adorned her neck. The shimmering gown, the sun's reflection on the agate necklace and her black hair, along with her radiant complexion and features – all these things seemed quite out of place in the dusty surroundings.

Burhan realised quickly enough that this woman was from the Jibreel family. Her clothes, so unlike those worn by the desert women, clearly reflected her life in the oases of the eastern frontier. He returned her greeting, went into his tent to fetch some cushions, which he placed on the straw mat, then invited her to sit down and courteously asked how he could be of service. She, though, hadn't come like other women for the benefit of his advice on spiritual matters, but to discuss something quite different. This she made clear as she sat under his shade at the far end of the straw mat, leaving the proper distance between them.

A fragrant scent wafted from her clothes, and her speech was proud. Burhan didn't resent her confidence. A woman as attractive as that had the right to display her charm in front of anyone! He listened to her in silence, putting in a word, just now and then, to show his interest in what she was saying. He gazed at her beautiful wide eyes, at her tempting lips and fingers dyed with henna. The henna lines and circles on her hands were beautiful, quite different from the patterns used by the women of his tribe.

Her name, she told Burhan, was Rabiha, and she was the sister of Yunus, who'd visited them in their camp with some of his relatives. She hadn't accompanied them on the visit, she went on, as she'd been busy preparing the tent in which they lived. She'd come to see him now because she'd heard how, that morning, he'd saved and healed a woman from a snake bite. This had made her curious, and she'd learned on inquiry that he was the camp's religious scholar and physician, as well as being skilled in writing charms and amulets for his patients.

She added that she was skilled too, though not in writing charms or amulets, or, being a woman, in leading prayers. She'd learned from her mother, before she died, how to make use of herbs and how to tell people's fortunes from the sands. As such she was responsible for advising the members of her family on what they should do, and they'd learned from experience not to disregard her predictions.

Once, she said, she'd advised the men of her tribe, including her late husband, not to work in the minefields, after the sands had revealed this would bring only evil and disaster. But the men had followed the agency's Maltese owner, who'd made them a tempting money offer. He'd gone into the minefield first to demonstrate his skill in defusing the mines, then shown the people how to extract the small pieces of platinum. This platinum he'd bought from them for a high price, and he'd also bought the iron from which the mines were made. They'd once been as poor as the mice that live in mosques. Now they made so much money they became rich. Still they'd worked on in the minefields, ignoring the dangers, despite her frantic warnings of a catastrophe predicted by the sands. When the finest men of the tribe, including her husband, were blown to pieces, the people at last realised the dreadful price they'd paid for ignoring her warning.

Burhan sat in complete silence after hearing of her husband's death, while Rabiha herself turned her face away, tears glistening in her eyes. Taking control of herself once more, she told him how she'd advised her relatives to travel to Jandouba where an abundant harvest awaited them. They'd heard, on the way, how they'd find nothing there but the bare stalks of the crop, but she'd refused to turn back or believe what they'd heard. She'd been aghast to see with her own eyes that there really was no crop and no barley, but the family had been delighted to find jerboas they could trap and eat. These, after all, were more nourishing than any grain.

Even so (she went on), it was no comfort to her that there was plenty of food for the people, who were catching and slaughtering and eating the jerboas. She'd promised her family barley, not jerboas, and the prediction of the sands was never false. And so she'd decided to go on looking for barley till she found it, sure it was somewhere here in Jandouba. Nor had she needed to look for long, for her watchful eye had led her to discover the barley was hidden just a few inches under the ground.

Rabiha paused to gauge the effect of her words on Burhan, who'd listened without comment, trying to affect an air of indifference about the whole matter. He didn't, though, make any effort to hide his admiration for her beauty, which had fascinated him from the moment he set eyes on her.

Rabiha then told him how she'd discovered the secret from the people of the camp, well though they'd guarded it. She'd seen no threshing floor, and she'd heard nothing about the ears of barley from anyone. Neither she nor any of her family had suspected a thing as they saw the people of Mizda digging under the *nabk* trees – they'd supposed them to be collecting firewood. But she'd been puzzled by the way the people of Mizda were staying on in Jandouba when there was no harvest to be reaped. They had brick houses, didn't they, in their village, with bedrooms, and a place for cooking, and basins of water to wash themselves? So why were they so intent on living in tents, in the midst of jerboas they hated and couldn't eat? And where, she'd wondered, did their food come from, when they owned no sheep or goats? This had led her on to wonder how the barley from all these wide fields had disappeared, how the jerboas could possibly have devoured the whole crop.

At this point Rabiha paused once more, gazing at Burhan with smiling eyes. He gazed back at her, then made a gesture of surrender with his hand to show her she'd won. He admired her intelligence, and told her that whoever had named her Rabiha (which means 'one who wins') had known what he was about. He urged her to tell him how she'd finally discovered their secret, and she said it had been revealed to her in a flash when, from a distance, she'd seen all the members of the camp, young and old, carrying bags and baskets to the fields and then back to their tents, several times a day.

Burhan stared at her, unable to conceal his astonishment – not so much at her cleverness in finding out their secret as to learn that this beautiful woman, still in the prime of her youth, was in charge of her family's affairs, respected and obeyed by men and women older than herself. Women had, he knew, equal status to men in the eastern desert, but that was only in the case of very old women. That a young and attractive widow, showing her superiority by wearing clothes more elegant than those of any other woman in her tribe, should be the tribe's leader – this amazed him. She'd refused to be treated as bedouin communities treated women, and that in itself astonished Burhan. He'd never heard, or seen, or imagined such a state of affairs!

He wasn't in the least upset that Rabiha had found out their secret. He even took a touch of satisfaction from it, since the barrier between them and the people of Jibreel would now be removed. This friendly visit from the family's leader must surely, he felt, herald a new stage in relations between her people and the people of Mizda.

As Burhan still remained silent, she asked him if he'd been upset by what she'd just told him. He told her, quite frankly, that he was still trying to recover from the astonishment he'd felt when he first saw her. He'd supposed she had come to ask for a cure for a head-ache, or for medicine for her child's eyes that had been infected with trachoma. He'd never dreamed a beautiful young woman would be the leader of her people, come to discuss agreements between tribes and villages. All this was quite inconceivable for someone like himself, who spent his day sitting on a straw mat gazing at nothing but fields of dry stalks and sand dunes. He was, he concluded, most grateful she'd chosen him as the person to tell of her discovery.

Rabiha told him she hadn't wanted to send a representative from her people, as he might not have been able to make the situation clear in the way she wished. On the other hand, she couldn't have gone alone to Sheikh Hamed, the leader of the camp's people. She'd chosen him, a physician, as someone who could meet with her openly, in this exposed spot, without embarrassment. She could then hear his opinion, and the opinion of his people, on the matter she'd just broached.

Learning that her family hadn't yet begun to collect the ears of barley, he asked why this was. She'd refused, she answered, to let them do so before she'd consulted with the people of the camp – they were installed on the land, and it wouldn't be proper to do anything before coming to an agreement with them. She also wanted to know if they'd divided the land among the families, as was customary in the harvest season, or if the ground was common for all. Her people didn't want to disrupt the scheme the villagers were following to collect the barley. They simply hoped they'd be given the chance to reap the crop alongside.

It didn't seem to Burhan that Rabiha and her people needed permission from the elders of his tribe to collect the ears of barley. He told her, accordingly, that she could send her people to dig the jerboa burrows and collect the barley whenever they wanted. Nobody could stop them doing that. All that would be asked of her and her family was that they should tell the secret of the barley to no one else. Also, they should store what they collected in their tents rather than piling it up in the open air, for if the secret came out they'd be overrun by hordes of people from all the four corners of the earth.

Rabiha said she understood the secret had now become her people's secret too, and that their joint interests obliged them to take the strictest precautions to keep things hidden. The matter, she believed, needed co-operation and association between the two tribes, and there must be an end to the hostile attitude on the part of the people of Mizda. She was sure both tribes would benefit from such co-operation, for they could thresh the barley together and go to the market together, so saving time and effort alike. The Jibreel family's experience as peddlers would also be an asset for the two groups.

Burhan welcomed this suggestion, and he admired, too, Rabiha's wish to pave the way for understanding and friendship between the two parties. Nevertheless, he asked her to give him time to meet the head of his tribe that evening, along with his companions, so as to pass on what she'd told him. Then, God willing, the outcome would be favourable.

Before Rabiha left, Burhan had wanted to learn more of the things the sands had predicted about herself and her own fortunes. But she'd simply laughed, then said fortune tellers could predict everyone's fortunes but their own, and she'd tell his fortune if he'd tell hers. Burhan explained he could write a charm for her that would make her loved by a particular person, another to protect her from the evil eye and a third to ward off nightmares. These were the limits of his spiritual powers, taken from books he'd studied, which taught the prevention and cure of certain diseases as derived from the Quran. As for telling a person's fortune, he said, God and God alone knows the future and the fate in store for all humans as recorded in the Preserved Tablet. He'd never himself practised soothsaying and had no faith in those impostors who cheated and lied to people instead of telling them their fortunes. He believed, however, that there were particular honest people beloved of God, who were granted knowledge of certain secrets. She, he was sure, was one of those, whose knowledge of secrets would bring joy to others.

Rabiha's face clouded somewhat as he mentioned his reservations, but decided, even so, not to hold back from reading his fortune from the sands, so as to prove to him how skilful she was. She took from her bag a number of kerchief straps and some pebbles, along with a small cloth bag with sand. She spread a kerchief on the ground, cast the sand from the bag over it, then took some pebbles, telling Burhan to clutch them tight and whisper to them the wish he desired to have fulfilled. Then she drew some lines in the sand, threw some more pebbles down and, after a brief silence, began telling Burhan of what had happened during his life, as though she were reading a set of facts from a book. Burhan was stunned, lost for words to express his amazement and admiration.

'As for the wish you whispered to the pebbles,' Rabiha went on, 'the time for such a wish to be fulfilled isn't yet here.'

Burhan, realising she knew what the wish was, smiled.

'Are wishes subject to time?' he asked. 'Doesn't a person have the right to wish for something, then leave it to the will of Almighty God? If He wills it, then it will be fulfilled; if not, it will remain unfulfilled.'

The sun was approaching the rim of the horizon, which meant it was time for her to return to the camp and tents of her people. But, before she could rise to leave, Burhan's family arrived – his mother, sister and two nephews, all carrying baskets filled with ears of barley. When his mother saw Rabiha, she tried to hide the baskets inside their tent, but Burhan told them Rabiha and her family were no longer strangers but partners in their search for the barley. His mother, not knowing what to say, invited Rabiha to stay for supper, and his sister, who saw Rabiha putting the sand back in the cloth bag, added her voice to this, in the hope of having her fortune told. But Rabiha couldn't accept the invitation. It was time, she said, for her to wish them goodbye and return home, but she hoped to see them again the next day.

The ecstasy Burhan had felt in Rabiha's presence stayed with him long after she'd left. He felt oblivious to all around him, as though he were sitting on a cloud that floated him along to where the setting sun adorned the horizon in gorgeous brocade. The world seemed a happier, brighter place, and, as he gazed out over the distant plains and grasslands, a feeling of peace and security wrapped him round.

When his mother asked him to go in and eat his supper of barley cooked with olive oil, he noticed the tent was full of insects he'd never seen before. Evidently storing the ears of barley in the tent over all this time, under cloths and among their belongings, had made some of it rot, and this had attracted ants, and grasshoppers, and worms, and beetles, quite apart from the jerboas that made such constant raids.

After finishing his supper, Burhan took a book from the box in which he kept his books, papers and herbs, and looked up the invocations for getting rid of crawling and flying insects. Then he recited these in a loud voice, so that all the insects and other pests of the plains would hear him and hold back from entering the tents.

❦ TWENTY-FIVE ❧

The people of Mizda had no choice but to accept the new situation, praying to God the newcomers would be the last to come to the place.

The Jibreel family had found out their secret, and that was that. Their task now was to face the new development and view the matter in proper proportion. Given the choice, they would never have let anyone come into the valley even, let alone pitch their tents opposite their own and discover the secret after just a couple of days. But there was nothing they could do now to change things, just as there was no way they could have prevented what had happened. These people had come from Bir Hakeem, the most distant spot on earth, to trap and eat jerboas, but they'd discovered the barley in the burrows and they now had a further source of food. Such had been the divine plan of Almighty God, which could not be gainsaid. The valley lay before the new people, and they could search everywhere, collecting barley from the countless crammed burrows, eating it night and day, on the sole condition laid down by Burhan – that they keep the secret.

But, while the people of Mizda were clear on this point, they wanted no further co-operation between themselves and the new-comers, no further involvement with this family of Jibreel that had made a woman its leader. That was, of course, their own affair, and Sheikh Hamed Abu Leila declined to discuss the matter, for he had no intention of entering into any dealings with these people. The customs of the women of Bir Hakeem, adopted from the easternmost point of the land, were unacceptable for the girls and women of Mizda.

'Let these people stay away from us,' Sheikh Hamed said. 'The way they live is against the customs and traditions of our own tribe, and we don't want them mixing with us. Members of a tribe have always been held together by blood kinship, until they become one great family, just as we have. We're all members of this family. How can we let a group of outside people invade our privacy, and how can we invade theirs? How can we possibly let our menfolk mix with their womenfolk, who aren't related to them in any way?'

He went on, speaking in a tone of disapproval to the people sitting around him:

'Have you ever heard of strangers wanting to mix with people who aren't their relatives? Every tribe has its own limits, excluding people who aren't part of it, and anyone who chooses to reject these rules and limits loses everything. Let everyone, I say, stay within his limits. There's no call to have any association with these people who'll corrupt us and open the door to sin.'

Such was Sheikh Hamed's reasoning on the matter, and Burhan, he decided, should convey the message to this woman who wished to create a union between the small family from Bir Hakeem and the large community, the wider family, come up from Mizda, with a view to their becoming a single community in this new land of Jandouba.

The task with which Burhan had been entrusted was no easy one, and he intended to pass the message on in a way that would create the minimum offence. He had no quarrel with what Sheikh Hamed had said – it was quite in keeping with the logic ruling the lives of tribal people in the small villages and plains. Nor would either group of people be harmed. Each person should live and work within the limits of his own tribe, and there was no need for the two groups to mix. The relations wished for and suggested by Rabiha would no doubt have led to all kinds of unforeseeable problems.

Even so, Burhan couldn't fight his heart's inclinations, and he decided he was entitled to protect his close relationship with Rabiha against any embarrassment in overall relations. Rabiha, he hoped, would return his feelings, and do her best to maintain the affection between them, in spite of the difference in attitude between their tribes. And so he didn't join in the criticisms made by the members of his tribe about the Jibreel womenfolk. He couldn't bring himself to do it after meeting Rabiha and talking to her – seeing, indeed, no sign of the immorality of which they'd accused her people.

Burhan had seen, in Rabiha, a woman proud and self-confident, who had a strong personality as well as being extremely beautiful. For all her womanly charms, she was clearly determined to preserve her chastity. And, on top of all that, she managed to command and lead all the men and women in her family, even though she was a widow who'd lost her husband less than two years before.

Burhan himself wouldn't, of course, have let himself be so drawn to Rabiha, or given his emotions such rein, had she not been widowed. He had no marital ties either, and he hoped the affection between them would develop into love, allowing him to marry her. This was the wish he'd whispered to the pebbles while Rabiha was telling his fortune, and she'd known his wish well enough.

The time, she'd told him, hadn't yet come for his wish to be fulfilled. Well, thought Burhan, so be it. There's no cause for worry there. If someone wishes for something before its time, that's better than wishing for it too late.

When Burhan had been to Fatima's home to ask her father for her hand in marriage, he'd found her cousin already there – the man had got in his request first. Her father and cousin had conspired against him; and, when he'd seen them shaking hands and reciting the opening verses of the Quran as a formal token of betrothal, he'd protested, in agonised tones, that he'd come to propose marriage himself. At that, Fatima's father had rebuked him, telling him he had no right to ask for a girl's hand in marriage when she was already engaged. What made everything worse was that Fatima's cousin had proposed marriage just seconds before Burhan's arrival. Those few seconds had cost him dear and taught him a bitter lesson. Just a merest moment's delay, he knew now, could ruin your chance of a happier life and better future. His most cherished dreams and hopes had been turned to ashes.

Could he, he wondered, after being cheated in his love for Fatima, find his compensation in Rabiha? Could he force life to give him back some small part of what it had stolen from him? Perhaps. And yet he couldn't be sure of anything after the frustrations and disappointments he'd known.

He longed to see Rabiha again the next day, but he was worried, too, how she'd react to Sheikh Hamed's message. Perhaps she was even aware of Sheikh Hamed's attitude before he told her – she could predict the future after all. Maybe that was why she'd said the time hadn't yet come for his wish to be fulfilled. 'But who says,' Burhan thought, 'that matters of love should be subject to the rules of time? Why shouldn't they make this moment the right one for their wishes to come true?'

Would Rabiha, he wondered, agree to his suggestion? Would she come closer to him or stay away from him? It wouldn't be anything new for him to have his feelings thwarted – it had happened with his love for Fatima. He didn't want his relations with Rabiha to be a repetition of that failure, to have his life become merely a series of frustrated emotions.

Ever since he'd been a young man, working on the Countess's estate, he'd suppressed the development of any emotions, however passionate. The world of the people living on the estate wasn't, he believed, his world. The lovely creatures who made his heart beat wildly, throb violently, had been created for people quite different from himself. And so he'd controlled his feelings, forced himself to stay calm. It wasn't that he felt any kind of barrier, tribal, or ethnic, or religious; these people had always treated him in a friendly, informal way. He'd known his limits even so, and realised what a gulf existed between himself and them. It was the gulf between poverty and wealth, for he was just a poor young man working to earn his living. All he owned was his shirt and his trousers, while they were part of the world of the Countess, who owned estates and palaces and cars.

Whenever the Countess had wanted to be friendly to the labourers who worked on her estate, she'd made a show of adopting their way of thinking. 'It's Fate!' she'd say. 'It's Destiny!' Her estate stretched over a thousand hectares, and her lands never suffered from drought because there were fifty wells on it, allowing irrigation for almond trees and orange groves and vineyards. A world war had been fought and Italian rule brought to an end. And yet, though Britain now ruled the country, the Countess, and her estate, and the society in which she moved, floated above such things as war, or drought or starvation, or a change of ruler.

What, Burhan wondered, had started him thinking about his work on the Countess's estate, just as he was about to lay his head on the pillow and fall asleep. Was it that he regretted, now, leaving a secure job in an evergreen world? When he'd made his decision to leave and go back to Mizda, he hadn't dreamed things would turn out so badly. His only thoughts had been that a person couldn't spend his whole life apart from his family, working as a labourer, taking orders from an Italian overseer, however fairly he was treated. You could accept a certain kind of treatment when you were twenty or so, but not when you reached thirty.

He spent over nine years of his life working on that estate, and not once had it occurred to him to wonder why the Countess and her family, and the other members of her society, lived such a luxurious life, filled with banquets and balls and receptions, while he and his like should remain deprived. It was fate and circumstances. The stars in their heavenly spheres allotted, throughout one's life, sustenance, and happiness or grief. People were destined to poverty or wealth, to health or sickness, misery or happiness, good or evil. Would fate, Burhan wondered, be kind to him this time? Would it fulfil the wish he'd whispered to the pebbles?

However late Burhan stayed up, or even if he suffered from sleeplessness, he always woke of his own accord a few minutes before the call to dawn prayers. Today he rose quickly from his bedding, remembering the reward that awaited him at the end of the day – the meeting with Rabiha. The circumstances preventing the call to prayers no longer applied. The newcomers had found out the secret of the burrows filled with barley, and there was no need to fear them any longer.

He decided to call dawn prayers that day, whether Sheikh Hamed agreed or not. They were all descended from Adam, and Adam was created from clay. Religion knew no tribal barriers, and so there'd be no barriers between them and the Jibreel family during the performance of prayers.

And so he made the call to dawn prayer just as he'd done before that other family had arrived. He was pleasantly surprised, as he welcomed the birth of the new day, to find the men of the camp coming to pray communally, including Abdel Aaly the woodcutter, who was there for the first time under his leadership. Sheikh Hamed and Haj Abu Hamama came too, with no sign of objection.

Then, as usual after dawn prayers, Burhan went to the fields to collect barley, before going to his shade to begin the day. He put on his clean white Arab suit, consisting of shirt, trousers and skullcap, along with a blue waistcoat over the shirt. Then he sat down on the mat with a long stick in his hand, waiting for the boys to come for their lesson, in which he taught them to recite verses from the Quran.

The problem was that, though it was customary at schools teaching the Quran for every boy to have his own wooden tablet, they had only one, bought by Hajja Khadija for her grandson Ali, and Burhan was obliged to use this for the whole class. It was rather as if someone had prepared a banquet for his guests but had only one small plate in his home. It wasn't enough, it seemed, that he'd volunteered to teach the young boys; he had to invent a new teaching method for them too. Instead of dictating the verses to them, as he would have done had they all possessed tablets, he had to use this one small tablet like a blackboard, for everyone to write on and read from.

For the first time Aunt Maryouma brought her son Miloud to Burhan's shade, so he could attend with the boys. Burhan wondered if poor Miloud could possibly understand the lesson, and if it was fair to make a man of thirty-five, even if he was mentally handicapped, sit side by side with ten-year-old lads. He voiced no objection even so, telling Miloud to join the others, for, like everyone else in the camp, he couldn't help feeling sorry for Aunt Maryouma. Shamed by the shocking exhibition her son had made of himself, she believed the only possible remedy for him in the world was the Quran. So she told Burhan. Then, while the boys were reciting the Quranic verses, she shouted:

'Only the words of God will solve my son's problem and calm that simple innocent mind of his!'

She didn't, naturally, mention to Burhan how one of the women of the camp had advised her to look for a wife for her son. This son, she knew, was a simpleton, who'd never be able to control any woman, let alone the one Suliyman's wife had suggested. Before she left, she made sure to ask Burhan to write a charm for him, to cure him of the outbreaks of sexual excitement that seized him from time to time.

The trouble was, the charm Aunt Maryouma wanted wasn't the only one he'd been asked to prepare that day. In fact he'd been asked to write numerous charms to cure an outbreak of a quite different sort: namely the sudden and widespread infestation of insects in the tents.

As soon as the lesson was over, the boys started running around, singing happily, and Burhan found himself face to face with his old love Fatima. Her pallor did nothing to lessen the beauty of her almond-shaped eyes, or her clear complexion, or her perfect features. On the contrary, it bestowed an air of peace and tranquillity. Burhan rose, happy to find she was better and had come to see him, but worried, too, that she'd left her bed before she was completely recovered.

127

'You should have stayed in bed for a full three days,' he told her.

Fatima told him she didn't feel sick or tired. As soon as she'd started feeling better, she said, she'd decided the first place she should go was there to his shade, and the first person she should see was the one who'd risked his own life to save hers. She was in his debt for the new life that had been destined for her, and, after giving thanks to Almighty God, she wanted to thank him. She also asked him to forgive her husband Abdel Aaly for not expressing his gratitude or making him welcome. She'd persuade him to make an apology some time soon.

Burhan told her he'd noticed nothing untoward in her husband's behaviour. And even if he had behaved as she claimed it wouldn't alter his, Burhan's, feelings for Abdel Aaly. Burham regarded Abdel Aaly as a brother, just as he regarded her as a sister. He was at her service at any time. She stood there in front of him, gazing at him and smiling without a word. From the start of their conversation Fatima had let the edge of the veil covering her face slip back, allowing him to see her smile and the expression in her eyes, as though rewarding him for having saved her life.

She saw a woman coming towards them from some way off, carrying an infant, and, not wanting to keep Burhan from his duties, she began to take her leave. But Burhan asked her to wait for a moment, while he finished writing a charm for her to hang around her neck and protect her from snakes and scorpions. Prevention, he said, was better than cure. Fatima raised a pair of eyebrows as perfectly curved as two crescents, amazed to learn such a charm existed, and wishing she'd had it before being bitten by the snake.

Burhan saw her off, then tried to muster all his faith and willpower to put out the small flame that had begun to glow once more in his heart, awakening his feelings for Fatima when he'd thought them dead. He would, he decided, focus his thoughts on treating the woman who'd arrived before Fatima's departure. The woman was carrying an infant who'd become a mass of swollen flesh from countless insect stings – further proof that these insects were becoming a serious menace to people's lives. He saw she'd brought a basket full of barley as payment for the treatment, barley she must have collected under the scorching sun. He asked her if this was so, and she confirmed it; whereupon he told her God helps those who help themselves and that carrying the infant in that blazing heat could have been fatal to him. Then he gave her some herbs to make an ointment, to smear on the infant's body during the night.

As she went off, Burhan saw she was barefoot, that she was lifting one foot after the other, for a few seconds, then bringing it down on the burning pebbles and stones. He pitied this woman who had nothing to wear on her feet, and came close to calling her back to return the barley she'd brought and give her some footwear. Then he realised he'd actually be increasing her pain by having her return over the burning ground, especially as she'd now almost reached the tent where she lived.

He followed her with his eyes, and finally saw her entering Uthman's tent with its crowd of boys and girls. The woman was, he guessed, Uthman's daughter-in-law, living there in his tent. Uthman's younger brother, Al Roumany, lived there too, and he didn't take part in any of the work – all he cared about was playing his bagpipes. It was hardly surprising this tent was not just the poorest in the camp but the poorest you'd find anywhere in the land.

It would still be several hours before Rabiha was due to come and meet him. He wanted to spend the time in something useful, so he prepared papers, quill and ink and busied himself writing charms for the people of the camp. Yet, in spite of his work, he looked out towards the fields every few minutes, so as to be sure of seeing Rabiha as she approached his shade. The moment he caught sight of her, he put his materials back in the tent and placed three cushions on the mat outside. Rabiha arrived carrying a basket full of barley, which she set beside her as she sat down on the cushions.

'This is the third basket of barley I've collected,' she said. 'When I work, I work, with no playing around.'

'If all the Jibreel family had your energy,' Burhan replied, 'the jerboas' burrows would be empty in no time.'

'We've a right,' Rabiha said, 'to make up for the time we spent here with you, knowing nothing about the barley because you refused to tell us about it.'

'We saw you eating the jerboas, so we thought you weren't interested in barley.'

Burhan couldn't hide his happiness at having Rabiha sitting with him there under the shade. He couldn't take his eyes from her, delighted at the chance to gaze at her beauty. But he also felt embarrassed at having to give her Sheikh Hamed's message. The best thing, he decided, would be to get it off his chest straight away, rather than just prolonging his embarrassment by telling it a piece at a time. In a few brief words he said everything he had to say, expecting an angry reaction followed by one of wisdom and shrewdness. But she only smiled.

'Do you know, Burhan,' she said sarcastically, 'your dogs don't try and harass us any more. In fact some of them even bark to welcome us. As far as I'm concerned, your dogs' friendly barking means more than your sheikh's message.'

'I'm grateful to the dogs for softening it.'

'Let's forget about the dogs, and the old men of your tribe. What's your own view about it?'

'You know I've lived away from the tribal system and the way tribes live. I spent nine years working for the Italians, and some of them have become my friends, despite all the differences of language, and country, and race and religion. So how do you expect me to behave with my own people, when I'm tied to them by so many bonds?'

'Well, let's put aside the view of the old generation and work together. According to new ideas.'

Burhan wanted to show he agreed with her without actually criticising what Sheikh Hamed had said. The sheikh's views might run counter to his own ideas, but it was the logic of his tribe, which had its followers and supporters, and they'd have to consider it before taking any further steps, before making mistakes that could harm both parties. But Burhan was stopped from going on with the conversation by the noisy arrival of his mother, sister and nephews. They'd come early because Rabiha had promised she would tell their fortunes. Actually Rabiha had no desire to tell anyone their fortunes unless they went to her in her own tent. But she didn't, in the circumstances, want to break her promise, so she told Burhan's mother her fortune and apologised to the rest of the family for not having the time to tell theirs at that moment. They were, she said, welcome to visit her in her tent whenever they wished.

Rabiha's tactic, Burhan realised, was to arouse people's curiosity to have their fortunes told, and so break the tribal and psychological barriers that stopped the people of Mizda visiting the family of Jibreel. Now Rabiha told them her people intended to celebrate the discovery of the barley, adding that this celebration would take place the night after next and that she'd like all the people of the camp, men, women and children, old and young, to come, so they could see the arts of the eastern desert for the first time.

Burhan saw now how Rabiha had already begun carrying out her plan to have the two tribes mingle fully with one another. She wasn't going to wait for Sheikh Hamed to give them permission to visit the tents of his camp. Instead she was going to entice the people of Mizda to visit the tents of her own family.

✺ TWENTY-SIX ✺

Two wise, ascetic friends lived side by side on the summit of the plateau, in a large cave made by nature within a rocky dome. One was a hedgehog, the other a spiny-tailed lizard, and sometimes they'd leave the cave and go to a small patch of level ground, like a terrace, on the plateau's edge. From there they'd look down on the valley and fields, on a scene of beauty and splendour where so many various creatures lived, pulsing with life.

The plateau of the Northern Mountains lay to the north-west, at the most distant spot the eye could scan. With its stony circles and its dusty brown colour, it lay between black patches of volcanic rocks, all of them nestling beneath the curve of the dark blue horizon. Tamarisk and *batm* trees grew on a slope, while, along the valley, stretched mile after mile of stalks and *nabk* trees. Also to be seen was a wilderness of sand and pebbles, marked by dry furrows made many years before by floods. Bushes of furze and lavender cotton and wormwood had grown there, but the leaves had withered in the heat.

In the centre of this wilderness, on the southern side of the valley, could be seen a number of black tents pitched in a single row, with a series of reddish sand dunes visible on either side of them, and with further dunes behind the tents and parallel to them. On the northern side of the valley, at the foot of the plateau, three grey tents were pitched. Between these motionless landmarks were to be found living creatures, which, from the high point of the plateau, could be seen going about their daily work. They included humans, dogs, donkeys and camels, all appearing as small dots against the vast expanse, and there were many other creatures too that couldn't be seen from the heights.

The hedgehog surveyed the scene sadly, putting out his head and hands from his prickly body, as he only ventured to do when he felt safe from all danger and thought his friend the spiny-tailed lizard wanted to enjoy his company in the early hours of the morning.

'What a strange place the world is,' he began. 'When you gaze on a scene like this, it seems to reflect every kind of well-being and love, of peace and beauty. You forget what a bitter conflict there is between its inhabitants, each moment of the day and night.'

'What's so odd about that?' replied the spiny-tailed lizard, who always went out of his way to avoid any conflict himself. 'Conflict's the rule of life, after all.'

The hedgehog, blessed by nature with a prickly shield to keep him safe from all harm, followed the spiny-tailed lizard's example, and he'd come here to live close to him. Like his friend, he'd chosen an ascetic life based on as little movement as possible and on food left uneaten by other animals that lived in the caves. They both rejected the false surface appearances with which so many creatures concerned themselves. They ate herbs that grew on the mountain, along with shrubs whose sap freed them from the need to drink water, and they enjoyed the peace and quiet and safety of the plateau summit, and the shadows that stretched from the large boulders, protecting them from the heat of the noon sun. The cool evening breeze refreshed them and they were quite free of the terror that afflicted creatures – some of whom had fled the valley and taken refuge on the mountain.

The hedgehog and the spiny-tailed lizard didn't let these un-expected events affect the seclusion in which they'd chosen to live. Nor did the ordeals of these other creatures change their fasting and their meditations on the universe and its Creator. They'd heard, often enough, the din of conflict in the valley, but they'd paid little attention to the dogs barking in Jandouba or the wolves howling in the caves of the distant mountains. Nor were they remotely concerned by the noise of humans, or the grunting of their camels or braying of their donkeys, and they cared nothing for the sounds of the children running and shouting in the valley, or the groans and laments of the creatures disturbed by these humans.

The spiny-tailed lizard made his comment on the throngs of creatures come to the plateau.

'We all strive after one aim,' he said. 'The aim of self-preservation.'

'And does self-preservation,' the hedgehog replied, 'mean we must have conflict?'

'Self-preservation,' said the spiny-tailed lizard, 'means the survival of the species. That's the crucial thing.'

'And can't that be achieved peacefully?'

'There's always the promise of passing happiness, like a tree growing in the distance, which everyone tries to reach first so as to win its fruit. The real winner, though, is the one who shuns such a contest, for the tree's a mere delusion.'

'The way those creatures in the valley behave,' the hedgehog remarked, 'gets on my nerves. From the noise they're making, and the terror they're living in, you'd think they'd never seen humans before. The truth is, they've always been in conflict with them, whenever they come to plough or reap the harvest.'

'Perhaps things are different this time – though I'm as surprised as you at the way these creatures never seem to see how life's journey is so full of lessons.'

'You're right. This journey, from birth to death, has so many happenings, so many ventures.'

'I'd rather be more hopeful – call it the journey of creatures from the past to the future.'

The hedgehog paused for a moment.

'I don't know,' he said, 'if we really have any right to blame these humans. They're attached to the particular world around them, and they've organised their lives by it – which means they've put themselves at its mercy. They plan their futures by the cycle of the seasons, just as jerboas and beetles and ants do. Other creatures toil in spring and summer, so as to store up provisions for autumn and winter. Or at least they did, before the humans invaded their lives and destroyed everything, separating one family from the other and making their children orphans.'

'Humans are creatures living in defiance of nature,' replied the spiny-tailed lizard, 'because God created them, yet part of them is owned by Satan. Nature answers other creatures, grants them what they need. But humans see themselves as masters of nature, devising the most fearful weapons to fight it. What can you expect from all this but conflict?'

'The other creatures,' the hedgehog replied, 'muster all their strength to defend themselves against these humans' encroachments.'

'But where's the point in waging war by attacking them face to face? They'll be the winners every time.'

'What's the answer then?'

'Has anyone come and asked for our advice? We would have given it gladly enough.'

As far as the spiny-tailed lizard was concerned, the creatures of the valley had only themselves to blame – they should have come to him to find a remedy for their trial, as they'd done before over personal affairs and family conflicts. It was as if their plight had scrambled their minds; they no longer thought to come up to the top of the plateau, to seek advice that would have delivered them.

❦ TWENTY-SEVEN ❧

The people of Mizda didn't believe Rabiha's promise that the arts of the eastern desert would provide something new and interesting. The family of Jibreel had asked Al Roumany to join them, and the people could see him from their distant camp, standing there in the midst of the family and playing his bagpipes. He was hugging his instrument as a mother might hug her child, and Matouq, one of the men in charge of the celebration, was skilfully beating his drum, with a novel, exciting rhythm. Apart from that, there was no kind of art or display that deserved to be called eastern, or, come to that, western.

Close to where Al Roumany and Matouq were playing, a group of this family come from the east were standing and clapping their hands. And if the rhythm of the music flagged, one of the women would ululate loudly to stir the players and their audience once more. Night had begun to fall now, and three kerosene lamps were hung in front of the tent nearest the place for the celebration. To light up the scene still further, a fire had been lit on a mound near their tents, and, throughout the celebration, they continued to feed this with wood.

Was there really anything to draw them to attend? So the people of Mizda asked one another, standing there on the other side of the valley and watching the preparations. Burhan, standing among them, was sure Rabiha would make a success of it, as part of her plan to attract the people of Mizda to her people's camp. He expected to see a more interesting display in due course.

135

At first only the children went to the celebration. Then the adults were lured to the other side of the valley by something they saw there. One of the women of the Jibreel family, wearing many bracelets on her arms, necklaces over her breast and anklets around her ankles, had begun to dance, swiftly and alluringly, as though a fire were burning beneath her feet. She danced and cavorted in a wide circle, the tinkling and jingling of the bracelets and necklaces and anklets, along with the rhythm of the drum, driving on to a high pitch and tempo.

Al Roumany was blowing on his bagpipes with all his strength, his fingers moving skilfully over the pipes, his tune keeping time with the dancer's feet and the beat of the drummer.

The audience were grouped in a half circle around the players and dancer, spurring them on with their frenzied clapping and singing a well-known song:

'How splendid the henna on your feet!

Beauty surrounds you, behind and before . . . '

This dance, so the people of Mizda had heard, was called the *hajjala*, and the clapping and the song were part of a kind of singing known as *kishk*. They began to feel the eastern arts were something exciting and interesting after all. And so, one group after another, they flocked to the place of the celebration, where the women gave them a hearty welcome. These women had used kohl to heighten the beauty of their eyes and the nectar of red flowers to put a flush in their cheeks, while the fragrance of desert herbs wafted from their clothes. Their hands and feet were dyed with henna. They wore strings of garnet around their necks and in their hair, which dangled and swayed as they moved to the rhythm of the music, as if the very hair was dancing. They walked about in the midst of the people, wearing no veils to cover their faces.

These women were carrying plates, too, of tasty food the people of Mizda had never seen before. They relished the pastry and loaves of bread made from desert herbs kneaded in with barley flour and boiled in oil – so much, indeed, that the women of

Mizda began asking how it was prepared, so they could make it in their own homes.

The hosts welcomed everyone, smiling – as the guests praised their food – insisting they should eat more of the pastry. The women of the family treated everyone, men, women and children, in the same friendly manner, and this cordial reception created an atmosphere of friendship and affection amongst all present. Everyone joined in clapping and singing, while the host women took turns in dancing the *hajjala* dance. Rabiha, too, danced briefly in honour of the guests, before returning to her duty of supervising the celebration, which went on till midnight.

The only people from the camp who didn't attend were the old men and women. Burhan, on the other hand, was at the head of those who'd gone, and he joined enthusiastically in the clapping as he sang. Rabiha had already made him one of her loyal followers. Now, he knew, this celebration would help fulfil the aims of the family of Jibreel.

The next day the people of Mizda found themselves divided into two groups. One praised the celebration of the night before and the hospitality of their hosts, and admired, too, their way of life influenced by the years they'd spent amid modern, broad-minded communities. The other group, though, was indignant, regarding what they'd witnessed as yet further proof of the immorality of these people, who'd abandoned the customs and traditions of bedouins in east and west alike.

Haj Abu Hamama, who'd travelled to the east of the country in the past and mixed with its people, said he'd never seen anyone there behave like the Jibreel family. He was convinced the family belonged to the wandering tribes that roamed the frontier lands, who people called gypsies. In fact, he referred to them as 'the gypsies' from then on. The reason, he added, why their leader Rabiha wanted to mix with them was to find a husband for herself and for the other unmarried women she'd brought with her on the journey. After that she'd bring more widowed women whose husbands had been killed in the minefields, with the same aim in mind.

Haj Abu Hamama's view seemed reasonable and convincing enough, especially as the people of Mizda had seen the intimacy, during the celebration, between the unmarried women of the Jibreel family and the unmarried men of their camp – an attachment that hadn't ceased even after the celebration was over.

In the days that followed people from these two unmarried groups would meet in the early hours of the morning, then go off in couples to collect the barley. They'd work side by side, on the pretext that the men were showing the women how to dig the burrows.

Rabiha's supernatural powers in predicting the future and telling people's fortunes became common knowledge. The women in particular would go to her tent during the midday heat, taking gifts of *makhdour*, and Rabiha would tell their fortunes and talk to them about matters they'd never before discussed or understood, about their relations with their husbands. She explained how to draw them and arouse their affection and passion, and how all this could be accomplished by making themselves more attractive. She'd noticed, she told them, how they neglected their looks, something which would end up ruining their relations with their husbands. Then she gave them dried carnation petals to mix with the water in which they washed their hair.

The simple women of Mizda left her tent fascinated by all the things she'd said and eager to use the dried carnation petals when they washed their hair the next day. The whole camp became suffused with the scent of carnation, and the women started addressing Rabiha as 'Mistress Rabiha' as a mark of respect.

The elderly people of the camp grew uneasy at the turn events were taking, yet it all seemed beyond their control. Haj Abu Hamama gave up supervising the collection of barley, as he'd done before when his people had been the only ones working in the fields. The work had become a free-for-all, and he decided he shouldn't hold back himself. In fact he entered the fray determined to collect, along with his family, more barley than anyone, and so show everybody that, for all his years, he was more efficient than most of the healthy young men.

In fact, had Sheikh Hamed not insisted on playing draughts with him each day before noon, he would have given that up too – not because he'd lost interest in the game, but because the new developments within the camp had ruined his peace of mind. He was anxious about his brother, Sheikh Hamed, on whom lay the responsibility for checking this serious problem.

During their pre-noon meeting under the *batm* tree Haj Abu Hamama brought up the matter of the men of the camp, who'd started pursuing the 'gypsy' women.

'I don't blame a man like Al Roumany,' he said. 'All he's capable of in the world, after all, is playing his bagpipes. I don't even blame Suliyman's silly, lanky son for running after these immoral gypsy women. But I do blame the man who's learned the Word of God by heart and teaches it to others – Burhan, that is, who's pursuing the most immoral woman among them all.'

Sheikh Hamed agreed. Then he added: 'Even so, what's happened to the men isn't as drastic as the change that's come over the women – going off in groups to be taught by these gypsy women.'

'Can't we stop them going there?' Haj Abu Hamama asked.

'None of our warnings seem to have had any effect on them.'

'Burhan's the one to blame, for all this immorality.'

'Maybe that fortune teller's cast a spell on him.'

'Strange, isn't it, that a man of God, bound by a solemn duty to save people from the evil of magic, should fall victim to this witch himself?'

At that point they heard Burhan's voice coming from the tree beneath which they were sitting.

'What magic are you talking about, Haj Abu Hamama?'

'You won't die young, Burhan,' Haj Abu Hamama said. 'The moment we mention your name, there you are.'

Sheikh Hamed intervened.

'Come and sit down, Burhan,' he said. 'You've come at just the right moment.'

Burhan knew the two old men had been discussing the way their people were mixing with the family of Jibreel, and he realised how the whole business must have disturbed and shocked them. In fact he'd come there that day to seek out their views on a connected matter. He now knew, though, that this was only going to complicate matters still further.

'One of your sons wants to talk to you,' he said. 'I'll call him now, so he won't have to stand there in the scorching sun.'

With that he called to Masoud Al Roumany, the bagpipe player, who came over and stood there in the shade, his eyes fixed on the ground as though he'd committed some dreadful act. Even when he sat, his head still hung down on his chest in embarrassment. With all possible speed, before he could be infected by Al Roumany's diffidence, Burhan told Sheikh Hamed and Haj Abu Hamama something about which they needed to be informed.

'People say,' he began, 'that poets and musicians have tender, sensitive hearts. Masoud's one of those people, and his smitten heart has followed a doe from the east. He wants to marry her according to the laws ordained by God and His Prophet.'

The two old men gazed at one another. Then they both looked at Burhan, as if to ask, resentfully, why he should be taking it on himself to intercede.

'Al Roumany came to me a short while back,' he went on, giving them no chance to speak, 'and asked me to recite the opening verses of the Quran to mark the engagement, and to write out the marriage certificate for him. But he doesn't want to do that before you've given your consent and blessing.'

'And why does he need our blessing, if he's already decided the certificate should be recorded tonight?'

Burhan laughed.

'Perhaps,' he said, 'he was afraid the girl might change her mind. The wedding, you know, isn't going to cost Al Roumany anything. No dowry, no gifts, nothing at all.'

He went on in a more serious tone.

'Al Roumany's asked his older brother Uthman, who's like a father to him, for permission to marry this girl. Uthman told him the matter was up to you.'

Uthman, Burhan knew, had no control over his younger brother, even though Al Roumany lived in his home and he provided for him along with his own children. Uthman it was, all alone, who'd dug and watered the land, sown the seeds and harvested the produce from the orchard he owned in Mizda, before the well dried up and the plants all withered. Al Roumany was good for nothing except sitting under a fig tree in the orchard and playing his bagpipes in the midst of his friends. It was even rumoured he'd made wine from the figs to drink with the comrades who came to visit him each evening.

'And who,' Sheikh Hamed inquired, 'is this pure, chaste maiden he's chosen?'

Burhan answered the question on Al Roumany's behalf.

'She's a divorced woman,' he said. 'Her name's Zuhra. She's one of the women who came to visit us with her brother, on the first day they arrived here.'

Now it was Haj Abu Hamama's turn to make an observation.

'Perhaps you don't know,' he said to Al Roumany, 'that Ruqaya, your grandmother on your father's side, was my cousin and one of the pure branch of the Abu Hamama family.'

'Of course I know that, Uncle Haj Abu Hamama,' he said, still hanging his head in embarrassment. 'It's a great honour for me.'

'Well, lad,' Haj Abu Hamama pursued, 'that's why I'm asking you to preserve that honour. You've seen for yourself how the women of that family walk around with no veils over their faces, letting their hair hang right down over their shoulders as they go here and there among men who aren't related to them. And you've seen how they dance in front of everybody, without a shred of embarrassment or shame.'

'And how are we to know,' Sheikh Hamed put in, 'just who these people are? Where does this woman come from? What's her family? She's divorced, you say, and she's been brought up away from her own land. All her family died in the war. Well, why did her husband divorce her, tell me that? Why did she leave her home and what happened to them? Do you know the answer to any of that?'

Once again Burhan intervened to try and help Al Roumany, who was confused and had not a word to say in reply.

'It's their custom in the eastern desert,' he said, 'for women to dance the *hajjala*. No one censures them for it or looks down on them.'

'I've been to the eastern desert,' Haj Abu Hamama replied furiously, 'and I've mixed with people from good families there. They never behaved in that disgraceful kind of way.'

Sheikh Hamed too resented Burhan's remark.

'Do you realise what you're saying?' he asked, in an angry tone. 'A pious man like you? You're defending this shocking business, recommending a woman who twists and turns her body in front of men, at night, and mixes with them during the day as though she were one of their family, not caring whether they're relatives or total strangers?'

With that Sheikh Hamed rose, and Haj Abu Hamama did likewise.

'Just let people remember,' Haj Abu Hamama said, raising his arm in a threatening gesture. 'I still have my rifle with me, and I won't think twice about using it on anyone who deliberately insults the members of this camp, or tries to sully the tribe's good name.'

The two old men went off, leaving Burhan dismayed and not knowing how to console Al Roumany, whose childish face suggested he was about to burst into tears, though he finally managed to control his feelings. He regretted now that he'd put Al Roumany in this embarrassing situation, for he was the one who'd brought him to Sheikh Hamed and Haj Abu Hamama, to ask their consent in a matter he'd known would be refused. Al Roumany had told him, in a few brief words, that he wanted to marry Zuhra and that she'd agreed. He'd added that neither she nor her family had any demands to make. All that was needed was a family meeting, during which the marriage certificate would be written by Burhan in his capacity as man of religion. Al Roumany hadn't actually meant to ask anyone's permission, but Burhan had persuaded him that anybody from their village who wanted to get married should first seek the consent of his family and of the chief of the tribe. If he didn't, he'd find himself a despised outcast. And so Burhan had brought him to see Sheikh Hamed and Haj Abu Hamama under the *batm* tree.

Burhan had decided it was his duty to help Al Roumany in his plight, and this could only be done after the man had told him the whole story of his involvement with Zuhra. It had, Al Roumany said, been love at first sight, during the celebration held by her family. After it was over, the family had asked him to stay and sit with them around the fire. They'd roasted some jerboa meat, too, having first dipped it in a mixture of salt and spices. When the meal was ready, they'd offered him a plate of pastry and herbs, knowing his family didn't eat jerboa. He, though, had surprised them all. They should, he said, regard him as one of themselves and allow him to eat some of the jerboa meat. He'd been tempted, by the smell of the roast meat dripping with fat and the way the people were devouring it, to join them in their feast.

Zuhra, Al Roumany went on, had been sitting there in front of him, and the flames of the fire had gleamed on the garnet necklace on her breast, reflecting its colour on to her face. His heart had thrilled with ecstasy, and he'd been able to see her buxom breast rising and falling as she laughed, her whole body quivering. She'd removed the veil from her coal black hair, which had been suffused with the fragrance of carnation petals and had glistened in the firelight like a heap of black pearls.

Here Al Roumany paused for a second before going on. What was still more important, he said next, was that she'd paid him the greatest attention, using all her charms to attract him. She even spoke his name as though she were fondling every letter in it. He'd heard his name spoken as never before! When he'd declared he was ready to eat the roast jerboa meat, she'd been filled with delight and offered it to him with her own hand. Then, when their hands touched, they'd stuck together because of the fatty meat, and he'd been filled with a passionate desire to hold her in his arms. His desire had grown fiercer, but he'd been powerless to do anything. And so he'd asked her to meet him the following morning.

Burhan listened intently, as Al Roumany went on to tell how she'd met him next day, and how she was as much in love with him as he with her. He'd taken her to a distant spot behind a large clump of *nabk* trees and tried to express his love for her in a practical way, but she'd refused to let him kiss her, or touch her bosom, or hold her in his arms. Nothing could pass between them, she'd told him, till they were married. She'd made it quite clear, too, that she wasn't demanding a dowry. All she wanted was his love, his loyalty and his manhood. She'd have no trouble, she assured him, in persuading her brother and the rest of the family to agree to the marriage. She'd been as good as her word. Next day she'd met him with a radiant face, telling him her family had raised no objection to the proposal, and that they awaited him that evening to ask for her hand in marriage.

Al Roumany concluded his account. He'd visited Zuhra's family to ask for her hand, and it had been agreed the marriage should be consummated that very day. Burhan remained silent for some moments, gazing, with a touch of admiration, at this young lad who'd shown a total disregard for all tribal tradition, taking on himself a matter as important as marriage in the twinkling of an eye. He needed to reflect in order fully to take in what the boy had said, and he needed to reflect on his own position too. Setting aside Al Roumany's reckless approach, there was a good deal of similarity between Al Roumany's situation and his own.

He considered what the boy had told him about his relation with Zuhra. Was it perhaps a fleeting whim, unfit to be the basis for a permanent, legitimate married relationship? That drew him on to consider his own feelings for Rabiha. Might they too be considered a mere passing fancy? Was his wild desire to bind his fate to hers just a daydream, destined to vanish like the dreams of the night?

'Are you honestly sure,' Burhan asked, in a serious tone, 'that Zuhra's a virtuous woman, who'll make you a good wife and be a good mother to your children?'

Al Roumany scratched his head but made no answer. Burhan found nothing strange in this, for Al Roumany came from a background where chastity and virtue were considered of vital importance for men and women alike, and where the belief had been handed down that women shouldn't mix with men. It was believed too that, however infatuated a man might be with a woman who flirted with him, he should never marry her, since he couldn't be sure she hadn't flirted in the same way with other men.

Suddenly the words shot out from between Al Roumany's teeth, in a tone that showed he was determined to speak frankly about his feelings.

'You wouldn't want me to do what that imbecile Miloud did, would you? I love Zuhra, and I want her, and I can't bear the thought of being apart from her.'

This, Burhan realised, was a real problem. Even though the head of the tribe had refused him permission to marry Zuhra, he was going to marry her anyway. Burhan asked him to wait just a few days, so he could talk to Sheikh Hamed and Haj Abu Hamama when they'd calmed down a little. He also whispered to Al Roumany that he could write a charm for him, which would pluck the love for Zuhra from his heart just as a hatchet roots up shrubs and grass.

But Al Roumany begged him not to do this. He didn't want an end to those emotions that had swept him away, nor did he want the flames of passion he felt to be put out. His love for Zuhra, he said, was the most wonderful thing that had happened to him in his whole life – he'd never tasted such happiness before. He swore, as well, that he would never stop loving Zuhra, or meeting her, or sitting with her around their fire on the other side of the valley and eating delicious jerboa meat with her. In conclusion, he declared that the old men – meaning Sheikh Hamed and Haj Abu Hamama – might as well agree, because neither they nor anyone else in the world would stop him marrying Zuhra.

⁖ TWENTY-EIGHT ⁖

After Rabiha had finished her rounds in the fields, and before returning at sunset to her people's camp, she picked up her basket filled with barley and went to Burhan's shade. Finding him in a state of meditation, she stood there in front of him and spoke in a joking manner.

'I heard you talking to yourself,' she said, 'and thought you must have friends in the mysterious unknown world – that you were maybe speaking to some beautiful girl there.'

'The life of pious, devout people like me,' he said, 'is one of praising God, and invoking and glorifying Him. That's why we never cease to converse with the creatures of the heavens – not with what you call creatures from the invisible world.'

The bonds of affection tying Burhan and Rabiha had become so strong they met twice a day now. Each morning they met in the fields and spent the first part of it collecting the ears of barley together, then they'd meet again just before sunset, when Rabiha went to Burhan's shade. There they'd enjoy the dusk breeze and watch the sun set, its red, transparent rays covering the lowlands and steppes, transforming the dusty land into what seemed part of some enchanted world.

During these meetings they'd exchange words expressing their affection for one another. Burhan, indeed, went further, telling Rabiha frankly how he wanted to spend the rest of his life with her. She didn't give him a direct answer, leaving him dangling between her consent and her refusal, but he felt sure she loved him even so. She'd hesitated to declare her love, he knew, because she was waiting for him to ask for her hand in marriage. She wouldn't be satisfied by talk of hopes and dreams. She wanted a commitment leading on to the full responsibility of marriage.

Rabiha looked over towards the sunlit summit of the mountains, then turned her gaze to the east, where she could see a silver moon rising slowly in the sky, waiting for the sun to make way, so it could bestow the beauty and grandeur of its light on the universe. Then she looked at Burhan.

'Do you know,' she said, 'that the time of the white nights is here?'

'Yes, I know,' Burhan replied. 'For three nights, from tonight, the moon will shine on till morning.'

'So, leaving out tonight, there are just two nights left.'

'What do you mean? Two nights left for what? My heart longs for some sort of adventure with you, in the moonlight.'

'These are the best nights for threshing barley.'

'I'm sorry. I forget heads of tribes like you never lose sight of reality. But tell me, in God's name, what you're thinking of.'

'You know, Burhan, my family doesn't own any camels to thresh our harvest. We'd like to ask your people to lend us two or three camels to thresh our own barley. If you don't agree, I'll have to hire camels from Jandouba.'

She was silent for a moment, then added:

'In which case it would hardly be our fault if the people of Jandouba found out the secret of the jerboa burrows filled with ears of barley. And since,' she added, seeing Burhan staring at her in amazement, 'the people of Jandouba actually own these fields, they'll be entitled to come and reclaim land and harvest together.'

Burhan couldn't fault Rabiha's reasoning, which he'd pass on to Sheikh Hamed and Haj Abu Hamama in the guest tent. They wouldn't, of course, be able to refuse her request, but even so he didn't want her to feel too elated with her schemes.

'I wouldn't go that far, Rabiha,' he said. 'The owners of the harvest, there in Jandouba, have been compensated by the mandate government, and very generously too. If any of them were to come looking for the harvest now, we could report them to the government, and the government would take back the money they'd been given. These people have their trades and their orchards. They don't need to compete with poor starving people like us, digging jerboa burrows to collect ears of barley.'

147

'Then tell me why you're all so panic-stricken if you see so much as a shadow of anyone near the fields.'

'That's because we like to cater for our needs discreetly, as the Prophet, blessings and peace upon him, instructed us.'

'Don't bring in the Prophet, blessings and peace upon him, to cover up your own tricks. Am I to understand, from what you said, that you're not prepared to lend us your camels here and now?'

'I'll give you the camel and everything on its back if I can just taste a handful of your barley.'

'God protect us from the talk of scholars – filled with poisons and mines!'

'And where's the poison, where are the mines, in what I said?'

'I know what Sidi Qinana meant as well as you do.'

Burhan was embarrassed to find Rabiha had grasped his reference. Sidi Qinana was the master of all the desert poets, ancient or modern, and the poetry he'd composed a hundred and fifty years before was still recited by people as though he were writing at the present day. How could he have been so naïve as to suppose she knew nothing about him?

'I know of Sidi Qinana,' he said, 'but I don't know any of his poetry by heart now.'

'Well, you know what he said about barley.'

Burhan certainly knew the piece about barley, which had been uttered by the poet's beloved. But he pretended not to, so as to hear it from Rabiha.

'All I can remember,' he said, 'is that the poet wanted to marry a girl he loved, but she refused him.'

'She taunted him with his poverty and insignificance,' Rabiha supplied, 'and answered his proposal by saying he'd never taste her barley.'

'But you realise,' Burhan said, 'I meant real barley – not what barley means in the poem.'

'There's nothing wrong with proper relations.'

'But Sidi Qinana's beloved didn't want any sort of relations – legal or otherwise.'

'At least she was able to decide for herself – what she wanted and what she rejected.'

'The man she'd refused,' Burhan said, 'was humiliated. He left the country, then prospered from his trade in the Sudan. He came back laden with ivory and silks and ostrich feathers, and asked for her hand in marriage a second time. She and her family accepted him, and they were married.'

'And then, instead of treating her as a bridegroom ought to treat his bride on their wedding night, he took his revenge on her. Isn't that so?'

'He behaved like any other man who's grown rich and arrogant. What else would you expect?'

'He waited till the poor girl had taken off her clothes, then recited the same verses she'd recited to him before. "I'm not your prey," he said, "and you're not my bird. You pretend to love me and you meet another." Then, before he swore the oath of divorce, he recited more verses. He swore he'd never touch her or come near her bed, then he turned her out of the house on her wedding night, with the henna still fresh on her hands and feet. Humiliated, she rode her camel through the wilderness till she reached her family's tents. Have you ever known anything crueller than the way men treat women in our country?'

'All that,' Burhan said, 'happened in the old, dark days, when revenge was still part and parcel of life. Sidi Qinana was one of those people, and he reflected his background.'

'And are things so very different now, Burhan?'

'How do you mean?'

'Well, look at what's happened to someone like Al Roumany.'

'Sheikh Hamed and Haj Abu Hamama could never have agreed to a marriage like that.'

'Why not? What business is it of theirs?'

'You know very well tribal custom and tradition give them the right to intervene in matters like this, so as to keep marriage within the tribe.'

'Well, where is the marriage in this tribe of yours? Sheikh Hamed's daughter has been promised to a man for years, and yet he cannot marry her. Maybe he won't be able to marry her till he's an old man. What *do* these people want?'

Burhan shrugged and pursed his lips, as if to say there was nothing he could do to change the customs of his tribe.

'Al Roumany,' Rabiha continued, 'came in accordance with the teachings of our faith, and the woman he chose accepted him, and her family agreed she should marry him. If he'd wanted to consummate the marriage that very moment, no one would have objected. Why do you have to complicate things?'

'I'm not the one complicating things.'

'You talk as if it's no business of yours at all. You say Sidi Qinana's poetry springs from times that were ignorant and unjust. So what do you call the time we're living in now, you and the heads of your tribe?'

Rabiha, Burhan saw, didn't approve of his hesitant, negative attitude to Al Roumany's marriage. But, before she left, he pointed out the big difference between a youth like Al Roumany and a man of experience like himself, respected by all his people. He knew the way, he added, to solve the problem, all in good time.

When it was time for the meeting in the guest tent, Burhan put on his shoes and set out, taking a short cut behind the tents and missing the usual clamour. He arrived to find the meeting already begun, the Captain sitting in his place making tea, the other men silent like mourners at a funeral, staring into space with gloomy faces. Burhan greeted them, then asked why the atmosphere was the way it was.

'Why should you need to ask,' one of them answered, 'when you're the cause of all the trouble?'

At first Burhan thought they meant the death of the infant who'd died of insect bites and stings two days earlier. He'd written a charm for him, but it had come too late to save him.

'What trouble are you talking about?' he asked angrily.

'You tell him, Uthman,' another man said.

Burhan hardly ever saw Uthman, and he'd certainly never come across him in a meeting like this. Even in Mizda he'd seen very little of the man, who'd lived as a virtual recluse in his orchard on the outskirts of the village, not mixing with the village people and never attending their celebrations. All Burhan knew of this tall, lean man was that he had skin as dark as burned coffee beans and black decayed teeth, and that he was the older brother of Masoud Al Roumany.

Uthman was sitting as still as a statue with his chest hunched down on his knees, which his arms encircled like a bundle of knotted bones. When he spoke, his voice sounded like the rasping of a grasshopper. His brother Al Roumany, he said, had told him that Zuhra had told him that one of the women from the family of Jibreel had told her how Rabiha and Burhan were planning to marry Al Roumany to Zuhra, in spite of Sheikh Hamed and Haj Abu Hamama.

Burhan realised just how serious this was; that what he'd whispered to Rabiha in confidence a few hours before had turned into a rumour, then become altered and distorted. He must defend himself against the storm that was about to break, put an end to the rumour even if it meant resorting to cunning. He immediately denied what Uthman had said.

'Do you good people really believe,' he said, 'what one man said to another man, reported to him by a woman who heard it from another woman? I'm the one who's actually concerned, and here I am standing in front of you. And I'm assuring you there's not a scrap of truth in Al Roumany's story.'

'What about your meetings with that woman every morning and every evening?' Haj Abu Hamama said accusingly. 'They're not a delusion, are they, Burhan?'

Haj Abu Hamama addressed Burhan as though he'd already begun investigating the matter. It was his regular role to intervene when his brother, Sheikh Hamed, felt too embarrassed to confront a problem. Burhan knew things could go badly for him if the two brothers were hostile, for he was relying on the people of the camp to be his patients and followers when he returned to Mizda.

He meant to establish himself there as a man of respected status – he was, after all, the religious scholar of the village, the imam of the mosque and teacher of their sons. How was he to prosper if the people of the camp were against him, if the chief men of the tribe condemned his conduct and sullied his good name? He'd find himself isolated, with no means of livelihood. Yet, at the same time, he didn't want to abandon his dream of marrying Rabiha; and so he decided to pray to God, invoking Him to help him fulfil these two wishes, without the one ruining the other. Surely Almighty God would grant him His mercy and aid, for he'd been a pious servant of God all his life.

'You know,' he told the expectant men, 'that her word's law with her people, and that I'm simply a messenger between her and you. If you want me to go on being a messenger, then I will. But if you want me to pass the role to someone else, then I'll do that too.'

'We don't want any links between her and us,' came the reply. 'We don't want anything to do with her or her people. So there's no need for anyone to act as messenger at all.' This was followed by a verse from the Quran: 'You have your faith and we have our faith.'

'Well,' Burhan answered, 'before I put my responsibilities aside, perhaps you'd like to hear the message she asked me to pass on to you, just a short while ago.'

'What is it?' they asked with one voice.

Burhan felt he'd managed to deflect their attention from his personal relations with Rabiha to more general matters.

'She needs camels,' he said, 'to thresh their barley.'

He went on to tell them of Rabiha's intention to hire camels from the fields' owners if refused the loan of theirs. They all grew furious at this, uttering threats in one breath, but that didn't disturb Burhan in the slightest, even when they swore there'd be battles and bloodshed if these people told anyone the secret of the barley ears. In fact their anger made it altogether easier for him to lead them towards more peaceful courses.

'They won't tell anyone,' he said soothingly. 'It's in their interest as much as ours for the secret to remain with all of us. Let's discuss the matter calmly, shall we, in a spirit of bedouin chivalry? What harm can it do us to lend them a camel or two to thresh their barley?'

'They're threatening to tell our secret if we don't lend the camels,' said one of the younger men. 'What we ought to do is refuse. Not be intimidated by their threats.'

Burhan turned towards Sheikh Hamed and Haj Abu Hamama.

'It's not really a threat,' he replied. 'They just want to thresh their barley, and they need camels. If we refuse to help them, what are they supposed to do?'

He paused, waiting for an answer, but nobody ventured one.

'Put yourselves in their place,' he went on. 'Tell me what you'd do.'

There was a lengthy silence, finally broken by Sheikh Hamed.

'If you want to lend them your camel,' he said, 'then do it. Maybe that will solve the problem.'

The old man looked at the men sitting around him, then asked: 'What do you think?'

Some were for the idea and some against. Burhan decided to wait till the clash of opinions had subsided.

Little by little those who'd refused to have anything to do with the Jibreel family began to change their minds in favour of a peaceful solution. It wasn't, surely, worth spending the last remaining days of their stay in Jandouba in conflict with people they'd met by the merest chance. These people had come from a distant part of the country, and soon they'd be going back. There was no chance of ever having to mix with them again.

Burhan pointed out that one camel wouldn't be enough to finish the threshing in a single night. Since, in principle, they'd agreed to help them in any case, it would be safer to lend them more than one. Their threshing could then be done in the one night, with no fear of the secret being found out by some passerby next morning.

Everyone in the camp knew the white nights would last for just

153

two nights more. They'd wanted to thresh more ears of barley themselves, but hadn't yet done so, dire though the need was.

At last they agreed to lend their camels to the Jibreel family for one or two hours at the beginning of the night, on condition they threshed their barley away from the camp of the people of Mizda, without mingling with them. During this time the people of the camp would prepare two large threshing floors. Then, when the camels had finished their work on the Jibreel family's floor, they could thresh their own. In this way all the threshing would be completed on the same night.

When the meeting was over, Sheikh Hamed whispered in Burhan's ear, asking him to remain after everyone else had left. Then the old man told him he hadn't meant to be harsh with him or Al Roumany, but that it was Burhan's duty, as a pious and responsible man, to dissuade a reckless lad like Al Roumany from falling such easy prey to a gypsy woman. The boy could never be sure, he added, if the woman would preserve his honour and the honour of his tribe, or whether she'd disgrace him.

Burhan did his best to explain Al Roumany's circumstances and the reasons for his involvement, trying to win Sheikh Hamed over to his side. Sheikh Hamed, though, surprised him.

'It's you I'm worried about, Burhan,' he said. 'There's nothing odd about their tempting a young lad like Al Roumany, and, even if they take him to live with them, our people won't be harmed. But it's vital you shouldn't be attracted to them. That really would be a disaster. I know you have a soft spot for this woman, this fortune-teller, Rabiha, but I ask you, in the name of your people, to fight your weakness and the feelings out of your heart. You know well enough that it's women who preserve a man's honour. If someone wants to harm a man, he'll use his woman as a weapon to destroy him. You must act with great care. The matter doesn't concern just you, but your whole people.'

Sheikh Hamed knew from experience what he was talking about. He'd seen Rabiha's influence on Burhan; and he himself, in his youth, had been caught up in something similar. He knew how a woman could enter a man's life and overwhelm his whole being, so that the world started spinning round him and wouldn't stop. Many years before, he recalled, when the Italians had first entered Mizda, a woman from the coast had come there with her husband, who'd been recruited as part of the Italian garrison. When her husband was killed in a battle in the desert, the woman had stayed on in Mizda, trying to find someone there who'd provide for her. Sheikh Hamed had helped her, and, after a few days, had fallen in love with her, then started sneaking out of his house in the middle of the night to sleep with her in her tin shack. He'd paid no attention to what people said, nor – being totally under the other woman's spell – had he cared about the feelings of his wife, whom he deserted night after night. So infatuated had he been that he'd wanted to marry the woman and leave Mizda, so as to escape the anger of his family, who condemned his liaison. But a short time later the battles between the Italians and the patriots had prevented Sheikh Hamed marrying her. When the patriots forced the Italian garrison to leave Mizda, the beautiful widow left with them and Sheikh Hamed never saw her again.

Burhan began defending himself, but Sheikh Hamed cut him short. There was no need, he said, since he wasn't making accusations but merely giving him the benefit of his advice, as an older, more experienced man. Then he asked him to recite some prayers and some verses from the Quran, so as to bless the tent and preserve it from pests and insects.

✿ TWENTY-NINE ✿

The moon shone like the sun at its gentlest and mildest, and the darkness of night was transformed into something like the pale light of warm winter mornings. The breeze wafted from the north – a sign that the task of winnowing the barley and separating it from the chaff would be an easy and successful one.

155

The threshing night showed every sign of being agreeable, and an air of friendship, affection and co-operation enveloped everyone. This was clear from the first minutes spent preparing the threshing floor. The family of Jibreel had placed all the ears of barley they'd collected on a small floor in front of their tents, and five camels, led by the youths and men of the camp, had gone off to thresh their barley.

On the opposite side of the valley, the people of Mizda had taken from their tents some of the barley they'd stored there. Now each family joined in preparing two large moonlit threshing floors. The two heaps of barley ears shone like gold, or rather, perhaps, gleamed and glittered like two stars descended from the heavens to settle on earth. The wondrous sight inspired Hajja Khadija to stand beside them, stretch her hands out before her and recite some verses from the Quran to protect them against the evil eye.

The beating of the drum and the sound of Al Roumany's bagpipes was heard in front of the Jibreel family's tents, announcing the celebration of the threshing, and straight away large numbers of people from the camp flocked to join them. They made a circle round the camels, within which the beasts would tread the ears of barley and thresh them. Then, to everyone's surprise, Zuhra entered the circle and started vigorously dancing the *hajjala*. In less than two hours the camels had finished their task, and the great heap of barley ears had become a mixture of grain and chaff there on the ground.

Yunus and two other men stayed to separate the barley grain from the chaff by winnowing it with the help of the breeze from the distant sea. Meanwhile the five camels returned to the other side of the valley, led, this time, by a larger group of people than had brought them to the Jibreel family's camp. A crowd of children had joined them, along with many men and women, making a noisy procession to where their own barley ears were heaped. They were all seized by a sense of joyous energy, led along by the drummer, Al Roumany playing his bagpipes and Zuhra dancing the *hajjala*.

The procession stopped near the two great heaps of barley ears, and the people prepared to drive the camels on to the threshing floor. It was as though the drummer and Al Roumany and Zuhra, at the head, wanted to perform some ritual to mark out the event. All three danced the *hajjala* now, whirling dizzily around and circling Zuhra. The tempo and rhythm of the music grew ever more intense, and they danced as though in a *zaar*.

A number of the camp people began imitating them, dancing and skipping and cavorting. Some of the young girls from Mizda joined in, to the fury of Haj Abu Hamama, who'd been standing outside his tent about to carry his ears of barley to the threshing floor. He ran towards the circle of dancing people, shouting and threatening. Then, when he reached them, he started beating the girls and boys with his stick, sending them yelling off from the blows. The scene of dancing was turned to one of confusion and abuse, and Haj Abu Hamama now switched his attack to Matouq and Al Roumany, trying to wrench the drum and bagpipes from them, since they, in his eyes, were the cause of the immorality. Matouq stood his ground and defended himself, clutching his drum to stop Haj Abu Hamama smashing it, while Al Roumany, for his part, ran off. As Haj Abu Hamama continued to grasp at the drum, Matouq pushed him away so roughly he fell to the ground. He got up again enraged, his clothes covered with dust, to take his revenge. The onlookers intervened to keep them apart, but then a quarrel broke out between Haj Abu Hamama's supporters and Matouq's, while the women of the Jibreel family ran off screaming and calling to their menfolk on the other side of the valley to come to their aid.

Yunus and two other men answered their cries and came up waving the tools they were using for winnowing the barley, showing themselves ready to use these as weapons. Meanwhile Sheikh Hamed had appeared and drawn Haj Abu Hamama away, while Burhan moved in to appease the other men, telling Yunus and his two comrades there was no call for such violence. Haj Abu Hamama, he said, had just been angry with his daughters and the daughters of his relatives, who'd been dancing in the midst of the men; he hadn't meant to upset anyone else. Then, seeing one of the men of the camp shaking his fist and muttering inaudible remarks, Burhan turned to warn him.

'Let's put an end to this fighting,' he said. 'God curses those who fan violence. Don't put yourself under a curse.'

Next Burhan asked Aunt Maryouma to help him calm Rabiha, who was furious at what had happened and had refused to listen to Burhan's apologies. Haj Abu Hamama, she said, was the one who should apologise, after deliberately insulting and abusing her people.

When the crisis was finally under control, Yunus and his two companions returned to the threshing floor on the other side of the valley, to go on winnowing the barley and separating the grain from the chaff, and Matouq and Al Roumany went with them to help with their work and pack the barley into sacks. Their women-folk left too, apart from Rabiha, who'd been persuaded by Aunt Maryouma to spend the evening with her in her tent. This had been at the request of Burhan, to whom she owed a debt of gratitude for looking after her son Miloud. She knew, too, how much Rabiha had come to mean to Burhan.

Some of the men from the camp, including Suliyman, Abdel Aaly and Amer ben Sheeha, did their best to finish the threshing, working together to keep the camels inside the circle of the floor, while the Captain and Samby helped collect the ears of barley scattered by the camels' hooves and fling them back on the floor. All this took place in a silence broken only by the sound of the hooves treading the barley and straw. There was no singing or ululating to spur the beasts on, as was the custom on such an occasion.

Most of the women had dragged their children off to the tents now, and only a few had accepted Aunt Maryouma's invitation to drink tea with her in their tent, treating the woman Rabiha courteously and doing their best to appease her. At last Aunt Maryouma and some of the women managed to break down the silence she'd maintained since entering the tent. They even persuaded her to compete with Aunt Maryouma in relating traditional folk beliefs.

Aunt Maryouma's feeling was that this lovely, robust woman felt no embarrassment at leaving her face unveiled because she was like the gypsy woman in the epic of Abu Zayd, who'd been the most beautiful woman of her Hilaly tribe and had managed to control both its men and women by her wisdom and keen perception. This belief was based in part on Rabiha's knowledge of the heritage of desert poetry, and its history and sayings, which she could quote by heart.

Aunt Maryouma contrived to win Rabiha's confidence, and wouldn't let her leave her tent till she'd promised to return. Rabiha would, the old woman assured her, be welcome with her and with all the other people of the camp, including Haj Abu Hamama. He had a quick temper, she went on to explain, but he was kind-hearted underneath and never bore grudges.

Before sunrise the threshing floors were massed with sacks full of barley, which Abdel Aaly and Burhan were loading on to their camels to take to the market of Abu Zayyan. The rest of the men helped place these on the nets on the camels' backs and gave them lists of the goods they needed. On the other side of the valley Abdel Aaly and Burhan could see Al Roumany loading his brother's camel, which he'd borrowed, with the sacks of barley of the Jibreel family.

Then the camels went off with their burdens, but with none of the air of rejoicing that usually accompanied such an event. In fact an air of gloom enveloped everyone on account of what had happened the night before. Nobody approved of Haj Abu Hamama's rash behaviour, but he was one of the leaders of the tribe and they couldn't blame him publicly for what had happened. At the same time they couldn't absolve him of all guilt, leaving him to sleep peacefully and come and go with a clear conscience, proclaiming how he'd done what he'd done to save the tribe's good name. They believed his action had actually harmed them, and some of them voiced that view in his presence. Others avoided him, failing to greet him when they saw him next morning.

As for Sheikh Hamed Abu Leila, he'd stayed silent, neither condoning nor condemning what had happened. He waited for

Haj Abu Hamama under the *batm* tree so as to give him his view on the matter. He was sorry, he said, there'd been conflict the night before, but he understood Haj Abu Hamama's motives even so. He further observed that what had happened hadn't been caused simply by the indecent and vulgar way the Jibreel family had celebrated the threshing night. It sprang from a whole series of events, beginning from the moment of the family's arrival in its ill-starred truck.

It had, he went on, been obvious right from the start that these people's behaviour and customs ran totally counter to the morals and traditions of the people of Mizda. He ended by pointing out that, while their own people might not actually be spending much more time alongside the eastern people, the latter's influence might not be so easily wiped out.

Haj Abu Hamama agreed, and he admitted it was these people's influence on the women of the tribe that had made him act the way he had. He wasn't, he said, so much concerned about the men, who wouldn't be disgraced by mixing with these women or even being seduced by them. But the women's reputations could be ruined if they let themselves be affected. He'd been horrified by the evil influence of these women on his daughters and all the other girls of the camp. Mizda had always had an excellent reputation on account of the villagers' good morals, which they'd not only preserved themselves, for generation after generation, but had actually helped spread to other nations in the wider world. Its ancestors had spread the faith and teachings of Islam to Kano and Timbuktu and Waday.

His objection to Al Roumany's marriage had, he confided, been based on these same grounds. Al Roumany would take the gypsy woman with him to Mizda, where she'd be like a rotten apple amid all the other apples, turning them bad too. And if Burhan really did mean to marry Zuhra's cousin, which he thought most likely, then the result would be disastrous. He feared on two counts. Not only was Burhan the religious leader of the people of Mizda, who were influenced by his advice and actions, he was also the one visited, in his home, by the village women, who'd ask him to write charms and amulets for them, and who'd go to him when they were ill to be cured by his medicines and herbs.

Sheikh Hamed didn't consider the men had any right to be angry with Haj Abu Hamama. They'd all agreed to have nothing to do with the family of Jibreel, and now yesterday's fight had ensured that. Someone had to take decisive action against this sudden danger threatening them, and Haj Abu Hamama had done just that. He'd acted because Sheikh Hamed, as head of the tribe, was responsible for many other matters only he could deal with.

Just before sunset the two camels that had taken the barley to Abu Zayyan returned loaded with goods needed by the members of the camp. There was one item, though, which no one had asked for but Burhan regarded as vitally important. When his written charms had had no effect on the pests and insects that had invaded the tents, he'd decided to pay out for a new invention he'd seen in the shops of Abu Zayyan – something with the power to kill insects on the spot. He'd seen its effect for himself when the shop owner had given him a demonstration.

The moment Burhan returned, he took this new invention to Sheikh Hamed and showed him how it worked. It was a small spray, sending out a liquid Sheikh Hamed thought must be kerosene, for it had that kind of smell. But Burhan told him it was an insecticide. He used it on a swarm of ants, which died instantly, then sprayed a large black beetle, which quivered, then died too. As for the flies buzzing in the tent, he worked it on them and they all fell dead on the spot.

Burhan gazed at Sheikh Hamed, proud of himself for having bought this magic spray. No insect that crawled or flew, he said, could face the new weapon and live.

'Are you sure,' Sheikh Hamed inquired, 'it doesn't kill people too?'

'The scientists have devised it to be harmless for humans,' Burhan told him.

Sheikh Hamed was suspicious of the new invention even so.

He'd never seen anything like it before, and regarded it with a mysterious fear. Surely God hadn't created all those insects just so people could kill them with this deadly liquid? If people used it too much, then worms, grasshoppers, beetles, butterflies, ants, flies and other insects would disappear from the earth, after Almighty God had created them for His own purpose. He wasn't sure such an invention was permitted by God. Use of the liquid might be a sin, and he expressed his fears on this score to Burhan, admitting he'd felt guilty when he first saw its effect on the swarm of ants. The reason was that the Prophet – blessings and peace upon him – had forbidden his followers to kill ants, which did no harm to anyone.

Burhan assured him the Faith permitted the use of such a liquid in self-defence or in order to gain one's livelihood. Sheikh Hamed, though, still felt uneasy, reciting to himself verses from the Quran that would drive off any evil involved, then begging God to forgive him for any sin that might come from it.

But the other people in the camp welcomed the invention with open arms, especially after the death of the infant from insect stings. This had terrified parents with infants of the same age, who'd feared a similar fate for them. Now they weren't afraid any more. The insecticide had put their minds at rest, and danger from that source was past as far as they were concerned.

The spray was passed from one man to the next, and from one tent to the next, with all possible speed. Before spraying, people took the ears of barley and placed them in heaps outside the tents, covering them with a cheap waxed material Burhan had bought for them from the market. They'd also swept out the numerous insects they'd found hiding under the barley.

The excitement of spraying with the insecticide, which stopped the insects invading their tents, was accompanied by another exciting matter not publicly announced – a secret not appreciated till everyone had retired to bed and it was time for intimate relations between husbands and wives. The husbands reaped the benefit from the sale of barley in the market, for Abdel Aaly and Burhan had bought scent to be used by the wives, along with oils to anoint their bodies and substances to remove hair from their private parts. The soap they used had a fragrance that suffused their bedding, and next day water was in great demand and the corners of the tents were screened off by curtains so the people inside could bathe and purify themselves.

The soap from the market also encouraged the women to take their washing to the well. They gathered barley only in the early morning, before taking a rest in the shade. Then they rode to the well on donkeys and spent the rest of the day washing their clothes and waiting for them to dry, before finally returning to the camp at the end of the day.

When they arrived back, they found a surprise awaiting them – whether or not it was a cause for rejoicing they weren't sure. They heard the sound of ululation from the other side of the valley, and, before they could send their children to find out the reason, they heard answering ululation from Al Roumany's tent. Then Al Roumany emerged in person, in the new clothes he'd bought from the Abu Zayyan market. He was wearing a white shirt that shone beneath the rays of the setting sun, along with the dark blue waistcoat traditionally worn by bridegrooms and a red skullcap. He had gleaming black shoes too, and he was accompanied by two women, one of them his sister, the other his brother's wife. They were carrying a woman's gown wrapped in transparent paper as a gift for the bride-to-be.

The small procession crossed to the other side of the valley, where the eight women of the Jibreel family were waiting to welcome them. They were singing and ululating to mark the occasion, and close by a new tent had been pitched, different from the others and made from the same waxed material used to cover the heaps of barley. This tent, small and low to the ground, was, from that night on, to be the home of Al Roumany and his bride Zuhra. This was his wedding night, which he'd insisted on celebrating that very night to show his defiance of Haj Abu Hamama, after the way he'd insulted and abused him and his guests from the Jibreel family. It wasn't possible for any of the

163

camp people to join in the wedding, which had sprung up as suddenly as the weddings of the jinn. Apart from Al Roumany's sister and sister-in-law, no one, man or woman, dared walk after him, now that he'd renounced and abandoned the traditions of his tribe.

The singing of the women across the valley grew ever louder, echoing over the wide expanses of plain through the first part of the night. The people of the camp heard it as a defiance of their own silence and refusal to take part in the wedding. The family of Jibreel sang:

'The eye says, welcome him
Who has brought with him the wedding gown!'

✌ THIRTY ☞

From time to time the spiny-tailed lizard and the hedgehog would receive a guest the two of them respected and admired. They were always happy to meet her, since they profited from her visits by learning new things about the history of the district, of the creatures that had lived there in times gone by and the disasters that had struck them. She'd lived through many generations, having spent more than a hundred and fifty years of her long and happy life moving about among the forests and tracts of sand. But she'd only ever left the plateau for the valley on certain days in spring, for diversion, or to meet her friends, or to enjoy the fragrance of the flowers. After that she'd return to her hiding place.

This welcome guest was the tortoise, who was a witness to her era and a living record of the battles fought between the creatures of the valley. She'd witnessed other battles too, forced on these creatures by groups of humans who'd come to these lands then gone on their way once more, leaving a string of disasters and calamities in their wake. She herself had passed through many trials, and, had Almighty God not granted her a strong shell to protect her from the many blows and falls, would have met her death. The distance between her home and the place where she met the hedgehog and the spiny-tailed lizard was by no means great, but the trip exhausted her, as she lived on much lower ground. Nor was climbing an easy matter for a tortoise of her age.

She arrived in the early morning and found her friends in their favourite spot, overlooking the valley with its trees and fields. They talked of how the humans had attacked and killed so many creatures living in the plains, of how they'd devised new kinds of trap and different means of extermination. Why, the tortoise wondered, hadn't the other creatures' means of resistance developed in the same way as the humans' weapons?

The spiny-tailed lizard replied that Almighty God had created these creatures with weapons in their bodies, as a means of defending themselves, but hadn't granted similar weapons to humans. Some creatures He'd created with horns, others with hooves, while other creatures still were created with talons, or fangs, or claws. God had also created small insects with the power to sting or poison their enemies. In fact He'd made all creatures, from the moment of their birth, with means of defence, like the hedgehog's prickles.

'And your shell too, my dear tortoise,' the spiny-tailed lizard went on. 'As for me, I have spikes on my tail, which I can use to strike deadly blows. But humans, having no natural weapons of defence, have had to invent them. Only, these weapons can be used for attack too, as they often have been and still are. But that isn't what we're here to talk about now.'

As the three friends were talking together, they saw groups of ants and spiders, grasshoppers, beetles, butterflies, worms, flies and other insects crawling or flying up to the heights of the plateau. They'd come, as delegates of their various species, to meet the spiny-tailed lizard, who was known as the sage of the plains, wishing to consult with him on the serious developments in the district and ask his advice on the best way of facing the catastrophe of the night before.

This disaster had wiped out great numbers of their families in a single night; just how many was still unknown. First estimates of casualties were that over ten thousand had been killed. Terror was written on their faces, horror rang in every word they spoke, for it had been a day of dread. Nor was the number of victims the sole reason for their terror. What was truly fearful was that, for the first time in their history, they'd been threatened by a weapon capable of wiping them out totally.

For all the insects' unease in the presence of the hedgehog, who'd often been known to kill flies, ants and fleas, their plight forced them to set aside fear of this traditional enemy and concentrate on the problem they'd come to discuss. They gave the spiny-tailed lizard and his two guests an account of the massacre that had taken place and of the new weapon the humans had used, able to destroy all the insects in the tents. The sole survivor, who'd managed to escape before being sprayed, had fled to his companions in the fields, dizzy and sick from the smell of the liquid. Trembling with fear at the recollection of the massacre, he'd told them just what had happened. The rest of the night they'd spent mourning their dead; then, as soon as dawn came, delegates from each species – within which widows and orphans were now in the majority – had made for the plateau to consult with the spiny-tailed lizard, as to how best they could survive such an ordeal.

A representative from the jerboas had come along with the insects, to express solidarity. Although the poison wasn't fatal to jerboas, one present at the spraying of the insects had been made dizzy and sick all the same.

The humans' new weapon was the most devastating of all they'd developed, one they could use thereafter to spray the creatures' hides and holes.

The spiny-tailed lizard asked why so many of them had been inside the tents, what they'd been doing there. They replied that they'd been carrying out a plan they'd all agreed in advance: a counter-attack to harm these humans who hadn't stopped harming them ever since their arrival in Jandouba. The aim of the plan had been to force them to leave the place.

The spiny-tailed lizard was astonished by this. Surely, he said, defending themselves didn't mean they had to attack the humans in their tents, digging their graves, as it were, with their own claws. Humans, he went on, would never have thought of using such a deadly invention if the insects hadn't stung and bitten them.

The spiny-tailed lizard then put to the tortoise his second question about this deadly weapon. Had she, he wanted to know, heard of any such weapon being used to kill insects in previous generations? Humans had, he knew, invented weapons of destruction before, but hadn't they up to now used them solely against other humans?

The tortoise said that, over all the long life she'd lived amid the events of the valley, along with what she'd learned from those who'd lived before her, she'd never seen or heard of anything like this devilish new weapon, devised by the great minds of humans as a means to still greater destruction and annihilation.

The spiny-tailed lizard's advice was explicit and firm. They should, he told them, put aside all thought of revenge and abandon all idea of retaliation, since this would only bring total destruction down on them. They should focus instead on one goal: to preserve themselves and their families by warding off the danger that threatened their species. They could be certain, he went on, that no humans would use this weapon to seek them out in their homes – they'd only used it to protect themselves in their own dwelling places. Moreover, the presence of the humans in Jandouba was merely temporary. If the other creatures avoided approaching them, and held back from attacking them for a certain period, the problem would solve itself.

If, he said in conclusion, they'd asked his advice when the crisis first sprang up, things would have turned out very differently. But they'd waited for things to grow serious and complicated before coming to consult him, and so dealing with matters now was a very different matter from making plans that would have guaranteed them success in the first place. Mistakes at the start always led to drastic consequences.

The creatures all listened to the spiny-tailed lizard's views with the greatest respect. They realised now that, if they were to avoid total destruction, they must avoid confronting their enemy. Even so, this wouldn't solve the problem of the jerboas, who had not only had their homes destroyed but were still being hunted and slain.

At this point the hedgehog entered the discussion – there'd never, after all, been any tension between him and the jerboas. He inquired after the progress of the jerboas' many plans to deal with their crisis, and was told these had all failed for reasons beyond their control. Every course they'd tried had been frustrated by some new development – their last plan, based on enlisting the help of other species to take their revenge on the humans, having been brought to nought by the new, deadly weapon. There remained only one solution, one they'd kept putting off, since, from the beginning of the crisis, they'd preferred to rise above the base means used by the humans themselves. Now, though, the dangers to which they were exposed had become critical. They had no choice but to fight them with their own methods and weapons, however contemptible, by seeking out the aid of those equally contemptible and vile.

The spiny-tailed lizard and the hedgehog listened closely to the plan that would, so the jerboas believed, put an end to their conflict with the humans, and end it in their own favour. They must enlist the city rats, known for the filth and squalor of their lives, and for their ability to spread diseases and plagues among people, to take revenge on these human tyrants. The jerboa chiefs should, accordingly, go to the city and explain their plight to the rats, asking them to use their experience in finding some virus that would infect the jerboa-eaters. This would result in their deaths, and would force the rest of the humans to leave Jandouba. There was nothing fanciful in all this, for the city rats had previously declared their willingness to strengthen the bonds of affection between themselves and their cousins on the plains, by offering their services. The jerboas had earlier disdained such a relationship, not wishing to have anything to do with these dirty, squalid animals.

The two wise creatures, the spiny-tailed lizard and the hedgehog, saw well enough why the jerboas should want to seek such a ghastly revenge. They objected strongly, even so, on moral and practical grounds alike. To start with, how could the jerboas guarantee the plague carried by the rats wouldn't infect other creatures and not just the humans? Indeed, other plagues that had broken out had not only infected the creatures of the plains but had struck at trees and plants too, had polluted water, food, even the air. It would mean exchanging one form of evil for another deadlier still.

The other point made by these two wise creatures was that, as the jerboas themselves had informed them, most of the jerboa homes had now been destroyed – which meant these people had almost completed their mission and would be leaving very soon. The two accordingly advised the jerboas to bide their time and wait for the people to go, rather than sully their reputation and their history by resorting to such base and contemptible means.

Soon the spiny-tailed lizard yawned, closed his eyes and rested his head on his shoulders, all of which indicated he was tired out and the consultation was at an end. But first he uttered some final words of advice to the delegates who'd sought his views. They all listened attentively to this sage of the plains, as he told them their ordeal wasn't the first, in the annals of disaster and calamity, to strike the inhabitants of this land, nor would it be the last. In the past they'd always come through such ordeals. Did they, he asked, know how that had been achieved?

The creatures remained silent, waiting for the sage of the plains to enlighten them, to reassure them and restore their confidence by guiding them towards their most important weapon of all. The spiny-tailed lizard smiled. The weapon, he said, was sexual intercourse. They must return to their homes, enter their bedrooms and pursue their relations vigorously; and they must call on all their species to follow their examples. Any engaged in other matters must abandon them in these difficult times, so as to reproduce and multiply. This would frustrate the plans of the humans who aimed to exterminate them with their deadly new weapon.

THIRTY-ONE

The chameleon has more than one face. In fact it assumes dozens in a single day. The chameleon's colour changes too, according to where it happens to be, seeming to become part of that place. And then, its appearance changes according to the way light reflects on it, and according to the sequence of night and day and the position of moon and sun.

One day Hajja Khadija spotted a chameleon climbing up the branch of a tamarisk tree. Its colour was as green as the tree's own leaves, and its body had patches of shining light reflected from the sun's rays, giving it a lovely, glittering appearance. The sight aroused the admiration of Hajja Khadija, who praised and glorified Almighty God for having made a creature so beautiful. She declared, too, that the tree in which it had made its home was a blessed tree, since the chameleon was a sacred creature, of lofty standing among the creatures fashioned by Almighty God. This belief was based on the views of many religious scholars, who had written of chameleons in their books.

God had created the chameleon with an amazing capacity for camouflage, and with the ability to kill poisonous reptiles with its spittle and use its tongue to kill noxious insects, so making a place clean and safe for humans. All these qualities increased people's respect for the creature, especially as it was mentioned in the heritage handed down from the older generations, marked out by high repute, great dignity and lofty standing.

Hajja Khadija had chosen the shade of this tree in which to rest at midday, along with other elderly women, like Burhan's mother Sadina, the aunt from Fezzan and Amer ben Sheeha's mother Saliha. Aunt Maryouma sat with them from time to time, but she never spent her midday rest in the one place, since everyone invited her to sit with them.

For all the tamarisk tree's gnarled trunk and bark, which proclaimed it one of the oldest trees in Jandouba, its branches were strong and its leaves green and flourishing. Hajja Khadija accordingly called it 'the palace', since it was as shady and comfortable as any palace could be. It was one of five large tamarisk trees the women of the camp had chosen as spots for their midday rest, bringing food and drink to enjoy in their shade. "The palace" was considered a blessed tree, as said, because of the chameleon that lived in it, and the creature had become famous among the women of the camp. They called it Hajja Sharifa as an expression of respect. Hajja Khadija would greet the chameleon each day, whenever she sat under the tree. Starlings and nightingales and other brightly coloured birds of good omen also perched on the branches, and this further strengthened the women's belief that the tree was indeed blessed. The woman from Fezzan brought green flags from her tent, and, with Samby's help, hung them on the branches, to ask for Almighty God's blessing and to be rewarded for the generous offering.

From a distance Amer ben Sheeha watched Zenab, who'd gone to the blessed tree with her mother and some friends for the midday rest. Rather than go to the place where he spent his own rest with the men, far from where the women sat, he hid behind an acacia tree where no one ever went, because it had no branches beyond a few bare twigs that gave barely enough shade for a rabbit. There Amer sat with his basket of barley ears, his bottle of water and a few dates for his lunch. And, as he ate, he kept his eyes fixed on the giant tamarisk tree.

For several days now he'd been waiting in vain for the chance to be alone with Zenab. Finally, that morning, his feelings aroused by Al Roumany's simple wedding that happened so suddenly and against the wishes of the chiefs of the tribe, he'd decided to see what he and Zenab could do on their own account.

The wedding should have taken place three years before, but, by ill luck, the past three years had been years of severe drought and famine. The lack of harvests had meant it had to be put off, for, if a man couldn't feed even one mouth, how could he feed the mouths of a whole new family? Nor could he have provided the customary banquets and feasts for the village.

Amer wished Zenab's father had agreed to the signing of the marriage certificate, even if the wedding itself had to be delayed until things improved. Then at least he would have been sure nobody else could marry her. Sheikh Hamed, though, hadn't wanted his daughter to be married on paper without knowing exactly when the marriage would be consummated, and so he'd refused Amer's request. The matter worried Amer and filled him with foreboding for the future. What if Sheikh Hamed decided to marry her to one of the young village men who'd found a regular job in the town and had enough money to hold a wedding feast, to pay a dowry and buy gold gifts for the bride? Especially as Zenab's beauty, and her status as the daughter of the village chief, made her a desirable catch for any young man.

Amer made a point that day of not letting Zenab out of his sight. Day after day he'd waited for the chance to be alone with her. Now, at last, he'd decided he must make his own chance, following her wherever she went. He dug by the *nabk* tree close to where she was, even though he knew the ground beneath had no jerboa burrows. He was waiting for her to leave her mother's side, so he could talk to her and tell her where and when to meet him.

During the early morning the Captain and Samby dogged his steps, chattering about what Al Roumany had done the night before, and about the women of the Jibreel family, together with the rupture between that family and themselves after yesterday's marriage. They'd sought his view on the matter, but received no answer- Amer had been too busy thinking how he could get rid of them, so as to carry out his plan to meet Zenab. He'd lost a lot of valuable time before finally escaping them and going to work near where Zenab and her mother were working. He'd wanted to talk to her, to make a sign of some sort that he'd like to meet her, but without success.

The whole midday break he'd spent closely watching every movement beneath the blessed tree opposite. Suddenly he saw

Zenab leave her mother, who was resting against the trunk, and go to a *nabk* tree on the edge of the valley. He quickly got up and followed, before anyone else could join her to dig for burrows beneath it.

In fact this tree, as he found out, had no burrows under it anyway. Zenab must have pretended to go and dig there to fool the others. And, if she'd done that, it must have been so they could meet. Since early morning she'd noticed Amer hovering around, and she'd noticed how he'd had sat, in the midday heat, under a bare, shadeless tree so as to remain close to her. Realising he wanted to meet her to tell her something urgent, she'd managed to persuade her mother to let her return to the fields to work alone. Her mother, she'd said, should stay there and rest. She, Zenab, was young and strong and could stand the heat.

So it was that Zenab had been able to meet Amer, though in fact she already knew what he wanted to say. Amer was delighted to hear her voice, and he knew her love for him was no less than his for her. Even so, he wasn't satisfied with this brief encounter in front of everyone. What he wanted was a meeting that would quench the thirst of his love for her. He wanted to be close to her, to whisper to her affectionately, as befitted a man and woman due to be married. He persuaded her they should find some distant spot where they'd be safe, where they could sit and talk together. She told him to walk ahead of her, towards a place he thought suitable. She'd follow at a distance to avert any possible suspicion.

With a light and happy heart Amer ben Sheeha walked swiftly to the west, where there were a few *nabk* trees. There were no jerboa burrows there, but sand dunes looming from the side of the valley. Zenab waited from a safe distance, then started following him as he walked. Whenever she saw the shadow of a man or a woman bending to dig a burrow or collect ears of barley, she'd avert her eyes and quicken her pace. Amer walked quickly on till he'd long left any places where people were working. Zenab started running after him.

'Slow down!' she said. 'Where are you taking us?'

'Where nobody can see us.'

'Well, nobody can see us here. We're far enough away now. Don't forget I'll have to fill this basket with barley before I go back.'

'There's a *nabk* tree over there. Near that mound of sand.'

'We don't have to go to the ends of the earth to talk to one another.'

'This isn't the end of the earth.'

'I mustn't be too late going back to my mother.'

Amer reached a red sand dune that looked like a mountain. Then, instead of going to the nearby *nabk* tree, he went round the sand dune, leaving the tents of the camp behind him. He sat down in the shadow of the dune, then, leaning on the sand, beckoned to Zenab to come and sit alongside, but Zenab simply stood there swinging the basket in her hand.

'Do you know any kind angel,' she said, 'who'll come and fill my basket with barley?'

Without a word, Amer stood up and emptied his own half-full basket into hers.

'Now,' he said, 'there's no excuse for you not to sit down.'

Zenab, accordingly, sat down close to Amer on the soft sand, facing the horizon with its range of mountains, beyond which lay the world of the north, its sea, shores and ancient cities. To their right was a large area of rocky land in the course of the valley, while the fields had dwindled to odd patches of ground where the *nabk* trees grew. On their left limitless expanses appeared before them, of grey, barren land marked by small furrows and grooves the floods had made, and dotted with gorse and other spiny bushes.

Zenab kept her eyes fixed on the ground, too embarrassed to say a word. She filled her hand with sand and let it run through her fingers. This was the first time she and Amer had been alone since she'd been promised to him, although they'd met often enough at family gatherings. They'd never been given the chance to discuss their future life together. Amer had known Zenab since she was a child, and he knew everything about her family, who were his

174

relations too. Even so, he knew nothing about her thoughts, about her likes and dislikes, or what she was hoping for in their future married life.

Amer loved Zenab, and he knew she loved him. He could even remember the exact moment he'd fallen in love with her, how this love had developed and grown after his mother had come from a visit to Sheikh Hamed's home and told him how Zenab had asked after him. She'd made the first move, and he'd responded, recognising his love for her, though he hadn't been aware of the depth of his feelings.

When Amer had sent his mother to seek out the views of Zenab's parents, he'd been sure Sheikh Hamed wouldn't refuse to marry his daughter to him. It wasn't just that they were closely related. His father had been a close friend of Sheikh Hamed. He'd owned a shop next to Sheikh Hamed's own, and, when Amer's father died, and neither Amer nor any of his brothers had been old enough to run the shop, Sheikh Hamed had supervised it along with his own – as though it were his own, indeed – with the help of the trusted Captain, and so kept it open. Then, when Amer had grown up, Sheikh Hamed had taught him the ropes, until finally he was able to stand on his own feet and run the place without help.

Amer gazed at Zenab's slender fingers as the sand trickled through them, jubilant at being alone with her in the open air. He laughed as he saw how the red streaks in her dress matched the colour of the sand dunes, so much so that he felt as though he was sitting on the hem of her dress, surrounded by an aura of radiance shining from her face.

'At last,' he said, 'we've managed to meet one another without any spies or guards.'

'Don't be too sure of things,' she said. 'There are plenty of people behind that sand dune!'

Zenab's mother hadn't neglected her daughter's education, and she wasn't illiterate like most of the village girls. She'd often asked her father to bring her books from town, so she could enjoy reading, but he'd only brought her religious books that taught her how to invoke Almighty God, and how to perform ablution and other rulings of the Faith.

'What would you say,' Amer asked, 'to living here, or having some other sort of bedouin life? Look, here in the open spaces you can live free, away from the walls of houses and shops.'

'And when did we ever live away from the open air?' Zenab rejoined. 'We only live in our homes for a while, then off we go to the desert, in spring especially, for ploughing and harvesting and shearing sheep.'

'Those were the things we did before the years of drought struck us.'

'Yes, and now the drought's made us leave our village and come to Jandouba. That's why I'd rather live in the city. I'd love to live in the city – I've read and heard so much about it. Why don't you like it? You've visited it often enough.'

'I think we've just had our first disagreement.'

'You know very well I'd live with you anywhere, even in a cave in the mountains.'

'I was only joking. I'll agree to anything you want. For your sake I'll find room in my heart for the city, as soon as we're married.'

Amer ben Sheeha realised they had only a very short time together. The sun had already begun its downward journey towards the horizon, like a ball rolling from the top of a mountain and disappearing finally behind the plateau, leaving the troops of darkness to begin their own swift descent to the sky and earth. He didn't let the mention of marriage pass.

'It's not fair,' he said, 'that we have to put our marriage off for so long.'

'Well, what can we do about it? It has to be like that, because of the way things are at present. There's nothing new in that, is there?'

'What's new is that a certain person's married without waiting three days, let alone three years like us.'

'And do you call Al Roumany's wedding a proper wedding?'

'He married the woman he loved, didn't he? Why do we have to make everything so complicated?'

176

'We're not making things complicated. It's just a matter of waiting for a better time.'

'I wonder if the jerboas' barley will back up your hopes and make a new life for us?'

' "The jerboas' barley" had become a standard expression, used by everyone in the camp. They'd used the term ironically at first, as a joke, then they'd gone on calling it that to protect it from the evil eye. But, whether the barley had been reaped by the jerboas, or wherever it had come from, it was still barley that had helped them raise the siege of hunger and drought that had encircled them. It was a source of food that would feed them for a full year, or even longer.

For that reason Amer believed there was no reason any more for Zenab's parents to put off their marriage. Zenab, though, asked him not to be upset if her father disagreed with him. This, she explained, wasn't her own viewpoint or wish – it was more important, after all, for a girl to get married than it was for a young man. A man could wait till he was forty or even older, while a girl, if she wasn't married by the time she was twenty-three, would be considered an old maid.

She rose suddenly, realising how late it was. The sun had reached the rim of the horizon, ready to vanish. She was very anxious now, for, even if she ran all the way back, she'd never arrive before dark. Amer took a small packet from his shirt. It was the size of a box of matches, and it was a gift he'd brought for Zenab from Mizda, waiting for a chance to give it to her ever since they'd arrived in Jandouba. Taking and opening it, she saw two silver earrings shaped like crescents and stars. It was a beautiful gift in these difficult days, but her delight in it was spoiled by her worry at being so late. The sun was deceptive. It had vanished quickly behind the mountain peaks, leaving streaks of light hanging above the horizon.

A young, dingy wolf come down from one of the flood furrows, and, as they left the dune behind them, Amer and Zenab found themselves face to face with it. It stood some way off, pricking up its ears and staring at them, then bared its fangs and shook its head from side to side as if about to attack. Zenab picked up a stone and flung it at the wolf, hitting it on the head and making it run off howling. Then, suddenly, it returned, howling more fiercely than ever. Zenab threw another stone, which made the beast more furious still. It howled and began to circle them. Zenab was about to fling a third stone, but Amer told her it would only make the wolf more angry. He told her, too, that the wolf was howling to call others to its aid.

Amer took Zenab's hand and hurried her on, before the other wolves could come and surround them. Suddenly he saw another running towards them, then a third. Letting go of Zenab's hand, he grabbed a long, thorny branch from a nearby *nabk* tree, as a defence against the beasts who were coming one after another, so that there were six now. Still they howled and moved around the couple. Amer took Zenab's hand once more and led her up to the top of the mound of sand.

Darkness began to envelop them, and the ring of wolves drew ever nearer, circling the mound. Zenab started weeping bitterly, while Amer whirled round, beating the air with the thorny branch to frighten the wolves and stop them climbing the dune and reaching them. One of the wolves leaped over the sand, and, dodging the blows of the spiny branch, opened its mouth, raised its two front legs, then sank its fangs into Zenab's body. Amer struck the wolf on the head with the branch, and, with his other hand, dragged Zenab away from the creature and held her close to him. He struck the wolf several times more on the head, and it retreated to the bottom of the dune.

Zenab's gown was torn, and she was wounded, the flowing blood making the wolves thirstier still. They all leaped up and began climbing the dune, ready to tear Amer and Zenab to pieces.

THIRTY-TWO

The trouble started when Haj Abu Hamama and Sheikh Hamed learned that Burhan had written the marriage certificate for Al Roumany.

Nobody in the camp had known anything of this, since no one had seen him when he went off to the other side of the valley or when he returned at night. As for Burhan himself, he'd told nobody of the matter, not even his mother or sister. Neither Sheikh Hamed nor Haj Abu Hamama would have known of Burhan's part in the marriage but for a talk they'd had with Uthman, Al Roumany's brother. They'd met him at noon the day after the wedding and blamed him for not stopping his brother marrying a wicked, immoral woman who'd bring disgrace on his family and tribe.

Uthman had tried to defend himself. He'd done his best, he said, to prevent the wedding. Uthman had warned his brother that, if the marriage to Zuhra went ahead, he'd have nothing more to do with him, and that the whole tribe would despise and curse him. But Al Roumany, foolish as he was, had insisted on doing as he wanted, having no notion where such a marriage would lead. He'd simply told his elder brother that he and he alone knew what was best for him, that no one else in the whole world could know better what was good for him. All he wanted from his family was to be left alone.

Uthman told the two old men he'd been helpless. If he had tried to stop his brother going out that night, there would have been a clash between him and his brother, sister and wife. The two women had already agreed to Al Roumany's pleas that they go with him to his bride's home on his wedding night.

According to his wife, he went on, it was Burhan who'd written and recorded the marriage certificate. This came as a shock to both men, and Sheikh Hamed could hardly believe a sane, responsible person like Burhan could have behaved so senselessly.

'Are you certain?' he asked Uthman. 'Did your wife actually see Burhan writing the certificate?'

'Yes, it was Burhan all right.'

It wasn't a suitable time to hold a meeting in the guest tent. Even so, Sheikh Hamed felt such a serious matter shouldn't be discussed under the *batm* tree. The afternoon was only just over, and the meeting couldn't be held at the guest tent without the Captain to prepare the tea. He stood up and looked around till he spotted the Captain in the field, then shouted to him to come at once. Seeing Abdel Aaly and Suliyman had been digging close to the Captain, he told him to invite them to come and drink tea with him.

As for Haj Abu Hamama, he raised his hands in astonishment, wondering how Burhan could ever have betrayed his people by committing such a dreadful crime. Abdel Aaly and Suliyman entered the tent in time to hear Abu Haj Hamama's condemnation of him.

'Thank God,' Abdel Aaly said, without waiting for details of the matter, 'you've begun to see the kind of man he really is.' Burhan might have saved his wife's life, but Abdel Aaly's old hatred for him still rankled.

For the third and fourth time the men asked Uthman to tell them of the role Burhan had played in his brother Al Roumany's wedding; whereupon the question rose as to why he'd done it and whether any further developments could be expected. Sheikh Hamed told the Captain to take a look at Burhan's shade from a distance, to see if he was there, and whether he had any visitors at this hour, and, if so, who they were. The Captain served the first round of tea, then hurried off on his scouting mission.

The men weren't used to drinking tea at this time of day, but it was always welcome, anywhere and any time. As for their relations with the Jibreel family, they'd hoped – before the latest unpleasant developments – to have as little to do with them as possible before the family went back home and they themselves returned to Mizda.

Most of the jerboa burrows had been dug now, and the ears of barley reaped by the creatures had been collected. Quite soon now they'd fold their tents and return home, putting an end to the encounter of the two tribes. But Al Roumany's irresponsible behaviour, which had resulted in his marriage, would cause definite complications. To accuse Burhan over the role he'd played might cause a split of opinion in the tribe, leading on to conflict.

The Captain came back. He'd seen Burhan, he said, giving the boys a lesson under his shade. Sheikh Hamed smiled ironically at this, for one of Burhan's pupils was his grandson. In common with the rest of his people, he'd trusted Burhan in this capacity, sending his grandson as they'd sent their sons, to learn the Quran and understand the teachings of Islam. How, he wondered, could Burhan go on doing all this after what he'd done?

He heard Abdel Aaly talking aside to Suliyman. They were making threatening remarks about Burhan.

'Don't let's judge the man in his absence,' he interposed. 'Especially as he's only a few yards away.'

Haj Abu Hamama disapproved of Sheikh Hamed's forbearance. Both Al Roumany and Burhan, he felt, had defied him personally. The only difference was that Al Roumany's defiance wasn't as important, or as dangerous, as Burhan's. Al Roumany had acted out of recklessness and ignorance, but the conduct of Burhan, as a sensible, responsible person, posed a serious threat. Something more, Haj Abu Hamama felt sure, was waiting to be revealed.

'With your agreement,' he said, 'I'll go straight to Burhan and confront him with his crime. Then I'll tell him to leave the camp and go over to the other side like his friend Al Roumany.'

Sheikh Hamed, though, felt a man like Burhan shouldn't be treated in this manner, that he had the right to defend himself. The whole thing might be a simple misunderstanding. Perhaps someone who looked like Burhan had written the marriage certificate. Perhaps what Uthman had been told by his wife, and had passed on to them, was untrue. The best way to find out what had happened, he said, was to hear Burhan's side of the story.

They should go and see him when his lesson was over and ask him to answer all their questions.

The noise of the lads running in front of the tents grew ever louder. Then Ali ran to where his grandfather was sitting, so as to be given some dates before he went to join his grandmother in the field. Sheikh Hamed asked him what the day's lesson had been about. They'd read, the boy answered, the chapter on *Al Kafirun*, or 'Those Who Reject Faith'. He wanted to recite what he'd learned: 'Say: O you who reject Faith, I do not worship that which you worship . . . '

His grandfather stopped him from going on to complete the recitation, as the last verse would have run counter to their argument: 'To you be your way and to me mine.'

Sheikh Hamed made a sign to the other men that, with the boys gone, the time had come for them to go to Burhan's shade. It wasn't a task he was relishing, but matters had to be cleared up.

From a distance they could see someone sitting with him, but they couldn't make out, till they came nearer, whether the visitor was a man or a woman. Then, as they approached, they saw it was none other than Rabiha, the head of the Family of Jibreel.

They stopped in their tracks, making a silent decision to turn back. But, before they could turn, Burhan noticed them. He greeted them and gave them a hearty welcome, standing up and walking towards them, having first bade farewell to Rabiha, who went off in the opposite direction to the one from which the men had come.

As soon as they were all seated under the shade, Suliyman slyly asked Burhan if the person who'd been sitting with him was Rabiha, the woman everyone talked about. Burhan nodded. He could hardly deny it was her, since he'd met her before on the grounds of mutual benefit for his people and hers.

Burhan realised that, with matters as they now stood between the two tribes, he must find some excuse for the woman's presence under his shade. He made the first that came into his head: that Rabiha had come to tell him she didn't wish the two tribes to part with bad blood between them. Each would soon be returning to its home, and she'd like them to part as friends.

'What's your view on that, Burhan?' Abdel Aaly asked dryly.

Burhan sensed a plot had been hatched against him, but was determined not to show any weakness.

'Only an ignorant fool,' he replied firmly, 'would prefer discord to reconciliation.'

Haj Abu Hamama couldn't resist the chance of a cunning dig.

'Especially,' he said, 'now the two tribes are related by marriage.'

Sheikh Hamed broke in before matters could get out of hand. Quietly and briefly he explained to Burhan why they'd come to visit him.

'I've heard something,' he said, 'that I refuse to believe unless I hear it from your own lips. Is it true you wrote Al Roumany's marriage certificate?'

Burhan was silent for a moment. Then he said:

'May God bless the Prophet.'

All except Haj Abu Hamama replied:

'And God's blessing and peace be upon him.'

Burhan noticed Haj Abu Hamama's silence, and sensed the man's hostility even before he began to defend himself. He asked why he'd wilfully refrained from asking God to bless the Prophet.

'I won't do it on any orders from you,' Haj Abu Hamama replied furiously.

'May God forgive me,' Burhan said simply, 'and forgive you.'

He went on, not answering Sheikh Hamed's question directly:

'As far as I was concerned, it wasn't a matter of Al Roumany wanting to marry Zuhra, a woman from another tribe. It was a matter, rather, of a man and a woman wanting to marry according to our religion and to the rulings of God and His Prophet.'

Haj Abu Hamama wanted to break in here, but Sheikh Hamed stopped him. 'A man of religion,' Burhan continued, 'is like a physician. Neither can refuse to perform his solemn duty if someone comes to request his services.'

183

'Does that mean,' Sheikh Hamed asked, controlling his temper, 'that you did write the certificate?'

'I didn't write it because I wanted to. They'd prepared everything for the wedding and insisted on consummating the marriage that night. They asked me to write the marriage certificate according to the rulings of Islam, and told me, if I didn't write it, they'd write it themselves. Naturally I was afraid I'd be guilty of a grave sin if I left them to write it in an ignorant, invalid fashion.'

Uthman's voice rang out triumphantly, for the truth of his story had been vindicated.

'There's proof of what I said. From Burhan's own mouth!'

Burhan shot him a disdainful glance, then said in a whisper, as though talking to himself:

'Why did Al Roumany have to have a brother like you?'

Haj Abu Hamama rose.

'Come on, Sheikh Hamed,' he said. 'There's no point in talking or staying here. Everything's clear enough now.'

Everyone followed Haj Abu Hamama's example and rose, including Burhan, who asked them to stay and discuss the matter with more understanding and tolerance.

'There's nothing left to discuss between you and us,' Haj Abu Hamama replied. 'A man who renounces his people, betrays them as you've done, doesn't deserve to be talked to or even greeted.'

'There's no call to abuse me, Haj Abu Hamama,' Burhan replied. 'I've done nothing to deserve what you've just said about me.'

'To be frank with you,' Sheikh Hamed said, in support of Haj Abu Hamama, 'I could never have believed you'd act as you have. You know well enough it's against the interests of our people.'

Then, before Burhan could ask what interests he'd violated, and who'd laid down such rules in the first place, Haj Abu Hamama announced the punishment Burhan was to receive for his actions.

'There'll be no further relations between you and us. From this day on no one will pray under your shade, nor will you teach the boys to recite the Quran. And we'll tell everyone in Mizda what you've done. Not a single person will pray under your leadership or take any medicines or charms from you.'

'And what sin,' Burhan asked, 'am I supposed to have committed? Is all this fuss simply because I wrote Al Roumany's marriage certificate?'

'You egged Al Roumany on! He wouldn't have done anything but for you.'

'Is it such a crime that he fulfilled the other part of his religion, by marrying? Where's the crime in that, tell me?'

'The crime's in the choice of the woman he married, and in the immorality defended by a man of religion. By you, Burhan!'

'You've no right to say that to me in my own home, Haj Abu Hamama!'

'I've the right to say more than that when morality's in question, and honour. We won't be surprised to find you acting the same way Al Roumany did.'

'When I want to marry, I shan't ask permission from you. And I won't hear any talk from you, either, about morality or honour. I'm more honourable, and more pious, than you are!'

The two men now lost their tempers completely, raising their hands to threaten one another, but the others rushed between them to stop Burham and Abu Hamama coming to blows. Sheikh Hamed, wanting to put an end to the confrontation, pulled Haj Abu Hamama away to a point halfway between the shade and the tents, where he began voicing his doubts about the nature of Burhan's relations with Rabiha.

Burhan, hearing this, pursued them, yelling at Haj Abu Hamama never to mention Rabiha's name again. He intended, he went on, to go to her family and ask for her hand in marriage, and he'd be honoured if she accepted him as her husband. Haj Abu Hamama should know, he said finally, that he wasn't afraid of him and cared nothing for his threats. He could take whatever stupid action against him that he wished.

The sun had vanished below the horizon a few moments before, and darkness, with its black, heavy curtain, had begun to envelop the camp. Many of the people, who'd spent their day searching out the last few burrows with remaining ears of barley, had returned to their tents and were standing in small groups watching the quarrel. Suddenly Aunt Maryouma rushed over, shouting at the top of her voice.

'While you're standing there quarrelling, there's a disaster in Sheikh Hamed's tent!'

Without waiting to hear further details from the old woman, Sheikh Hamed rushed towards his tent. Samby and the Captain ran ahead of him, while the rest of the men followed, wondering what could have happened. As for Burhan, he returned to his shade, cursing the devil in muttered tones.

Sheikh Hamed found his wife in tears, with a number of the other women trying to calm her down. Her daughter Zenab hadn't yet returned to the tent. Her mother said she'd been with her most of the day and had only left her after their noon rest, when she'd gone on ahead to work in the fields. The mother had meant to follow her to the field, then return with her to the tent as they did each day. She hadn't, she went on between her sobs, found her daughter there, and a number of women had searched for her in all the places she might have been, till sunset, but they'd found no trace of her. The distraught mother had asked everyone in the field, men and women alike, if they'd seen her, but no one had any idea where she might be. It was dark now, and everyone had returned to the tents. Zenab would never have been so late by her own choice. Something dreadful must have happened to her.

Everyone in the camp was getting ready to start the search, when the dogs began a loud, fierce barking in answer to the howling of wolves not too far off. It was coming from the west, and Hajja Khadija sensed straight away that the howling had something to do with her daughter's absence. She insisted, through her tears, on going with the dogs to investigate the matter herself, but her husband told her to stay in the tent. She couldn't possibly see her way in the dark, he said, and this was a job for men. But still she rushed off, heedless of what her husband said.

The men had sprinkled a few drops of kerosene on to some dry tree branches they'd cut, then lit them to use as torches to light the way. Now they all rushed off together, to the spot where the dogs and the wolves were already fighting. Despite the rough, rocky track and thorny bushes, the men moved quickly, no one lagging behind. Hajja Khadija herself was at the head of the throng. As they approached the place where the animals were fighting, the howling and barking grew ever louder, and, when they finally reached the spot, they found a number of dogs from Jandouba had joined their own, and that, together, they'd managed to defeat the wolves and send them fleeing towards the distant plateau,

By the light of the torches they could all see Zenab lying there, her clothes so ripped they covered scarcely any part of her plump body, which was covered with wounds from which blood was gushing out. She tried to get up, moaning faintly. Close by her lay Amer ben Sheeha, the blood from his wounds covering his body and face, his clothes torn to shreds except for a few tattered pieces covering his private parts. Only a slight tremor of his hand on his head showed he was still alive.

The women shrieked in terror. Then, from the middle of the crowd, a shot rang out from the rifle of Haj Abu Hamama, who'd wanted to shoot Zenab and Amer on the spot, in front of all the people who'd witnessed the scandal. But Hajja Khadija flung herself on her daughter to protect her and cover her exposed body, while Amer's mother likewise threw herself on her son's body.

A number of men surrounded Haj Abu Hamama and pulled the rifle from his hand. He, for his part, went on with his threats that he'd kill Amer and Zenab and complete what the wolves had left unfinished. They deserved such a fate, he cried, for bringing such disgrace on their families.

❧ THIRTY-THREE ❧

Between the town and valley of Jandouba, above a wide section of flat land made by the wind between seven sandy plateaux, was the spot chosen by the dogs of Jandouba and the dogs of the camp to hold a celebration on the occasion of their great victory over the wolves. They'd fought side by side in the battle, and there'd been a high degree of co-ordination between them all – between those who lived in Jandouba and those come from the south.

Marzouq, the camp's head dog, had fought bravely, and, as was the custom of dogs on such occasions, his due was to be honoured and rewarded with the most beautiful female dog. She was to be his companion that night – the selfsame lovely dog that had been sent as a delegate of the Jandouba dogs when those of Mizda had arrived some weeks before. She had a mellow voice, attractive black eyes and seductive crimson lips, and Marzouq had fallen madly in love with her the moment he saw her.

In response to the audience's demands, Marzouq had made a short speech to inaugurate the celebration, delivered, he said, in honour of the beautiful female dog who'd been the cause of his success; for, as the saying went, behind every great dog was a female. Such a female must, he went on, be as noble, lovely and alluring as this one before them. From the moment he'd set eyes on her he'd been determined to win her love, and that had spurred him on to fight so courageously in the battle, and to triumph for the sake of her beautiful eyes. His inestimable reward now was to spend this whole night in her company, enjoying her irresistible charms. He would refrain from speaking at greater length, since he wished to begin his night of happiness immediately.

Without further ado Marzouq descended from the platform, took his darling female dog in his arms and began dancing with her to the music played by a group of Jandouba dogs. Thus began the celebratory dancing, in which singing and embraces between the lovers went on till the following morning.

That same morning, in the fields, a strange event took place, one passed on in every detail, by those witnessing it, to the rest of the creatures living in the plains.

Everyone saw the chameleon leave the great tamarisk tree where she'd lived among the starlings and other birds, and the green flags. She walked slowly, in stately fashion, towards the fields, till she reached the bank of the valley. Next, turning neither left nor right, she crossed the valley, then veered right towards the plateau. She reached the foot of this, and began slowly, steadily climbing.

The reason this was so strange was that the chameleon had spent her whole life in that giant tamarisk tree, day and night, winter, spring, summer and autumn. She'd made her home in the verdant tree, known to be the oldest in Jandouba. The chameleon had adapted herself to life there in every type of circumstance, in the company of birds and animals, and even humans who visited the tree. No one had ever seen the chameleon leave the tree before the dawn of that morning.

Ceaselessly the creatures of the valley and fields asked one another what could have happened. Whatever the reason, they could find no explanation. Most of the creatures, like the insects, had already sought out the plateau as a refuge from the injustice and injury to which they'd been subjected at the hands of the humans. The chameleon was held in respect and esteem, and all the creatures of Jandouba now welcomed her, holding celebrations in her honour. They too regarded the tree where she lived as a sacred tree, for people prayed beneath it and draped green flags on its branches.

The other matter of interest to them all was that the chameleon had spiritual powers, and a keen perception that enabled her to predict events before they occurred. Thus she could know things of which others knew nothing, see things others had no power to see. What, the other creatures asked one another, had the chameleon known, or seen, or sensed, that had made her leave her home and climb to the plateau? And a further question followed all these others. Who was the chameleon intending to visit, and was her visit a temporary one or was she going to settle on the plateau?

These were all pertinent questions, for never had the chameleon ascended the plateau except when she wanted to meet with the sages there, on matters concerning the future of the district and the welfare of its creatures. On her way she passed the home of the tortoise and asked her to come along, as the chameleon was going to call on the rest of their friends. Next the chameleon knocked on the doors of the hedgehog and the spiny-tailed lizard, who welcomed her. Then they all went together to the terrace over-looking the plains and fields of Jandouba.

The meeting between these friends encouraged many other creatures to climb to the plateau, to see for themselves why the chameleon was making this visit to the highlands. They saw the chameleon sitting in the midst of the hedgehog and the tortoise and the spiny-tailed lizard. She'd turned her face to the east, where the sun was just rising, and its bright, glorious colours reflected their beauty on her, just as the redness of the sky reflected on the silvery granite rocks. In that moment the chameleon's body had absorbed the colours surrounding her, so that she seemed to be wearing a robe in which the colours of sunrise and the silver of the rocks were blended.

Sitting with her friends on the high terrace, the chameleon learned that the worms and beetles and grasshoppers, the lizards and butterflies, the sparrows and mice, and all the other creatures seeking refuge on the plateau, had heard of her visit and had come to meet her, along with the other creatures who'd followed her up from the foot.

They all asked the chameleon what she'd seen in her crystal ball, concerning the troubles that had begun with the arrival of the human tyrants, and whether there was to be an end to all the misery. The hedgehog and the spiny-tailed lizard, the sages of the plateau, had advised them to endure their trial in patience, and they'd followed that advice with no result as yet. Now they were eager to learn, from the blessed chameleon, just how much longer their ordeal was to last.

'Salvation will come very soon,' the chameleon replied.

She'd come, she went on, to tell them the good news, according to the vision she'd seen. Although she herself was on the best of terms with the humans, she deplored their cruel, unjust treatment of the valley creatures. Her fate, she accepted, was bound up with the fate of humans; but she'd heard a voice at dawn that morning telling her and all the creatures living at the foot of the plateau to seek safety on the heights. And so she'd come, in obedience to the voice, and she asked all the other creatures to follow her example if they wished to be delivered from the unknown.

❧ THIRTY-FOUR ❧

Burhan wasn't able to treat Amer and Zenab. His herbs would have been no use for their condition. The wounds from the wolves' thrusts were deep, and the beasts had struck as they always did, with human and animal alike. They'd torn at the throat, a most vulnerable part of the body, and at the breast.

Zenab and Amer had both lost a good deal of blood, and their condition was so grave Burhan decided to act before it was too late. He must, he decided, go to the central hospital in Gharyan and fetch the medicine, antiseptics and bandages to treat their wounds. He'd describe their state to one of the doctors there and have him prescribe the proper medication.

Burhan sat up with the couple that night and eventually managed to stop the bleeding from the wounds, assisted by Aunt Maryouma, who was experienced in nursing. Then, as soon as he could leave the patients, he mounted his camel and headed for Gharyan. Before going out of the camp, he assembled a number of men to guard the tents where the couple lay, in case Haj Abu Hamama should try to come and kill them. He left Aunt Maryouma to sit up and care for them for the rest of the night.

Before midday he was back with the medicine, ointments, gauze and bandages he'd been given by the Italian doctor. He had described the patients' condition, explaining how he hadn't been able to move them to the hospital. He treated Amer's wounds in his tent, where Amer's mother was now tending him, then went on to Aunt Maryouma's tent, where Zenab had been moved by her mother, away from the neighbouring tent of the girl's uncle, Haj Abu Hamama.

Haj Abu Hamama had accused Amer and Zenab of sin, and of bringing shame and disgrace on their families. The only remedy, so far as he was concerned, was to shoot them both. Hajja Khadija and Saliha, Amer's mother, had wept, begging him to let their children be treated and saved from certain death.

Aunt Maryouma had raised her voice too. This wasn't, she insisted, the time for threats. Haj Abu Hamama should wait till he'd calmed down, till his furious rage had subsided, before he did anything. In any case, his suspicions were unfounded – what had happened was actually the opposite of what he imagined.

When morning came, Aunt Maryouma went to see Sheikh Hamed Abu Leila in the guest tent to which he'd retired. Haj Abu Hamama's accusations, she told him, were quite untrue. She'd seen Amer ben Sheeha before sunset, digging by himself. Zenab hadn't been with him or even close by. He hadn't seen Zenab, or met her, before she was attacked by the wolf that had stopped her returning to the camp. When she'd flung a stone at it, it had howled to fetch other wolves that came and surrounded her. Then, when she'd screamed for help, Amer had heard her and rushed to protect and save her.

It didn't matter too much to Sheikh Hamed whether Aunt Maryouma's story was true or not. What was vital was that the people of the camp should be convinced it was, so he'd be spared the shame and disgrace of Haj Abu Hamama's slur. The story must be spread among them all, to let them know what had happened and stop them gossiping about his daughter. Aunt Maryouma's account would, he hoped, pacify Haj Abu Hamama and stop him taking his revenge on Zenab and Amer, which would only stir up scandal.

But Haj Abu Hamama wasn't convinced by the story, even when Sheikh Hamed invited him to his tent to hear it from Aunt Maryouma's own lips. There was no reason, he said, why Zenab should have gone so far off, all alone, and stayed there till sunset when the wolf attacked her. And why, besides, had Amer ben Sheeha been the only one on this earth to hear her screams?

Aunt Maryouma heard him out, then went off, leaving the two sitting there in the tent. Sheikh Hamed said he understood why his brother had acted as he had, for the man who failed to protect his family's honour was bereft of all honour and decency himself. If he himself, he went on, had had his rifle with him when they came upon the scene of shame, he would have acted just as his brother had done. When, though, he'd recovered from the shock of seeing his daughter in such a situation, he'd been convinced of the truth of Aunt Maryouma's account. He knew Amer very well, and he trusted him, for Amer had been like a son to him. He was sure, too, of his daughter's virtue. He was certain they would never have done anything to disgrace the family.

He paused for a moment, then went on.

'They're engaged to be married,' he said. 'Everyone knows that. Their wedding's been constantly put off because of the drought. After what's happened, I think they should be married as soon as possible.'

Haj Abu Hamama wouldn't accept his brother's viewpoint. A speedy marriage, he said, would actually be a reward for their sin, after the wolves hadn't managed to kill them and his own bullet had missed them. They'd only been saved at all because the men had stopped him firing more bullets. The only way to wipe out the disgrace was to send Zenab to his relatives by marriage in Fezzan, marry her to one of the family servants and so bury her shame there. She must never return to Mizda. As for the sinner Amer, his life shouldn't be spared, and Haj Abu Hamama himself would never cease to hunt him down. The only way Amer could save his life was to leave Mizda and live somewhere far off, never showing his face in the village again.

This time Sheikh Hamed was firm in refusing Haj Abu Hamama's demands. No sin, he insisted, had been committed at all. What had happened was just a tragic accident, and everyone would accept the fact. It was Haj Abu Hamama's behaviour that had turned the matter into one of disgrace. The best remedy now was to let things die down, so that everyone could forget and get on with their own affairs.

Haj Abu Hamama was furious. He didn't know, he said, as he left the tent, how he was to face the people, and he couldn't stay here any longer. He'd leave it to Sheikh Hamed to deal with matters as he thought fit. Meanwhile he himself would leave his sons to thresh the harvest and go straight back to Mizda.

After leaving the guest tent, Haj Abu Hamama went to his own tent, took his saddle and set it on his horse's back. Then he put on his cloak and mounted his horse, waiting, before he rode away, for Samby to bring him his water bottle and food for the journey, which he hung from the saddle. Then he dug his heels into the horse's flanks and galloped off in a cloud of dust from its hooves.

The jerboas, meanwhile, went on digging new burrows to replace the ones that had been destroyed. But the people of the camp and their neighbours on the other side of the valley destroyed these new homes too, in their search for ears of barley that were becoming scarcer by the day.

Sheikh Hamed remained in his tent and devoted himself to prayer and worship, seeing no one.

As for relations between the people of the camp and the family of Jibreel, these gradually returned to normal after a few days of deadlock, as people began to talk to one another and visit one another once more. The women of the Jibreel family felt no embarrassment at visiting Zenab in her father's tent, to which she'd been moved back after her uncle had left. They visited the other

194

women of the camp too, with no objection from Sheikh Hamed, besides spending many evenings in Aunt Maryouma's tent.

Rabiha and Aunt Maryouma had become the centre of attraction for the women of the two camps. Both told interesting stories, recited poetry and talked of the history of their ancestors, while Rabiha was always ready to tell the fortunes of anyone who asked her. The sky, she once told all the women present, had closed its gates in their faces, but soon it would open those gates once more and send an abundant bounty, bringing great benefit to the people. But just as, she went on, any form of evil is usually accompanied by some good, so the benefit to come would bring some harm along with it. She ended her prediction by saying they must wait, rejoice, but be careful too. She herself, she told them, would be the first to profit from the coming good fortune, since her marriage to Burhan – God willing – would take place before the Great Night of the Threshing.

This Great Night was due to come in three or four days, and, since there were no more ears of barley to be collected, there was no longer any need for secrecy when threshing them. The people of the camp prepared seven floors, on which they placed all the barley not yet threshed, while the Jibreel family prepared two large floors for their own harvest.

Burhan had wished for a quiet wedding, in which they'd read the opening verses of the Quran before he then took his bride to his tent with no processions, or singing, or dancing, or music. This, he'd argued, was his own third marriage and Rabiha's second. They'd both held celebrations at their previous weddings and there was no need for one this time. Indeed, such festivities were usually reserved for people's first weddings.

But the people of the camp and the family of Jibreel insisted on a celebration, so as to express their happiness for the bride and bridegroom. The arts of the eastern and western desert were on show, along with the singing of *kishk* songs accompanied by Al Roumany's bagpipes, Matouq's drum and the dancing of the women. Aunt Maryouma also brought three young girls from the camp, who swayed their hair from side to side as part of the celebration,

Except for Sheikh Hamed, who remained in his tent, everyone attended the wedding. Even Zenab and Amer ben Sheeha were there, though their throats and shoulders were still being bandaged, Zenab sitting with the women and Amer with the men.

Aunt Maryouma composed a new song especially for the wedding, which everyone joyfully sang:

> 'Oh what joy for this village of many a brave knight,
> On this, oh Burhan, your night of most delight!
> From Barqa they come, bearing a gift for you,
> People they are of goodness, of hearts honest and true.'

Suddenly, from the far western horizon, a dazzling flash struck out, rending the screen of darkness, lighting up the whole district for a moment. Then it vanished. Further, repeated flashes shot through the sky, but no thunder or rain followed.

☙ THIRTY-FIVE ❧

The next day brought a shock for everyone. They'd all stayed up long into the night. The wedding of Burhan and Rabiha had been one of the happiest they'd ever attended, and they'd enjoyed all the different forms of entertainment. There was no reason for them to wake before dawn, as they'd done before, for the jerboa burrows were now just black, empty holes in the plains and valleys of Jandouba. For that reason they'd seized every joyful moment of the wedding celebration. In another two days it would be time for the tribes to go their separate ways. They'd thresh the ears then return to their homes laden with sacks full of barley.

It's hard to disturb people's sleep in the early hours of the morning. And yet a strange happening jerked them awake. All the animals in the camp had woken together, sending out cries of terror. The grunting of the camels, the barking of the dogs, the braying of the donkeys were all mingled, confusedly, with other sounds coming from the unknown.

The shrill calls of birds, the buzzing of invisible insects surrounded them. The people rushed from their tents to find the cause of the inexplicable terror that had struck the various creatures. Never, in all their journeys, had they known anything so strange, nor could they see anything to account for the state of panic. Some thought thieves must have crept stealthily into the camp, others that the pack of wolves that had attacked Zenab and Amer had struck at fresh victims.

But neither of these suspicions was confirmed. Apart from the terrified cries of the animals and the buzzing of the insects, everything was quite normal on the two sides of the valley, just as it had been for thousands of years. The sun, a crowned queen, reigned as sole monarch over these lands, over plains, valleys, highlands, mountains, and over every creature living in burrows or dens or caves. The sun ruled over all that walked on the earth, or beneath it, or flew in the sky, or lived in trees and other haunts. The sun tormented where it willed and was merciful where it willed. It could be cruel or gentle, it could approach or withdraw as it wished, in accordance with its long journey from the eastern to the western horizon. Slowly it began its ascent, across the eastern horizon, as it had done each day from time immemorial, to fill the four corners of the earth with its radiant light.

Now, too, the jerboas began acting in the strangest manner. The camels and dogs and donkeys of the camp had cried out in dread, scattering in all directions. Now the jerboas woke, left their burrows and dens and began jumping and leaping about everywhere, in great numbers, some of them bumping against the rocks, or the tent poles, or people's feet. They even, in their frenzied panic, collided with one another. It was as if they didn't know what to do now that their homes, where they'd taken refuge in any crisis before, had been destroyed. Even more confusing was the noise they made, like the creaking of old doors. Never before had the people of the

197

camp heard these strange sounds. The women called out to their menfolk to do something to keep the hordes of leaping jerboas away from them.

The people of the camp were stunned by all this, finding no explanation for the confusion around them. Even Burhan left his tent and his bride, astounded by the things he saw and heard, unable to answer the questions of people like Amer and Suliyman and Uthman.

Sheikh Hamed Abu Leila left his tent and stood there before them with his cane in his hand, his white beard longer and heavier than before. The people ran up to him, hoping he could tell them what had happened. But all he said was that it was a portent of some great event. Then, fingering his rosary, he resumed his invocations to Almighty God. The people stood there alongside him, scanning the horizon, as if awaiting some giant magician about to put on a new performance.

After a few seconds they heard a rumbling sound, like thunder, but they couldn't tell where it was coming from. It hadn't come from the sky above, or from the earth on which they stood. Still the rumbling went on. They knew now it wasn't thunder. It seemed to be coming from some unknown source, and there they remained, anxiously waiting. Then they saw Burhan pointing and shouting:

'There it is!'

They all looked in the direction he'd pointed, to the west of the valley, and saw mountains of water racing towards them, and before these mountains pillars of dust churned up by the water's onward rush. This was the reason for the rumbling they'd first taken for thunder! The force of it made the earth on which they stood shake violently.

Startled cries warned those standing in the valley, or alongside it, to flee the oncoming flood. Only the Captain and Samby had gone to the fields at that early hour, and both managed to leap clear. The roaring flood surged on, capped with foam, its waves enveloping the trunks and branches of the trees it had torn up. The clouds of dust it raised hung in the air like smoke, and the dust and earth turned the water to a reddish brown. The water splashed as it surged, sending out a drizzle like fine rain.

It was an extraordinary sight. No one had expected to see such a powerful torrent at this time of year, with no sign of a cloud or a drop of rain even. The flood rushed before them under a clear sky, in which the sun blazed on with all its strength.

Years had passed since they'd seen such a sight. Years had passed and no valley had been blessed with rain. Indeed, a flood coming with this kind of power, out of season like this one, was something quite unique in the life of everyone witnessing it.

The people noticed how their animals had ceased their terror-stricken noises, having fled to places further than the eye could see. They'd seen great numbers of jerboas too, leaping from the fields towards the banks of the valley, just in time before the flood reached them, as though they'd realised the danger of staying in its path.

The people moved from where they'd been standing in front of their tents, towards the valley, so as to receive the spray sent out by the flood, enjoying the feel of the water that sprinkled their faces and clothes, breathing in the wonderful smell of the torrent as it churned the earth and uprooted plants.

With a vigour and enthusiasm he'd never felt before, Sheikh Hamed walked at the head of a group of men. The rain that falls in summer, he told them, was generally the most abundant, its flood the most powerful.

The surge was like the legions of a mighty army moving towards the sun, sweeping all before it, carrying with it plants and branches and roots. And in its path, too, it swept tents and belongings torn to shreds, sheep and goats that had had no chance to leave their barns, because their owners had never expected a flood at this time of year.

However violent, however turbulent the flood might seem, it came from the rain of which they'd constantly dreamed, for which they'd always longed, to revive the land, cause the plants to sprout and bring them food and bounty. Rain coloured the season of spring, transformed the days of poverty and want to days of plenty, joy and sufficiency. Only by the kindness and bounty of the rain are the granaries of barley and wheat filled. Only where there is rain are great feasts and celebrations found. And until it rains weddings are held back.

Aunt Maryouma, beside herself with joy, sent out a long and loud ululation, greeting the valley and its surging flood, upon which the other women followed suit, sending out ululations still louder and longer. The women of the Jibreel family, standing with their menfolk on the other bank of the valley, joined in with joyful happiness.

The people were exultant. They'd finished collecting the ears of barley from the jerboa burrows before the flood arrived. Had it come earlier, it would have swept away barley, burrows and all, destroying their chance of profiting from the bounty they'd gathered.

Rain had poured down on the high peaks of the Atlas Mountains beyond the frontier, sending its precious gift to this parched land. It was this blessed flood the animals had sensed before it came.

A long time passed, and still the flood surged on. The sun had advanced some way in its journey across the sky, and was starting to send its burning rays on to the earth's creatures. Gusts of refreshing air, stirred up by the movement of the flood, blended with the spray to counter the sun's heat. Such a flood, with its torrents surging so long, must have covered the vast desert that stood between it and its final destination at the sea. Midway it would meet the wide valley through which it passed to the coast, bordering on the desert at Sert.

Sheikh Hamed had explained to his people the route the flood would take. He knew all about these valleys, their sources and estuaries. He expressed concern, though, over the sheer power of the surge; for the strength of a flood is mostly in its first rush, as it sweeps before it all that stands in its way, be it soil, sand or trees, so that the water behind can flow calmly. What had happened here was almost the opposite of what usually happened, for the power of the flowing water had increased rather than growing less. His fear was that the defiles and passes between the mountains, through which the water flowed, might not be able to withstand the rest of the water, which was still increasing steadily.

Sheikh Hamed didn't need to elaborate. The people, gazing at the scene, could see for themselves. The valley, spacious though it was, couldn't hold the floodwater, which surged and flowed still, filling every groove and furrow till they too became part of the torrent. Then, after covering the sides of the valley, it began to flow in a wider course.

The people rushed back, to leave a distance between themselves and the water, supposing it would settle in its new course after rebelling against the old path through which it had flowed for generations. But the flood was beyond holding to any course now. The surging onflow rose, higher and higher, till it flowed out of the valley. Sheikh Hamed told them to run to their tents and save whatever food and belongings they could carry away. But, before they could act, the flood reached their tents. Their fear was for their lives now, and the lives of their children. The most any of them could do was stop and save one of the camp children, bundling him up to stop him being swept away and drowned. The tents were carried off one after the other, their belongings first floating on the surface, then being borne along to the distant sea.

As the people fled, screaming, behind the sand dunes that kept the water from them, they didn't realise at first that the torrent had robbed them of their most precious possession of all. Only after they'd stood there for a few moments did they see the flood rushing on to the threshing floors, where the ears of barley were piled in heaps that toppled just as their tents had toppled, before being swept off by the waves.

They gazed in horror at the dreadful scene, their eyes clouded with tears, utterly powerless to save their barley. They knew they'd lost everything, and now the water was beginning even to pierce the barriers of sand. They must run for their lives. The Jibreel family started climbing up towards the plateau the water was even now surrounding, till they reached a safe spot above the flood level. As for the people of Mizda, they could do nothing but wait for the water to recede from where they were standing.

Sheikh Hamed felt very grateful to Burhan, who'd stayed by his side and helped him cross the dunes, leaving the Captain and Samby to take care of the children and the old people. Meanwhile Rabiha, Burhan's wife, had stayed all the way alongside Aunt Maryouma, the old woman's ululations turning to wails as she realised her son Miloud, who'd been playing by her side when the flood first surprised them, had disappeared. She didn't stop wailing till several people had assured her he was safe, that he'd climbed a *batm* tree as the flood surged towards him. She looked around her and saw him sitting on the top of the tree, dangling his legs on the branches.

The flood settled, at last, in the new, wider course it had made for itself, forming a number of lakes and rivulets in the lower areas and between the sand dunes. The people of the camp had stopped their flight. Some of them were sitting on the ground, others resting on high mounds of sand, catching their breath and watching as the flood abated and ceased to threaten them.

Sheikh Hamed sat on a mound, and, having regained his strength, asked in a firm voice, above the children's screams and the wailing of the women, if everyone in the camp was safe. Then, when no one said otherwise, he broke into a beaming smile for the first time since his daughter and Amer had been attacked by the wolves.

'Do you see, Burhan?' he said. 'We haven't lost anyone in the flood.'

Burhan, greatly relieved, took a deep breath.

'Thank God, Sheikh Hamed,' he said. 'All our people are safe and sound.'

'Yes,' the old man replied. 'Yes! We may have lost our harvest, our tents, our belongings. Our camels and donkeys and dogs have run off heaven knows where, and they'll never come back maybe. But everything can be made up, so long as we've all survived.'

Then, in a remark that signalled his approval of Burhan's

202

marriage, he said: 'Rabiha's family are safe too. I saw them climbing up towards the plateau.'

'Yes, they are, Sheikh Hamed. All's well, as long as everyone's alive.'

This was no consolation, even so, for Suliyman, who was still panting from his exertions. He couldn't believe all his toil in reaping the barley had simply been blown away.

'We can bear everything,' he said, 'except the loss of the barley.'

Burhan, as if to make light of the loss that seemed so heavy to Suliyman, answered:

'You mean the jerboas' barley?'

The people of the camp all repeated the phrase, 'the jerboas' barley', as though they'd just heard it for the first time, especially as Burhan had uttered it with all the gravity and dignity of a scholar of religion. Sheikh Hamed was astonished too.

'What was that you called it?' he asked. 'The jerboas' barley?'

He turned to his wife.

'Did you hear that, Hajja Khadija?' he said, laughing. 'They're calling it the jerboas' barley!'

He went on laughing and repeating the phrase till he infected the Captain, who was seized by helpless laughter in his turn.

'Ha, ha, ha!' he roared. 'You said it, Burhan! Ha, ha, ha! You're right, Burhan. It *is* the jerboas' barley!'

Still the Captain went on laughing and spluttering, till his laughter finally infected everyone, even the women and children who'd been weeping and wailing, and now started laughing, then wailing again.

Suddenly they all noticed the hundreds of jerboas leaping around them. These creatures had fled the water just as they had, as if their two fates were bound together. Countless numbers had come, in great hordes, seeking safety just as they had. Some of the jerboas were wailing, just as the women and children were. It was a mournful wailing, lost amid the clamour of the people's cries and the roaring of the flood.